**He wore red swim trunks. And nothing else.**

It was kind of ironic, really, that her mouth went entirely dry, because there seemed to be a lot of water sliding off the contours and planes of his hard, lean body as Alex left the pool and walked toward her.

"Maya."

She simply nodded. What with her tongue being stuck to the top of her mouth and all.

"You brought me books?"

Then there was that deep, rumbling voice. And that smile. She felt her own mouth curl up. "Um, yeah." *What was the question again?*

Alex was standing really close. Not close enough that she could lean slightly and lap up that one drop of water right in the middle of his chest, but close enough that she was able to see the light stubble on his jaw and the way his wet eyelashes clung to one another.

"Thought we were going to e-mail," he said, his voice gruff.

"We were going to e-mail," she agreed. "But you had so many questions, I thought maybe this would be better."

"There's only one problem with that theory," he said. "Now that you're here, talking about books is not even in the top three of the things I want to do."

Lust flashed through her. "I'm hoping that at least two of them match up with my top three."

"You have a top three for what you want to do right now?"

She shook her head. "More like a top ten."

# ACCLAIM FOR ERIN NICHOLAS

"Sexy and fun!"
—Susan Andersen, *New York Times* bestselling author
on *Anything You Want*

"Erin Nicholas always delivers swoon-worthy heroes, heroines that you root for, laugh out loud moments, a colorful cast of family and friends, and a heartwarming happily ever after."
—Melanie Shawn, *New York Times* bestselling author

"Erin Nicholas always delivers a good time guaranteed! I can't wait to read more."          —Candis Terry, bestselling author of the Sweet, Texas series

"Heroines I love and heroes I still shamelessly want to steal from them. Erin Nicholas romances are fantasy fodder."
—Violet Duke, *New York Times* bestselling author

"A brand-new Erin Nicholas book means I won't be sleeping until I'm finished. Guaranteed."
—Cari Quinn, *USA Today* bestselling author

"Reading an Erin Nicholas book is the next best thing to falling in love."          —Jennifer Bernard, *USA Today* bestselling author

"Nicholas is adept at creating two enthralling characters hampered by their pasts yet driven by passion, and she infuses her romance with electrifying sex that will have readers who enjoy the sexually explicit seeking out more from this author."
—*Library Journal* (starred review) on *Hotblooded*

**Also by Erin Nicholas**

*Completely Yours*

# Forever Mine

# ERIN NICHOLAS

FOREVER

NEW YORK  BOSTON

Copyright © 2017 by Erin Nicholas
Excerpt from *Totally His* copyright © 2017 by Erin Nicholas

Cover design by Elizabeth Turner. Cover illustration by Blake Morrow. Cover copyright © 2017 by Hachette Book Group, Inc.

Forever
Hachette Book Group
1290 Avenue of the Americas, New York, NY 10104
forever-romance.com
twitter.com/foreverromance

First Edition: March 2017

Forever is an imprint of Grand Central Publishing. The Forever name and logo are trademarks of Hachette Book Group, Inc.

The publisher is not responsible for websites (or their content) that are not owned by the publisher.

The Hachette Speakers Bureau provides a wide range of authors for speaking events. To find out more, go to www.hachettespeakersbureau.com or call (866) 376-6591.

ISBNs: 978-1-4555-3967-3 (mass market), 978-1-4555-3969-7 (ebook)

Printed in the United States of America

OPM

10 9 8 7 6 5 4 3 2 1

*For Nikoel... I want to be more
like you! You make
everything better.*

*For Mari and Stacey... for
always being just one text
message away.*

*For Liz... I don't know how I got
so lucky. I still have that first
e-mail from you. That
was a very good day.*

*For Lindsey... What would I do
without you?*

*For Alex... for making it
all shine.*

*And for Nick, Derek, Mom, Dad,
Shannon, and all my friends who
lift me up and keep me grounded.*

# ACKNOWLEDGMENTS

I wrote a book several years ago in which a character treats a little boy with hemophilia at one point in the story. The scene is important for that character, but it's a small portion of the overall story, really. But after that book came out, I got a lovely e-mail from a reader who is the daughter of a hemophiliac and has her own hemophiliac child. She was so grateful that I'd mentioned hemophilia—and gotten the details right ☺—and she'd shared the book with her support group of mothers with children living with hemophilia. She was thrilled to read a book about a condition that affected her life greatly and that not many people know much about.

I can't tell you how touched I was by that. I kept that e-mail for a very long time, and when I was getting to know Alex for *Forever Mine* and realized that he was going to have hemophilia and it needed to be a big part of his story, I wrote that reader again. She became my primary resource on living with hemophilia, as a patient as well as a family member and caregiver. So a huge and very special thank-you goes to Karla Brown for being my go-to expert! Thank you for sharing your knowledge and experiences, time, patience, and heart! I also want to thank her friend Brendan Hayes for also sharing knowledge and experiences that made the story so much better.

Hemophilia A occurs in one in five thousand live male births. The number of people with hemophilia in the United States is about twenty thousand, according to the National Hemophilia Foundation. It is a rare but life-altering condition. It is even rarer for a girl to have hemophilia. In a case like Charli's, where her father is a hemophiliac, the girl is a carrier for the condition. However, some carriers have a blood factor that puts them in the category of hemophilia, and they can have symptoms and require treatment like a true hemophiliac.

I truly found everything I learned fascinating, and I hope that Alex and Charli's story will help others understand a little more about this condition.

For more information about hemophilia please visit:

The National Hemophilia Foundation
    www.hemophilia.org
The Hemophilia Federation of America
    www.hemophiliafed.org
The World Federation of Hemophilia
    www.wfh.org

# *Forever Mine*

# CHAPTER ONE

The answer to his prayer came in bright-purple leather.

He hadn't been expecting that.

Alex didn't know if the woman was supposed to be a superhero or what, but he was definitely in need of a little saving.

Along with the leather pants and vest, she wore a black tank top and black boots that went to midcalf. And then there was her big stick.

She was battling a guy with an equally big stick. It was a staged fight, part of a bigger demonstration of the techniques taught in the classes at Active Imagination Martial Arts and Fitness Studio. Still, the strength and skill it took to wield the weapons were obvious.

Even to Alex, who had never given two seconds of thought to what it would take to wield a weapon.

A flyer had been thrust into his hand at the mall entrance. When he'd seen the words *kids* and *superheroes*, Alex had assumed the kids would be the ones playing superhero. But not one of the fifty or so watching the demonstration, ranging from about age four to nearly twenty, was dressed up.

The seven adults demonstrating various martial arts, stage fighting, and weaponry techniques were, however. One guy looked like an Indiana Jones impersonator, another was clearly a Superman knock-off, cape and all. A couple of others also wore leather, though none as well as the woman in purple.

"Self-esteem is how you feel about yourself, no matter what other people say," the woman said, finishing the battle and addressing the crowd as she had been doing periodically throughout the demonstration.

Alex glanced down at the pamphlet in his hand. Maya Goodwin. She was the owner of the studio and taught a few of the classes. It offered classes to adults too, but it seemed that Maya specialized in working with the kids. The Super You class, where the kids dressed up as superheroes, was apparently her specialty.

Which made her exactly the person he needed to meet today.

"It's knowing who you are, no matter what's going on around you," she went on. "It's the person you want to be in good times and in bad."

Her voice was as sexy as her ass in the tight purple pants. And that was saying something. She couldn't have been more than five six or five seven. Her hair was nearly black, with deep-red stripes through it, and stopped at her ears. Her eyes were also dark, shining brightly from swoops of black and purple that looked like a mask but were clearly painted on. She was trim, the pants and her sleeveless top and vest showing off the contours of muscles that spoke of regular workouts. Her outfit also did nothing to hide the jagged scar that ran from below her jaw on the left down her neck, disappearing under a few inches of leather and then reappearing to join three others traveling down her upper arm to her elbow.

Alex could have told himself that it was his medical degree that made him curious about the injury that had caused those scars, but he knew better. That was the kind of disfigurement that made everyone curious about what had happened. But the scars simply joined the list of things he found fascinating about her.

For instance, she seemed so much bigger than she was. Her voice was strong, her smile confident, and the way she moved her body and handled her weapon was mesmerizing. Or something.

Alex couldn't explain it. He'd stopped at the demonstration because it made him think of his nine-year-old daughter, Charli, and her obsession with the huge movie franchise *Galactic Renegades*. Something Alex knew next to nothing about. He'd intended to grab a registration form, ask a few questions, and be on his way. That had been twenty minutes ago. During that time he'd found himself moving steadily closer to the raised performance platform.

Now he stood at the front of the crowd, only a few feet from Maya, probably blocking the view of a bunch of little kids, unable to take his eyes off her.

He'd known when she first noticed him. Their eyes had met, and for just a moment, she'd faltered in what she was saying.

This woman didn't falter. He had no idea how he knew that, but he did. The big-stick battle might have been part of a show, but her passion and confidence were not. And ever since he'd come to the front of the group, she hadn't made eye contact with him again. Alex found that as intriguing as the rest. Did he fluster her? And if so, why was that the best thing that had happened to him in some time?

"You can be anything, but first you have to imagine it," Maya said to the crowd. "And that's what our classes are about. Yes, it's martial arts and self-defense and weapons work, but it's more than that. It's about figuring out what makes you feel strong—not just physically but emotionally. That answer is different for everyone. We all get our strength from different places.

"Some of the kids will come and find a group of friends. Some will come and find an adult mentor to look up to. Some will come and find their inner strength from doing something that's hard, that they never thought they could. And some will come and find their strength in letting go, in having a safe place to play and imagine and pretend.

"Yes, we dress up," she said, with a light laugh that made Alex feel as if he'd just taken a shot of brandy. She gestured to the people in capes and spandex. "And we encourage the kids to become a character in class. We want the character to represent the things they love most about themselves, along with some traits they want to develop."

Maya was moving across the stage, addressing the crowd, talking to the kids as well as the parents. Her enthusiasm was clear and contagious, and she was obviously quite comfortable as the center of attention.

Alex knew what it was like to have a hundred pairs of eyes on him at once. He was a nationally renowned expert in genetic disorders and regularly spoke to groups of patients and caregivers as well as lecturing to medical students and to colleagues from multiple fields. But he was never completely at ease in front of a crowd.

Maybe because he was always hiding something.

Maybe he needed a costume.

"We spend the first two classes helping them develop their character," Maya continued. "We have teachers and a counselor on our staff who work with the kids by asking them questions about what things they like about themselves, what they admire about others and why, what powers they most wish they had, and more.

"Then our amazing artist, Kiera"—she pointed to another woman who was dressed as some sort of warrior princess. The princess raised her hand and smiled—"sits with each child and helps them sketch how they want their character to look.

"Then one of the top costumers in Boston, Sophie"—this time she pointed to a curvy blonde dressed in a white jumpsuit—"comes in and helps us put the costumes together. Their time and expertise make this program truly unique and utterly wonderful."

If her words hadn't been enough to get people pulling out their pens to sign up and write checks, the smile she gave them would have been.

Damn. Alex shook his head. If she ever turned that smile on him, she could have anything she wanted.

"Kiera and Sophie are going to bring around some sign-up sheets while Ben and I do another bo staff demonstration," she said as her sparring partner stepped forward. "And then we'll take some questions."

Bo staff. That's what the big stick was called. Alex

pulled his phone from his pocket and typed in a note. He'd have to look that up later. Right now his eyes and brain seemed unable to do anything but watch Maya Goodwin.

She and Ben positioned themselves several feet apart on the platform. She was on the side closest to Alex, which meant he couldn't see her face. They did a little bow and then they went at it. The sticks clacked against one another as they moved together, then away, thrusting and blocking and turning. It was almost like a dance—if you were constantly trying to knock down your partner while you tangoed.

Alex watched her intently, noticing that there was a limit to how high she could raise the arm due to the scars and that she most often swung and thrust with her right arm, perhaps due to a lack of strength on the left. She continued to use the arm, wincing as she did, but not giving Ben a single advantage. They turned in a wide circle and finally she was facing Alex's direction.

As far as marketing techniques went, this was brilliant. Put the hot girl in leather to get the dads to pay attention. Show off her kick-ass bo staff techniques to get the kids' attention. Have her use buzz words like *self-esteem* and *fitness* for the moms. And then pass out sign-up sheets.

Alex was ready to sign up himself.

His head and heart had been spinning for the past two months, since he'd found out that not only did he have a nearly ten-year-old daughter with a woman he remembered only as "the cute blonde who liked butterscotch schnapps," but that his daughter was sick. Because of him.

Ironically Rachel, who hadn't touched schnapps since

that night, had found him only because of Charli's condition. She'd read an article he'd written about hemophilia for a parenting magazine. She'd recognized him from his photo and tracked him down at Boston Children's Hospital with the help of his bio at the end of the article. Otherwise he still wouldn't know his daughter.

And if he could untangle his emotions about missing ten years of Charli's life and the guilt over being the reason for her condition in the first place, he could get closer to her and be a real dad to her.

His first step in proving that Charli was the most important thing in his life was bonding with her over the things she loved. *Galactic Renegades* and superheroes, to start. He could ask her all about them, of course, but he couldn't deny that a part of him wanted to impress her by already knowing a few things when they talked.

The first time Charli had initiated a conversation with him, it was to ask him who his favorite *Galactic Renegades* character was. His initial reaction had been *Well, shit.* His second had been to answer Beck Steele, the tough-guy fighter pilot Alex had heard of only because one of his favorite actors played the character. But he'd known that she suspected he was lying.

He knew nothing about superheroes or sci-fi space sagas and was apparently no good at faking it. He'd been watching one *Galactic Renegades* and superhero movie after another ever since. He was still unclear on whether the renegades were considered superheroes, but he wasn't sure it mattered. If Charli liked *Renegades*, then Alex was going to become a *GR* expert.

He watched the woman in purple and wondered what she knew about *Galactic Renegades* and Piper, the newest young heroine in the movie franchise. The first three movies had come out about five years ago, but now they were doing a next-generation kind of thing, and Charli was all in. That meant Alex needed to get all in.

Just then Maya pivoted and lifted her staff into the air. But just before Ben struck, her gaze swung to Alex. They made eye contact for less time than it took him to suck in a deep breath. But it was enough to cause a reaction.

Ben's staff came down swiftly, but instead of blocking with her staff, the woman flinched. Ben's stick hit her on the shoulder, and she went to her knees.

There was a moment of stunned surprise from the audience and the performers alike before she got to her feet and swung to face them with a big smile.

"We work on things like concentration and focus as well as getting up again after you've been knocked down," she said. "And with that, I'm going to let Sophie take my spot, and she and Ben are going to show you some sword work."

The blonde in white looked around quickly, and someone thrust a sword and scabbard into her hand. It seemed obvious to Alex that Sophie hadn't been prepared to step in, which made him think that Maya was taking herself out of the demo unexpectedly and might be hurt.

She moved to the side with the rest of the demonstrators, rolling her shoulder forward and back. But she didn't seem in distress, and Alex made himself stay put. He wasn't her friend, and while he was a physician, he certainly hadn't done any acute injury care recently. Or ever. He'd gone to medical school for a very specific reason, and his focus had gotten him the residency at Boston's Children's Hospital. He'd been there ever since.

Though she talked and smiled at her fellow super-heroes, Maya was also scanning the crowd—and avoiding looking at Alex again. He smiled. He was either distracting her because she was attracted to him or because she thought he was a stalker. And he'd be very happy to get close enough to assure her he was not stalking her. Which would seem stalkerish.

He should just focus on the whole Active Imagination presentation and staff. Any one of them could probably help him with the plan he'd started forming for Charli's birthday.

But if he'd been thinking about what he'd need to do to keep Charli safe while she took part in a class where she could be the one who got smacked by a bo stick, he would have missed Maya slipping off the edge of the stage and making her way around the side of the crowd of people.

Alex turned and saw two teenage boys talking to a girl about their age. The girl didn't seem pleased. She yanked her arm out of one boy's hold and tried to pass them, but they stepped together, blocking her way. Alex frowned and noticed Maya heading in their direction. He slipped to the side and then headed around the back of the crowd, who were oblivious to any drama unfolding behind them.

The girl finally managed to push past the boys, and she walked quickly down the east corridor of the mall, turning into a clothing store after about twenty yards.

The boys followed. And so did Maya.

Alex headed in that direction as well, picking up his pace. She probably knew the kids or something. Maybe they'd been in one of her classes. Still, something told him to follow.

Or maybe it was just that he wanted a few minutes of time to talk to Maya privately. Or that once she'd left the stage, the demonstration had lost most of its appeal for him.

Maya made it to the storefront a few strides in front of him. She glanced at him, startled, as he came up beside her. She opened her mouth, but before she could say hi or ask if he was a stalker, something in her peripheral vision inside the store drew her attention. Her brows slammed together, and she headed in.

Alex was right behind her.

\* \* \*

The last thing she needed was the hot guy from the demonstration distracting her in here. But Maya couldn't take time to get rid of him. She had to make sure the girl she'd seen being harassed was okay. So she headed into the store and tried to ignore him.

The store was deserted except for one young female clerk at the register on the far side of the store. The boys had the girl in a corner behind several racks of clothes. The one in the green hoodie had a hold of her wrist, and she was clearly trying to get loose.

Maya went straight for the kids, but the guy who had followed her hung back. He pretended interest in a table of T-shirts, but he was close enough that he could hear everything. She didn't know what his deal was, but as long as he stayed out of the way, it would be fine.

"Leave her alone," Maya said firmly as she approached from behind the boys.

The boy in the black denim jacket glanced over his

shoulder at Maya. "This is none of your business," he told her. Then he got a good look at her. He straightened and turned. "It's not Halloween, babe."

Maya planted her hands on her hips, her feet spread. "I said leave her alone."

The other boy and the girl both stopped struggling and focused on Maya.

The first boy, who couldn't have been more than seventeen, laughed. "You a big, brave superhero or something?"

Maya's eyes narrowed. "Or something. Like Boston PD."

"Yeah, well, everything is fine here," the kid in the black denim said, disdain dripping from his voice. "We're just talking to her. We're not doin' nothin' wrong."

"I saw you stop her outside and then follow her in here. Guessing she's already turned you down," Maya told him. "So how about you back off?"

"I'm not hurting her. We're friends."

"I don't care if you know her or not," Maya said. "No means no."

"Tell her that you didn't say no to me," the kid in the hoodie said to the girl.

The girl winced, and Maya assumed the boy had squeezed her wrist. Maya started to step forward when she heard, "Can I be of some assistance?" from right behind her.

She turned. It was the guy. It made sense that he had a sexy, deep voice. It totally fit.

She shook her head. She could *not* be distracted by him right now.

The boys swung to face him, which drew their

attention away from Maya. She took the opportunity to move in closer.

"No, you fucking can't," the first kid said. "You can mind your own damned business."

"How about you lower your voice and let go of the young lady?" The guy's tone was authoritative, and he drew himself to his full height—which had to be at least six two—and his gaze hardened.

She wasn't getting distracted. But damn, he looked good being all big and bad and heroic.

The kid in the hoodie straightened as well and took a step forward, dragging the girl with him. "How about you stop harassing me?" Green Hoodie asked. He looked at Maya. "I'd like to file a complaint."

"Too bad. I don't have any forms with me, and my memory is terrible if I don't write things down," she said blandly. She also wasn't on the force at the moment, but he didn't have to know that. "I guess it would end up being your word against mine about what happened."

"I'm not afraid of you," the kid said.

"That's because you're stupid," Maya told him bluntly. "Which is also, no doubt, one of the many reasons that she wants nothing to do with you."

"Okay, everyone relax," Hot Hero interrupted, stepping closer. "Do you know these guys?" he asked the girl, who had been standing there, her eyes wide.

She glanced at the boy holding her, then looked at Maya. Maya gave her an encouraging smile.

"No," she said. "They just came up to me outside."

"And do you want to be with them?" the guy asked.

Her eyes still on Maya, the girl shook her head.

"Let her go." He delivered the words in a tone that

should have made the two teens' knees shake. Even Maya felt her eyes widen.

Green Hoodie's hand loosened on the girl's wrist, and he took a step forward. "Who the fuck do you think you are?"

"I'd like to be the guy who's going to make you understand that you can't put yourself into other people's space just because you want to," he said. "But no matter what else, I will be the guy who's going to make sure this girl leaves the mall without you."

The girl suddenly jerked her arm and pulled free from Green Hoodie's hold. Maya moved quickly to put herself between the girl and the two boys. "Are you hurt?" she asked the girl.

"No."

"You need help getting home?"

"No." The girl worried her bottom lip. "I still need to buy what I came for."

Maya glanced at the boys. "I'll make sure they don't follow you. If you want, I'll shop with you."

The girl looked at the boys, her expression hardening. "You don't have to." She took a deep breath and looked at Maya again. "But I'll be at Daniel's looking for a dress. If you have time."

Maya relaxed slightly and smiled. "I'll meet you there." There was no reason this girl should have to leave the mall just because these two jackasses had insinuated themselves into her day.

As the girl left the store, the boys started to move too. Maya spun, her smile gone. "No way. You're not leaving yet," she told them.

"The fuck we're not," Black Denim said.

"You're going to wait until security gets here to throw your asses out of the mall," she told them.

"We're not leaving this mall until we're damned good and ready," Black Denim said.

Maya was unfazed. "I'll follow you around the entire time you're here."

"And do what?" the boy challenged.

"Nothing. Unless you decide to be assholes again."

The kid balled up a fist and took a step toward her.

Maya braced herself, readying to block any attack.

But she didn't need to bother.

"Stop right there." Hot Hero grabbed the kid's shoulder.

The kid swung around and pulled his arm back, but as soon as his attention and center of gravity shifted, Maya moved in. She wrenched his arm behind his back and put him on his knees.

"Goddammit!" The kid started to turn. "I'm going to—"

Maya put a knee in the middle of his back and pushed him onto his stomach. She pulled his other arm behind his back and held his wrists pinned together.

"I'm pressing charges with the Boston PD!" the kid shouted.

"Well, good luck with that. They can't fire me twice," Maya told him.

She hadn't been fired. She'd been given a desk job after her injury. But she simply wasn't made to sit in an office all day, so she'd left and started the studio. But she didn't owe this kid any explanations.

"You're not even really a cop?" Black Denim asked, writhing underneath her.

She put more of her weight onto him. "Well, consider this a lesson in consequences. You mess with someone who doesn't want you, and you could get messed with by someone you don't want."

Suddenly there was a sharp pain in her side. "Dammit!" The kid in the hoodie had punched her. The dick. The surprise of it made her let up her pressure on Black Denim. He tried to roll, but she leaned on him again, as Green Hoodie turned toward her hero and the store employee he was talking to. She opened her mouth to yell at him but the kid kicked him in the side of his knee before she could make a sound. Holy shit.

The guy swore, and his leg buckled. Maya instantly started to move toward him, but Green Hoodie swung around and grabbed her hair, pulling her off his friend. He shoved her, and she went to her butt, her head colliding with the display stand behind her. Stars danced in front of her eyes, and she had to work for her next breath.

Just then two security guards showed up. "Alright, what's going on?" one asked, coming around the racks of clothing.

Hot Hero immediately got to his feet. He grabbed Green Hoodie by the front of his sweatshirt and lifted him onto his tiptoes before turning and shoving him toward the security guards. Then he lunged for Black Denim as the kid spun toward Maya. He got a hold of the denim jacket and started to pull, but Maya drew her leg up, kicking out and sending the kid sprawling.

She scrambled to her feet, and she couldn't avoid gasping and grabbing her side. She started forward, but one of the guards and two other teenagers who'd come into the store were on Black Denim first.

But she forgot all about the kid when Hero Guy tried to put weight on his leg and grimaced. "Hey, you okay?" she asked, ignoring the stabbing pain in her side. Son of a bitch. She'd fractured ribs less than a year ago at Comic Con, and it felt as if the kid had hit her in exactly the same spot.

The guy opened his eyes. "Yeah. I'm good."

"Doesn't look so good," Maya said. He had straightened his leg, but he had sucked in a quick breath as he'd done it.

"I'm fine. You could have a concussion," he told her. "Let me take a look."

He was going to take a look at her? She shook her head, then winced at the pain it caused. "No nausea, no dizziness, no ringing in the ears, and I remember everything that happened." She frowned. "Even the first time you distracted me and I stuttered, and the second time you distracted me and Ben got a shot in, and the third time when that kid was able to get a hold of me."

The guy actually smiled. "Those were all my fault?"

She nodded, then winced again. "I never get distracted."

His grin grew, but he asked, "You know the symptoms of concussion?"

"I do martial arts," she said. "We fall down sometimes." Her whole staff knew first aid and had experience using it. Working with weapons required it. "How do you know how to do a concussion check?"

"Doctor."

Huh. "What kind of doctor?"

"Pediatrician. So yes, your head is bigger than the ones I'm used to dealing with." He gave her a cute smile. "But it's basically the same thing." He glanced around, then took her by her upper arm and pulled her to a chair that sat outside one of the changing rooms.

"You're kind of grabby," she complained, but she found she didn't really mind. He had nice hands. Big hands. Strong hands. And he had, after all, jumped into the fight with her.

"Yeah, the Hippocratic oath is so inconvenient at times," he said drily.

That amused her. "You just can't take my word for it?"

"Sorry."

He put her in the chair and then started to kneel to look her in the eye. He frowned as he bent his knee, however, and stopped with his hands on his thighs instead, putting his face right in front of hers.

He was really good-looking—sandy-blond hair cut short, deep-green eyes, a deep voice that rumbled right through her.

And she was suddenly just fine with him taking a look at her. She'd show him whatever he wanted to see. "I'm not familiar with this concussion test," she said softly as he continued to just look at her.

"This is turning out to be more of a test of my willpower than of the condition of your head," he told her.

Oh, she liked that. "I thought maybe it was some kind of medicinal magic."

"Not being able to take my eyes off of you?"

"Well, my head suddenly doesn't hurt anymore." Wow, she hadn't flirted like this in a long time.

They just paused there, smiling at one another in a way she couldn't remember ever having smiled at someone. Just smiling. For several long seconds.

"What about that?" he finally asked, pointing to where she was pressing her hand against her side.

She sighed. "A rib, I think. He punched me in the side."

Big Bad Doctor's eyes hardened. "He *punched* you?"

He straightened and turned toward where they'd left the kids with the security guards. Maya had the distinct impression he wanted to go after the kid who'd hit her. And that did funny things to her stomach. Security was on the way out the door with them, though.

"Let me check your rib," he said, focusing back on her.

"You're not in great shape yourself, Dr. Wonderful." She gestured to his knee, which was clearly bothering him. "I've had cracked ribs before. And worse." She indicated her shoulder with a small smile. His gaze followed the line of her scars. "Besides," she said, dropping her hand from her side and straightening in the chair, "I have a dress to shop for." The girl was probably waiting for her in Daniel's Boutique.

"That was really nice of you to offer."

She shrugged. "A girl shouldn't shop for a dress alone. I don't know where her friends or sisters or mom are, but the least I can do is be sure she looks for something in red."

"Red?"

"She'll look great in red," Maya said.

"And you're also going to talk to her about being safe? Not shopping alone?" he asked.

Maya frowned. "No. There's no reason she can't shop alone. That's crap. Those guys had no right to harass her."

He nodded his agreement. "But you're not just going to shop and blow it off." He said it as a statement, not a question.

She had no idea how he knew that, but no, she wasn't just going to shop with the girl. "I'm going to talk her into coming in for a few free self-defense classes," Maya admitted. "Next time she'll be the one with the knee in the guy's back."

"Not worried about her cracking a rib?"

"The only reason that happened was because a certain good-looking doctor distracted me," Maya said. "As long as she stays focused, she'll be okay."

He almost looked smug for a moment. "Maya, I—"

He was cut off by a chorus of "Oh my God!" and "There you are!" and "What happened?" as Kiera and Sophie swept into the store.

But she didn't miss that the guy knew her name. She had no chance to say anything else to him. Or to find out his name. Or even to say thanks. Or good-bye.

By the time she'd been hugged by her friends and was looking around for him, he was gone.

# 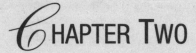CHAPTER TWO

i."

Rachel looked tired. But she smiled as she noticed the takeout bags in his hands.

"Hi. Thought I'd be in charge of dinner tonight," he said.

"You're my hero," she said, stepping back and opening the door wide.

"It's just tacos."

"There's no such thing as 'just tacos,'" Rachel said with a laugh.

Rachel had invited him to have dinner with Charli and her every night to help Charli get used to him and to start building their family unit. Rachel was a great cook, but she was also working full-time providing day care for special-needs kids, still unpacking their little house, and dealing with Charli, who wasn't exactly thrilled about the move to Boston. Alex figured that in a real family, the parents took turns with things like dinner. So here he was with tacos.

Rachel led the way down the hallway to the kitchen. "Charli! Your dad's here! Dinnertime!"

Alex wondered if he'd ever get used to the sharp twinge of emotion he felt in his chest every time he heard the word *dad* in relation to himself.

He hoped not.

He heard her footsteps coming from the living room and braced himself for the stronger twinge that always came when he first saw her. He also wasn't getting used to that.

Charli came around the corner. Her hair was stuck up under a pale-green stocking cap. She was wearing a pair of tan pants that had been cut off at the knee, the ragged ends still dangling. She wore black boots that went to about midcalf, and a white T-shirt. She had draped a long red scarf over her body from one shoulder to the opposite hip. She was also scowling.

The twinge was as sharp and real as every other time.

He'd never wanted kids. He'd understood early on that any female child of his would at least be a carrier for hemophilia. And Charli was. But more, she was a carrier who actually had symptoms of hemophilia. He hated that. He'd have done anything to change it. Except not have her. Now that he knew her, he couldn't imagine not having her. But he'd never pictured himself as a father and had had no idea that there was an emotion that was a combination of pride, protectiveness, joy, and fear and was so strong that it could take a man's breath away.

"Hey, Charli," he greeted her, resisting the urge to scoop her up and hug her.

He had yet to do more than touch the top of her head.

She was well behaved and friendly when he was around, but she was definitely not interested in hugs or cuddles from him. Yet. He knew it was too soon to expect that. But he held out hope.

"Hi." She gave him a little smile but then went right back to scowling at her mother.

She really was beautiful. She had Rachel's bright-blond hair, her nose, her face shape. But she had Alex's eyes. And the current stubborn set to her jaw definitely came from him.

"I need a black scarf," she told Rachel.

"I don't have a black scarf," Rachel said. "I think that one looks nice." She pulled the tacos from the bag and started distributing them among three plates.

"It doesn't look nice. It's red," Charli told her. "Piper wears black."

Alex could, in fact, verify that. He'd watched the *Galactic Renegades* movies featuring Piper more than any of the others, just because he knew Charli loved that character.

"You need a black scarf to dress up like Piper?" he asked.

Rachel shot him a look that clearly said, "Don't you dare offer to buy her a black scarf."

He and Rachel weren't a typical couple. They weren't in love. They hadn't raised Charli together for the first ten years of her life. But apparently he could read Rachel's looks already. He supposed that was something.

"I need a whole Piper outfit," Charli said, climbing up onto one of the stools that sat at the island in Rachel's kitchen. "But Mom says it's more creative to make it myself."

Awesome. He was already being torn between going along with Rachel's rules and wanting to please Charli. "I met a woman who makes costumes," he said, reaching for one of the plates. "I wonder if she could do Piper."

Rachel gave him a frown.

"We could have someone make a Piper costume?" Charli looked as if he'd just told her he knew someone who could make her a flying pony.

Okay, he hadn't actually met the woman who did costumes for the Super You class, but he'd seen her, and he knew how to get a hold of her. Of course that would require him to call or stop in at Active Imagination. And he wasn't sure that was a good idea.

"I think so," he said carefully. He tried to give Rachel a look that said, "No worries. I've got this."

Rachel's frown deepened. So his look hadn't gone through. Maybe they weren't that great at the wordless communication yet.

"That would be amazing!" Charli exclaimed.

*Amazing* was one of her favorite words, but so far Alex hadn't heard her use it in regard to something he'd done. It took only one time and he was addicted.

He grinned at her. "I'm glad you think so. Let me see what I can do."

What he could do was go to Maya Goodwin's studio and hire her friend to make the costume. That seemed simple enough. But he'd been around Maya for about an hour total, and he already knew that he shouldn't go to her studio. Because he'd want to keep going. And he couldn't do that.

He was not in a place to start something with Maya. Or anyone. The two females he needed to concentrate on were in this kitchen with him right now. Yes, Charli needed him. But so did Rachel. She'd raised his amazing daughter on her own while going to school and working. The least he could do was give her his time, and support, and attention, now that she was back in his life.

"I just really think it's more fun if you make the costume yourself," Rachel told Charli, handing her three tacos with the lettuce removed.

Alex made a note that Charli didn't like lettuce. At least on tacos. As he'd learned about strawberries the other day, her not liking them on top of yogurt did not mean she didn't like them in other ways. He'd been making a lot of notes—mental and actual—over the past couple of months.

"But this is red," Charli said with a sigh, dropping the scarf on the floor. She picked up a clump of cheese and ate it, seemingly devastated about having the wrong-colored scarf.

"Then maybe you can find something that's black that you can use instead of the scarf," Rachel said, giving Alex a look over Charli's head.

He understood that look too—"Leave it alone."

Alex diverted the conversation, making small talk with Rachel, listening raptly as Charli told them about school and an upcoming science project her class would be working on.

"Speaking of projects, I was hoping you'd help me with an art thing I want to do with the kids next Wednesday," Rachel told Charli, gathering up the taco wrappers and sauce packets from their dinner and sweeping them into the trash can. "I got a bunch of glitter glue on sale."

"Okay," Charli said with a shrug. "But Toby doesn't like glitter."

Rachel turned back, drying her hands on a dish towel. "He doesn't?"

Alex had been paying attention to—and actually inputting notes into his phone as soon as he got in the car every night about—the subjects Rachel and Charli talked about, along with Charli's food preferences, her favorite TV shows, and anything else he learned in his time with them. He knew that Toby was one of the kids Rachel babysat after school every day. He had cerebral palsy and was in a wheelchair full-time. He also didn't speak, but Charli insisted he communicated with her, and Rachel didn't seem to doubt it.

Alex hadn't met any of the four kids Rachel cared for. She had two for only a couple of hours after school, and two she had all day while their parents worked. They had a variety of diagnoses, but all had needs that made Rachel, with her nursing degree, a perfect caregiver.

He felt a familiar twinge of guilt. After their night together, he'd gone off to finish college and medical school. Rachel had gone off to have a baby alone, who she'd had to raise alone, who had then been diagnosed with a rare bleeding disorder that she'd had to manage alone. And still, today, she was a kind woman with a nursing degree who provided care for special-needs kids.

He really should fall in love with her.

Alex sighed. If only it were that easy.

"So what do you think Toby would like?" Rachel asked Charli.

"He wants to make swords," Charli told her.

"Swords." She shot Alex a look.

Charli nodded. "So we can have a sword fight."

Rachel sighed. "Is it Toby that wants that or you?"

Rachel had told Alex how great Charli was with the other kids. She played with them and read to them after school and helped her mom with some of the caregiving tasks, like snacks and washing them up when the pudding got all over. Alex was so in love with his sweet, big-hearted daughter. Rachel had done a great job.

This was all so complicated. He wanted to want Rachel. Clearly they'd had a physical attraction at one time. He remembered the sex being good. Being around her now was no hardship. Still, he felt nothing even close to the spark he'd felt for Maya Goodwin the moment he'd seen her—a total stranger dressed as a superhero at a mall.

But maybe over time he would fall for Rachel. Hell, people had made long-term relationships work based on less than he and Rachel had right now. And even if he didn't desire her and wasn't in love with her, he owed her. Big-time.

"I want to make swords and have sword fights," Charli confessed, climbing down from her stool. "But Toby does too." She crossed her arms, a stubborn look in her eyes. "He loves *GR* as much as I do. But when we play, he's Conner, and I'm Piper."

Conner was another of the new young heroes in the series. Alex was glad he'd bought the box set. And the fan guide. And the *Galactic Renegades* encyclopedia.

"Well, we can't make swords," Rachel said, again looking at Alex. "I don't think a day care is an appropriate place for that. And when you and Toby have your sword fights, you'll need to use imaginary ones. Promise. I don't want you pulling out long sticks or kitchen knives or something."

Alex felt a shudder go through him. He didn't want to think about a couple of kids swinging knives around and possibly cutting each other. That could be a devastating injury for anyone, but especially Charli. He cleared his throat. "I agree with your mother."

Rachel looked relieved, and he belatedly realized she'd been trying to get him to join the conversation. Yeah, they definitely needed to work on reading each other's looks.

"Nothing hard or sharp," he told Charli.

Charli sighed. She was nearly ten. She knew the risks. She just didn't heed them all the time. She thought her mother was overreacting. Alex knew exactly where Charli was coming from. And that she was wrong.

"So pillow fights," Charli said, pouting.

"I didn't even love your last pillow fight," Rachel said. "You were climbing all over the furniture, jumping off of things, and swinging hard enough that you were all knocking each other over."

Charli rolled her eyes and looked at Alex. "I can't even have pillow fights."

Alex lifted his brows. So she was suddenly comfortable enough to appeal to him for help winning an argument with her mother? He gave her a small headshake. Even he knew disagreeing with the mom in front of the kid was a no-go.

"Falling against a table and hitting your head would be a very dangerous situation," Rachel went on. "Being hit in the face with a pillow hard enough to bite your tongue or get a bloody nose is also very dangerous."

Charli threw her hands up theatrically, swiveled her

stool, and jumped to the floor. "I guess I'll just go look up arts and crafts and get used to a lot of glitter glue in my future," she said as she slumped from the room, the very picture of dejection. Or at least of put-on dejection.

Alex shook his head and looked at Rachel. "Wow. That was dramatic."

She laughed. "Get used to it. At least some of that was fake drama. She knew I'd say no to swords. There are times when it's all real drama, and she can get really loud about how mean I am."

"When has she gotten loud?" Alex asked.

"When I wouldn't let her play soccer with her friends. When I said she couldn't do gymnastics. When she couldn't take karate." Rachel wiped a paper towel over the countertop absently, even though the surface was clean.

His heart ached. "I'm sorry. I know it's tough."

She nodded. "One good thing about the move, even though she does not see it this way, is that we moved away from her friends who were getting to do all this cool stuff that she can't. It helps to feel like she's missing out because she moved instead of missing out because she can't do the stuff they do."

Alex fucking hated that Charli was going through that. He remembered it all too well.

"Alex—"

He knew what was coming.

"—you have to help me discourage this stuff. You know how she throws herself into things. Getting her a Piper costume means she'll be running and jumping around this house, making things into swords and pretending to take on the galaxy."

He blew out a breath. To date he'd gone along with 99 percent of Rachel's decisions. But he was about to put his foot down. He looked Rachel in the eye. "Rach, I respect the hell out of you. And I'll continue to defer to you on most of the parenting stuff. But I'm getting her a Piper costume. This is my first birthday with her, and I'm going to go overboard. This is your warning."

Rachel took a deep breath. "Fine. But you can't encourage this weapons fascination."

"I'm going to give her sword fighting lessons too."

Rachel's eyes widened. "Excuse me?"

He nodded. "We can't just constantly say, 'You can't do that' or 'Be careful' or 'No.' There are doctors for that. We're her parents. We need to at least try to help her find a way to do the things she wants to do."

Rachel's mouth actually dropped open. "And you, of all people, think our daughter, who has a bleeding disorder, should have a sword?"

"With modifications and treatment, she can do a lot of the things she wants to try," Alex said firmly. He had been thinking about it—among other things—since the mall demonstration.

"Alex..." Rachel was clearly having trouble wrapping her mind around it.

She was overprotective. He understood. He'd met many parents like that. There were a lot of things kids with hemophilia could do, but some activities were riskier than others, and parents had to be the ultimate decision-makers.

But he was one of Charli's parents and he wasn't budging on this. When he was growing up, his overprotective, anxious mother had made everything about his hemophilia. She'd told coaches, teachers, and his friends' parents all about it. She would tell strangers in the line at the grocery store. And every single time, people looked at him differently after they knew. His condition had been part of everything he tried growing up—or the reason he didn't get to try. He wasn't doing that to Charli. He would find a way to help his daughter do the things she loved.

"You have to trust me, Rachel," Alex told her, his voice low and even. He was trying to be reassuring, but he'd made up his mind. "I will help you raise our daughter. But you have to let me do things my way sometimes. I will do dinner, I will help with homework, I will take her to practices. And I will keep her safe. But she won't hear, 'You can't do that' from me."

Rachel looked at him, chewing the inside of her cheek. He got her hesitation. Rachel had always been Charli's only protector. Until now.

"I love her, Rach," he said. "Let me do this."

Finally she accepted the determination in his gaze. She nodded. "Okay. Fine. I trust you."

She wasn't thrilled, but he'd prove it was all okay. He'd never let anything happen to Charli.

"Thank you." That meant a lot to him.

Rachel made them coffee, and they headed into the living room together. It was about an hour until Charli's bedtime, and she usually worked on homework at the coffee table. If she didn't have any, or got it finished, they all watched TV until it was time to go upstairs. The routine had become well established over the past two months, but Alex was still amazed by how great it felt to sink into the corner of that overstuffed couch, stretch his arm along the back, and just be there. He would help with her homework or ask questions about the TV shows Charli liked. It seemed she enjoyed filling him in on the plots and characters, and he would ask questions just to hear her talk, not actually caring one bit about the sitcoms.

But tonight it felt different. It felt as if he was really a part of this now—a real part of Charli's life. He was giving input; he was making decisions; he was advocating for her. And he was going to make some of her dreams come true. That was being a dad.

He settled back as one of Charli's favorite shows started. It was a comedy about a young teenage girl and her best friends who ran a smoothie stand on a beach in California. Alex didn't think that the State of California would actually give a business license to a bunch of kids no older than fourteen, and it seemed to him that they were off having kooky adventures far more than they were actually at the smoothie stand, but Charli giggled throughout, and that was all he needed.

* * *

"Bring your hand up higher," Maya coached Sophie as they turned on the mat. They were facing each other, their weapons drawn. "When I swing up, you cut down, and it will look completely smooth."

Sophie huffed out a breath. "I thought I did that."

As the owner of a small theater and a playwright, Sophie knew the importance of practice, but she was also a fan of improvisation here and there for authenticity. And fun. Maya didn't worry about Sophie's ad-libbing. Maya's skills with the weapons they used for their workouts and performances were far beyond Sophie's. Still, the sai—the metal batons with one long prong and two short—were sharp.

"Hand higher, Soph," Maya said.

Sophie sighed and lifted her hand.

They went through the move again and then repeated the portion of the routine they had so far from the top.

"Then I think she should sidestep and thrust," Kiera said from the side, where she was sitting on the floor with her legs crisscrossed and the choreography they'd written on her lap.

"Okay," Maya agreed. "Then I'll act like she connected and stagger back, she can jump forward, we'll go to the floor, roll, I'll lose one of my sai, and she'll end up on top."

Kiera nodded and scribbled the notes down.

"You want to go through that part or go from the top?" Maya asked Sophie.

"From the top," Sophie said. "I can't believe I'm working up a sweat here."

Maya grinned. Sophie didn't like to sweat. Or breathe hard.

"You're barely glowing," Kiera told her from the sidelines.

Sophie pressed a palm to her forehead and withdrew it, showing them both that it was damp. "Sweating."

"I'll show you sweat, Soph," Rob said as he came into the studio. "How about you thrust and roll around with me for a while?"

They all laughed. Rob lived next door to them in the other unit in the old house Kiera had inherited from her grandmother. And he was only a friend.

"Thank you, no," Sophie said. "Sweating is overrated."

"Maybe you're not sweating right," Rob said with a wink as he dropped down next to Kiera.

Sophie sighed. "Actually, I barely remember sweating like that."

Maya laughed. And tried to keep her thoughts from going to the hot doctor from the mall. That had been happening with annoying regularity ever since she'd looked around the clothing store and found him gone.

It wasn't that she minded being attracted to him. He was good-looking, had stepped into the tumultuous situation to help, and had even gotten hurt doing it. He'd been amusing and mildly charming. But then he'd disappeared. Which had her more intrigued than she wanted to admit. Especially when Kiera had said, "All the best heroes disappear before the heroine can thank them. Spider-Man never sticks around."

Maya had been thinking the same thing.

It was silly and fanciful, but she appreciated silly and fanciful once in a while. It could be very therapeutic. Glancing around her studio now, she had to smile. She was a twenty-eight-year-old woman who spent at least two nights a week doing weapon work with her best friends in a room that was covered in framed superhero posters, and no less than one night a month with them around their dining room table making costumes, masks, and weapons—out of plaster and foam board, of course.

Fanciful was right up her alley. She fully embraced it. Ever since the injury that had taken her off the force, it had been a bit of a coping mechanism.

So if she wanted to think of the hot doctor as a superhero, she would.

"Arm up, Maya."

Maya looked up to find Sophie smiling at her with an eyebrow arched. Oh, she'd spaced out there in her daydream for a second. Oops.

She raised her hands, a sai in each. "Bring it."

Sophie brought her weapon down in a wide arc as planned, and they moved around the mat, turning, twisting, ducking, and swinging in a perfect pattern.

Until movement at the doorway to the main room caught Maya's eye and she glanced over.

Sophie sidestepped and thrust as written, but Maya didn't move fast enough to avoid the sharp tip of Sophie's sai. The point pierced the soft cotton of her tank and the skin along her side. It wasn't deep, but it definitely stung.

And bled.

"Maya!" Sophie dropped the sai and lunged for her. "Oh my God!"

Maya pressed her hand against her side. "I'm fine. It's no big deal."

"You said we wouldn't need protection tonight," Sophie scolded, planting her hands on her hips. "Dammit."

"We didn't need protection," Maya said about the thick leather vests they sometimes wore to practice when they were using things that could accidentally cause, well, blood and stuff.

"What happened?" Kiera was beside her, pushing Maya's hand out of the way and lifting Maya's shirt.

"I didn't move fast enough."

"Yeah, I noticed," Kiera said drily. She prodded the skin around what turned out to be a small cut. "But why? You knew it was coming."

The sound of someone clearing his throat made them all look toward the door. It was Rob. And he was pointing at...the hot doctor.

"That's why," Maya said.

"Oh." Kiera straightened, seemingly forgetting about Maya's injury completely. "Oh."

Sophie was also staring at him. "Is he the one—"

"He is," Maya interrupted, pushing between them on her way to where the doc was standing. "Hi," she said, stopping in front of him.

"Hi."

Wow, he was good-looking. In a totally not-at-all-her-type way. Sure, he had a little hero in him. He was a doctor, after all. A pediatrician even. What woman wouldn't pay at least a little attention to those green eyes and a love for kids?

Maya realized they were standing there just looking at each other as they had in the store two weeks ago. She glanced over her shoulder to find Rob, Kiera, and Sophie watching them with interest, and decided to find a little more privacy. She grabbed the doctor's wrist and pulled him down the hallway around the corner.

"You're a little grabby," he said as he followed her.

She looked up and grinned at his use of her words from the other day. And just him being in her studio. On purpose. "Sorry." She stopped and dropped her hold.

"Don't be." He didn't smile. He was frowning, in fact. "You're hurt. Again."

"You distracted me. Again." She pressed her shirt against her very minor wound that had, amazingly, stopped stinging.

He looked down at her sliced shirt. "Thought you said that doesn't happen."

"It doesn't." And she couldn't explain it now. Yes, he was good-looking. But for God's sake, she met good-looking guys like him every day. Okay, maybe every week. Well, once a month for sure. Probably.

"Sorry."

She didn't want him to be sorry. She didn't want him to be sorry for coming to see her. And she didn't want him to stop doing it. "How's your knee?" she asked.

He frowned again. "Better. Fine."

"Good." She waited. He'd come to her, so surely he'd tell her why if she gave him a chance. But she wasn't a patient person, so it was only about twenty seconds in before she asked, "What are you doing here?"

That seemed to pull him out of whatever thoughts had been going through his mind. "I'm here to sign up for a class."

Oh. That was almost as good as him being here to ask her out. Almost. "A class?"

"The Super You class," he clarified. "I need to know everything there is to know about superheroes, *Galactic Renegades*, and sword fighting."

"Well," she said slowly, "that class would cover some of it."

"So I'm here to sign up."

"But...you're not a kid," she said. "And you don't have a kid with you."

His lips curled at one corner again. "Is there an age limit on the classes? I didn't see that in the fine print."

No, because who over the age of twelve would want to dress up as a superhero and take a class with a bunch of kids? "I can honestly say this has never come up," she told him. "And you know that makes you sound kind of creepy, right?"

He chuckled. "And yet here you are in an empty hallway with me."

She lifted a shoulder. "I think I mentioned the distracting thing."

His smile didn't dim. "Yeah, tell me more about that."

Her lips twitched, but she stared him down. "How about I tell you that my combat skills don't always require a sharp blade or a big stick."

\* \* \*

Alex laughed. He liked Maya. The thought hit him directly in the gut.

Maya smiled brightly, and he admitted that he was intensely attracted too. Now fast attraction—that he'd experienced before. But it had been a long time since even that had happened.

"I'm Dr. Alex Nolan. I'm on staff at Boston Children's Hospital. I'm on their website if you want to look me up."

Maya suddenly frowned. "I can't believe I didn't think of that."

"Of what?"

"Googling pediatricians and finding out who you are after the mall the other day," Maya said.

Alex raised an eyebrow. "Wouldn't that be a little creepy?"

"Probably," she agreed. "Maybe that's why I didn't do it."

He laughed. "Well, to further decrease the creep factor,

I do have a kid," he said. "A daughter. Charlotte. We call her Charli. She'll be ten next month. She's very into superheroes, *GR*, and swords, and I know nothing about any of that. I liked the demonstration at the mall and thought I'd come check out your studio."

"So you're wanting to sign her up," Maya said with a nod. "Okay, not creepy at all."

"Uh…" Alex knew this was going to sound strange. "Actually, I want to take the class myself."

Maya frowned. "These classes won't teach you about superheroes exactly," she said. "They are kind of a combination of stage fighting and martial arts and self-esteem workshops."

"I know." He'd been on the website. Which was how he'd found out more about the studio. And where he'd stared at Maya's photo before looking up more about her on the Internet. Which was how he'd found out that her classes had won some local awards, she'd been a brilliant cop—who had not, incidentally, been fired for beating someone up—and she regularly blogged about superheroes and their fandom and the psychology of that fandom. He'd bookmarked her page immediately.

He could learn a lot about superheroes and *GR* from the movies and Internet fan sites, but what he needed to know was the why. Why were superheroes so popular? What was with the obsession that pulled even people like Maya in? Her blog was a gold mine. Now all he needed was to learn the sword techniques.

"And the things you do in class sound like the perfect bonding activity for Charli and me. I'll take the class and then go home and teach her."

Maya looked puzzled. "Why not just bring her to class?"

"She..." He swallowed. Charli would love Maya. Hell, if she saw Maya with those pointy weapon things, she'd want to be Maya.

But Alex had seen Maya only twice, and he'd already witnessed her get hit with a bo staff, punched in the ribs, and cut with some kind of sharp hand weapon. Which reminded him that she'd been bleeding.

He looked down, but the bleeding had already slowed or stopped. Which was what happened when a person with normal blood got cut. But Charli didn't have normal blood. She didn't bleed faster, but she would bleed longer—because of the genetic mutation he had passed on to her.

He'd told Rachel that Charli should be able to try whatever she wanted. But he'd also told her he'd keep Charli safe. If Charli took classes here, he would have to fill Maya and her staff in on the hemophilia and precautions and treatment...

No. In his experience, the words *bleeding risk* made people nervous. Maya would look at Charli differently. She'd start treating Charli differently. She'd think about Charli differently. He wanted the weapons work to be fun. Safe, but fun. It could be that way only if the person teaching her knew all about hemophilia and didn't get overly anxious about it, and if that person could make the necessary adjustments without Charli even knowing there were adjustments to be made. Obviously the only person who could teach her was him.

"She has some special needs," he said, cringing a little as he said it, knowing that Maya might easily jump to conclusions that were not at all correct. But it didn't matter what she thought. This was the right thing for Charli.

But Maya didn't even blink. "Okay," she said. "I understand. Maybe..." But she trailed off while watching him thoughtfully.

"Maybe what?" he asked.

"Maybe I could teach you and your daughter a private Super You class."

He was surprised at her offer, but more—he was tempted. Which meant he had to say no. The timing for meeting a gorgeous, intriguing woman couldn't have been worse. "I think a class with lots of other people, especially kids, would be better."

"Why?"

Maya was direct. He liked that. And he could return the favor. "Because you look just as good in workout pants as you do in leather."

Her eyes widened in surprise for just a beat before her smile widened. "And that's a problem?"

"It is when I'm trying to give all of my extra time and attention to my daughter."

She studied him for a moment. "Okay," she finally said with a nod. "And once you see the class, if you change your mind, she's always welcome."

Alex relaxed. "Thanks."

"You're not going to feel funny taking a class with a bunch of kids?"

"I love kids," he told her.

"What about the tights and cape?"

"Tights and cape?" Alex repeated.

"The costume," she said with a nod.

"Thought the participants all helped create their own character," he said, realizing she was messing with him.

"They do."

"Well, there's no way in hell I would create a character that would wear tights."

Maya's gaze wandered over him, from head to toe, before she said, "Too bad."

# CHAPTER THREE

$\mathcal{I}$s your costume under your clothes?"

Maya felt a smile tug at her lips as she watched Alex look down at the eight-year-old boy who had just asked the question. She'd really been hoping Alex would show up for the Super You class, but when he'd walked in almost an hour ago, dressed in a suit and tie, she'd actually caught her breath. Then he'd searched the room, as if looking for something, and when his gaze landed on her and his mouth curved into a big smile, she felt her stomach flip.

"No," Alex told the boy. "Why?"

Ethan inched closer to Alex and lowered his voice. "It's okay. I wear mine under my clothes at school sometimes."

Maya was making her way around the room, checking her students' technique as they practiced the bo staff spins she'd just taught. But she lingered in the area where Alex and Ethan were paired up. Not only had he showed up for class, but he'd taken his place with the other students as if he didn't tower over them and weren't getting amused and puzzled looks from everyone in the room.

"It helps me remember my superpower," Ethan told Alex.

Alex merely nodded as if that made total sense. "What's your power?" Alex asked.

"I'm funny. I make people laugh."

Alex grinned at him. "That's a really great power to have."

"Yeah?" Ethan asked.

"Definitely. Laughter is the best medicine. And I should know. I'm a doctor."

Ethan's eyes widened. "You are? So your superpower is healing people."

Alex's grin dimmed slightly, and Maya felt a twinge in her chest. That was weird.

But Alex said, "I am. And I'm still working on that power."

Maya didn't realize she'd stopped stock-still in the middle of two other students until one asked, "You okay, Maya?"

She glanced down, shaking herself out of the hot-doctor-induced daze. "Yeah. Yes, I'm fine. Sorry." She got out of their way so they could keep spinning. And avoided looking in Alex's direction again.

Damn. Distracting. But watching him interact with little kids was making her melt, and then there had been that little moment where his smile faltered...She shook her head and glanced around. She found Jill, one of the studio's best instructors and a child psychologist, standing with Ben, watching the class and talking. She made her way over to them around the spinning and swinging staffs.

"It's stupid that paper beats rock," Ben said.

Jill rolled her eyes. "I don't make the rules. Stupid or not, you lost."

"Let's do best three of five."

"No way. I beat you three-for-three ten seconds ago," Jill told him.

"What are you guys talking about?" Maya moved to stand next to Jill and turned to face the room. And her eyes immediately went to where Alex was now talking to Ethan and two more little boys, Jacob and Matthew.

"We did rock-paper-scissors to see who gets to interview Alex," Jill said. "I totally won."

Maya frowned at her. "Interview Alex?"

"Yeah, we need to do his character interview," Jill said.

"I called dibs," Ben said, "but then Jill made me do the rock-paper thing."

"You called dibs? I think the little kids are rubbing off on you," Maya told him. "Besides, no one's interviewing him." But she wasn't fully focused on the conversation. Alex was distracting her. Still. What were they talking about over there? They were supposed to be practicing the bo staff stuff.

"Why aren't we interviewing him?" Jill asked.

"Yeah, he's a student in class," Ben said with a chuckle. Apparently he was still vastly amused that Alex was actually participating.

"He's a grown man," Maya said. "He's doing this so he can teach his daughter."

"But you said he wanted to bond with his daughter, right?" Jill asked. "This is perfect. He can do the interview with us, and then it will give him some talking points to discuss with her."

That sounded good. Probably. Maya wasn't sure. She was straining to hear what Alex and the kids were talking about.

"So you pick. Which of us do you want interviewing Alex?" Ben asked.

Maya looked at them both. "You really want to interview him?"

Ben laughed. "Do I want to spend an hour one-on-one talking to the first guy to have your panties twisted up in forever? Hell yeah."

Maya ignored the panties comment. She didn't want Ben interviewing Alex. Ben would not keep the topic to superheroes. She glanced at Jill. "Why do you want to interview him?" But she already knew. Jill was young, cute, and single. So was Alex. And Maya felt the distinct urge to call dibs on him. Maybe the little kids were rubbing off on her too.

"Seriously? I think my ovaries swooned the minute he picked Ethan to be his partner," Jill said.

Yeah, that had been a good moment. Maya caught herself just before she sighed. Sighed, for God's sake. Over a guy. But it really had been sweet. She didn't know if Alex knew that Ethan felt left out a lot of the time at school, but when he'd turned to the little boy and said, "Want to be my partner?" Ethan had lit up as if Alex had just announced he was Santa Claus. And Maya had definitely felt...something. Could ovaries actually swoon? She didn't have a better explanation for the feeling. She'd never felt it before, that was all she knew.

"Please let me do the interview," Jill said. "A hot

doctor who plays superheroes with little kids?" She sighed. Just the way Maya almost had.

"No. No one's interviewing him."

Two more kids—a nine-year-old girl, Abby, and another boy, Carson—had joined Alex and his little fan club. What were they talking about?

"Not even you?" Ben asked.

"I don't do interviews," Maya said. She let Shannon, the grade school counselor, Ben, and Jill handle those. But she really would love to know who Alex Nolan's favorite superhero was and why. "Be right back," Maya muttered to her employees, and headed for Alex and the kids who were being drawn to him like bees to honey.

"Have you ever touched a real brain?" Matthew asked Alex.

He nodded. "Oh yeah. Cut one up even."

Six pairs of eyes widened at his answer, including Maya's.

"In medical school. On a cadaver," he added.

"What's a cadaver?" Matthew asked.

"A dead body." Alex delivered the answer with a straight face, but Maya could see that he was enjoying himself.

"Whoa!" Matthew exclaimed. It seemed he spoke for the whole group.

"Have you touched an eyeball?" Ethan asked. "Does it feel like the gummy eyeballs?"

Alex shook his head. "No. More firm than that. Like a grape."

"Cooool," Ethan breathed.

Maya saw the corner of Alex's mouth twitch, and her crush got a little bigger.

"Do you know that there are two hundred and six bones in the body?" Abby asked.

"I did," Alex told her.

"I broke my arm one time," Jacob was quick to say.

"I broke my leg one time," Matthew said.

"If you stab someone in the heart, will they die right away?" Carson asked.

"Okay!" Maya interrupted. "I don't see anyone getting better at bo spins over here."

The kids all looked at least slightly sheepish. Alex did not. The kids went back to their spots. But not before Jacob called to Alex, "My uncle got his whole entire finger chopped off one time!"

Alex gave him a thumbs-up.

Maya propped her hand on her hip. "You're distracting to more than just me, it seems, Dr. Nolan."

He grinned. "Sorry."

She laughed. "No, you're not."

"We need to get to practice," Alex said to Ethan, "before we get in trouble with the teacher."

"You're already in trouble. I'm going to need to see you after class," she told him, her heart flipping a little at the idea of keeping him after hours. Alone.

He gave a dramatic sigh and looked at Ethan. "Great. Now I'm going to be late for dinner."

Ethan gave him a sympathetic look, and Maya had to stifle another laugh.

They finished class ten minutes later, and Maya stood by the door as she always did, saying good-bye to each kid. Alex brought up the rear.

"Detention?" he asked.

"Something like that," she said with a nod.

The door closed behind the last kid and her parents, and Maya glanced around. Her staff was still in the building, cleaning up, and Kiera would be by with her boyfriend, Zach, soon. They were going to work on some hand-to-hand combat moves Kiera was teaching him.

But Maya had a few minutes alone with Alex. She turned to face him. "You have a fan club on the very first night. Impressive."

"They're kids," he said, but his smile said that he'd enjoyed the class.

"I'm not a kid, and I'm impressed with you."

"Stop," he said, shaking his head.

"Can't," she told him honestly.

He watched her for a moment. Then he took a deep breath and blew it out. "Thanks for class."

"You're leaving?" she asked.

"Yeah."

"Chicken."

He nodded. "A little."

"Why?" She really wanted to know.

"You're ... tempting."

"Good." She gave him a big smile.

"Not good," he said. "Maya, I—"

"We haven't done your interview yet," she said before he could complete his thought.

He paused. "My interview?"

"Your character interview. You're a student in the class." She shrugged. "You deserve the whole experience."

He studied her eyes, not saying yes, but also not saying no immediately.

"And if you're going to be so distracting in class, we might have to talk about the private-class thing again," she added.

"I didn't mean to distract the kids," he said, with another of those grins that told her he'd had a great time being the center of the kids' attention. "And they'll get over the thing about me touching dead bodies and guts and brains."

Maya felt her smile growing. "Yeah, well, I wasn't talking about you distracting the kids."

His eyes heated slightly, and she knew she was right to push this. He was interested, and Lord knew she was interested. She at least wanted to get to know him better.

"Let's have dinner," she suggested. "I can do your interview, and we can talk about some of the things Charli's into." He wanted to know more about superheroes and *Galactic Renegades*, after all. She was doing him a favor here.

"I can't have dinner with you," he said.

But there was a note of regret in his voice that made her unwilling to give up.

"It's just dinner, Alex."

"It wouldn't be just dinner."

The combination of his words and the way he said them made her forget what she'd been about to say. And how to breathe for a second. Yeah, she was definitely going to go for this. "Fine. We'll stay here and order pizza. My friends will be working out right down the hall."

"Chaperones?" he asked with a half smile.

"Right. That way no one will take their clothes off while we talk."

Just one of his eyebrows went up. "I think I'll be able

to keep my clothes on while we eat pizza and talk about *Galactic Renegades*."

She shrugged. "Then that makes one of us."

He moved in closer. She wasn't sure he was even aware of it, but suddenly he was a few inches into her personal space. "*GR* and pizza get you going?"

Maya had to swallow before she could answer. "Yeah. But it was compounded by how sweet you were with the kids and the way you handled your staff." She realized a second too late how that sounded. "Your bo staff. Of course."

The corner of his mouth quirked. "Of course."

"Your hands were great...I mean, I'm not used to watching such big hands on the sticks...Your handling was..." She stopped, took a breath, and was finally able to say, "You did well in class." But her cheeks felt a little warm. She hadn't thought she was capable of blushing.

"Thanks. I like a woman who can tell me exactly what she wants from me."

Maya heard the humor in his voice, and she rejoiced inside that he was flirting back.

"So my friends will be here to be sure I behave," she told him. "Which is what you seem to want." But given the slightest hint of permission to misbehave...

Again regret flickered in his eyes. "I wish I could—" He stopped and clenched his jaw for a moment. Then he said, "Charli's mom was a one-night stand. Eleven years ago. Rachel brought Charli to meet me two months ago. I'm behind on...everything...fatherly. I'm trying to catch up as fast as I can. I can't get distracted. Charli deserves the best of me."

Wow, there was a lot of information in those few

sentences. But two things were clear to Maya right away: Alex needed her help even more than she'd thought. And she liked him even more now. His love for his daughter was so apparent that it made Maya ache a little.

Okay, three things were clear—Alex might be attracted to her but he wasn't going to act on that.

She nodded. "Got it. And clearly you have to stay for pizza. You need a crash course, and I'm the perfect person to teach you all about the things Charli loves."

He didn't respond for several long seconds, but finally he said, "I'll text Charli's mom and let her know I won't be there for dinner tonight."

"Great."

He chuckled softly. "Do you always get your way?"

She smiled up at him. "Oh, Alex, this is your way. I'd have you down shooting tequila and dancing with me at Ricki's if it was my way." As soon as she'd said it, she realized she was still pushing. Kind of. She couldn't seem to help it. *Back off. Teach the guy about* GR *and stop thinking about his big hands on the staff…and all the other things you'd like to see his hands on…* She cleared her throat. "Don't worry, Alex. I'm doing this for Charli too."

"You are?"

"Of course. She's a fellow *GR* lover. I need to be sure her nerdy interests are fully nurtured."

Alex gave her a smile that made her stomach flip. "I get it. You're trying to increase your numbers."

"My numbers?"

"The number of beautiful geeky girls in the world."

Maya laughed. "Yes. That's one reason."

"Well, thank you," he said. "Charli is—" He broke off,

as if it was hard to explain what he wanted to say. "I've been working with kids for a long time. But I don't get to really fix things for them very often. Charli is mine. With her I can actually make things better. Some things, anyway."

Oh wow, yeah, she definitely wanted to take her clothes off with this guy. It was good her friends would be here, for sure.

"That sounds pathetic, probably," he said.

Maya shook her head quickly and made her mouth move—and not say, "I've never been so turned on in my life." "Actually, that," she said, pointing her finger at his chest, "is the other reason I'm doing this."

"Why?"

"You."

Maya shouldn't have been surprised when Alex took a hold of her finger and pressed her hand against his chest. There had been chemistry zinging between them since the first second she'd seen him standing in the crowd at the mall two weeks ago. But she was surprised that he touched her without hesitation. And there wasn't one thing creepy about it.

Dang, his chest was nice and hard. And hot. Her palm was warm and tingly.

The rest of her was pretty warm and tingly too, as a matter of fact.

"Thank you," he said. Sincerely. No flirtation.

She found that even more tempting.

"You're welcome."

She should probably ask Alex to produce some proof of this daughter he claimed to have. But she knew he wasn't lying. There had been something in his eyes when he talked about her that was impossible to fake. It was a combination of love and panic that she'd only ever seen in parents.

Besides, she simply couldn't waste a single second of time with a guy who looked like this, made her feel like this, and wanted to know all about one of her favorite topics. Because seriously, once he got her going on the Avengers, she might never see him again.

"Okay, let me change and tell everyone what's going on." She pulled her hand away and her brain started functioning again. "Do you like Jerry's pizza?"

"Love it." His gaze swept over her from head to toe.

"What?" She smoothed her hand down the front of her tank.

"Just taking in the view before you change."

She felt her body heat.

This was not just about superheroes. No matter how much either of them thought it should be.

Still, she headed to the locker room to change clothes. Maya pulled her clothes out of her locker with a sigh. All she had with her were jeans and a white World of Leokin tank top. World of Leokin was actually Kiera's obsession, and it wasn't about superheroes—per se. It was a video game. But the characters used awesome weapons, and Maya didn't mind an occasional visit to the online world.

She stepped out of her yoga pants and ran a hand through her hair, wishing she didn't look as if she'd been planning to hang out at home with her roommates tonight. But hell, she'd been dressed in purple leather and face paint when Alex had first met her. The jeans and tank were fine. She pulled her workout top off and had just pulled the clean tank over her head when Kiera and Sophie swept into the room.

"You should start with Marvel and then go to DC," Kiera said of the two most popular comic book worlds, where the best-known and most beloved superheroes came from.

"I didn't even know you were here," Maya said.

"Yeah, you were a little preoccupied," Kiera said with a wink.

She definitely had been. There was no sense in denying it.

"And you were eavesdropping?" Maya asked, not even a bit upset... or surprised.

"Of course we were," Sophie said.

Of course they were. The girls had the kind of friendship that automatically required keeping each other informed of all huge, amazing occurrences—when their favorite bakery brought back its seasonal lemon-blueberry bars, when fabric and foam board went on sale at one of their favorite hobby stores, when a kid in one of Maya's classes did something they hadn't been able to do before, when one of Sophie's plays got a good review, when one of Kiera's game graphics won an award... and when they developed huge, crazy crushes on hot guys they had nothing in common with.

"He wants to know about *Galactic Renegades* too," Maya said.

Kiera smiled. "One date won't be enough."

It wasn't a date. But Maya didn't feel like pointing that out. Because it kind of felt like a date, and if she could spend more time with him after tonight, she was just going to enjoy it.

She sighed. "He's a dad," she told her friends.

Sophie's smile was bright. "You love dads."

"No, I love kids."

"You love kids. But you also love dads," Kiera said.

Okay, she did. Maya was fascinated with dads and their interactions with their children. She'd been raised in a loving home with two parents, but both of her parents were women. She hadn't had a dad of her own, so she knew very well that a kid could grow up and turn out fine without a dad in the picture. But she found the dad-and-kid relationship interesting. And it wasn't as if she were looking for a guy with kids. But being a good parent automatically elevated a person's status in her opinion, and if a guy was a single dad, yes, that made him more attractive to her.

Now not only to meet one who was trying to get involved in something that interested his daughter, but for it to be superheroes? Alex Nolan could have had a hunchback and bad breath, and she still would have liked him. Because it was clearly way out of his wheelhouse, but he was trying anyway.

She almost wished he did have bad breath. But no, he'd smelled damn good in every way.

Not that it mattered. Alex wasn't looking for a woman who could get him into the special edition room at the local comic book store or who could write intelligent but controversial blog posts about how comic book writers have the best grasp of human psychology of any writers. Then again, he'd been pretty clear that he wasn't looking for a woman, period.

But that was fine. Maya really preferred hanging out with guys who already knew all about the backstory of the Winter Soldier and who appreciated the nuances of Black Widow's complex character.

"He's staying for pizza. I'm going to give him a crash course in superheroes and then send him on his way," Maya said.

"For tonight," Kiera said.

Maya shrugged. "We'll see." She wanted to see him again, and she hadn't even had a full conversation with him.

"Well, we're going to hang around," Kiera told her. "Zach's on his way over, and Rob might swing by."

Maya rolled her eyes. Of course Rob would swing by. She was sure Kiera and Sophie had told Rob the same thing they'd told Zach…*Maya has a guy here!* All her friends would be here within thirty minutes.

But she was glad they were going to hang around. Not because she was afraid Alex might do something to her. Because she was afraid she might do something to him.

Sophie gave her a smile. "Don't look so worried. It's pizza and superheroes. You're an expert in both. Just have fun."

"You think?" Maya asked, wondering if her friends realized how drawn to Alex she was. If they did, they would know how unusual that was. Even the guys who were her type hadn't been doing it for her lately.

She gauged her interest in a guy and her engagement in the relationship based on one criteria—would she rather be with him than at the studio? She hadn't been able to answer yes to that with the past four or five guys she'd gone out with.

"He was all Captain America for you the other day," Kiera reminded her. "Enjoy it."

"He was not." Maya frowned. She didn't need saving. She was quite proud of that fact. She was the saver. That was part of who she was. So it shouldn't matter at all that Alex had stepped in the other day. It should probably even irritate her that he had assumed she needed help.

But it wasn't working that way. Being saved didn't totally suck all the time.

Kiera laughed. "He so was."

"Yeah, well, you know Peter Parker is more my style. I like the wounded-hero thing," Maya said.

Kiera and Sophie both laughed at that.

"You say that all the time," Kiera told her, "but we know you. You totally go for the good guy with the moral compass pointed due north and the unwavering loyalty."

Maya shook her head. "Peter is more complex. He has the constant struggle between the easy way and the hard way. He's—"

"I know," Kiera said. "I've read your blog posts. But I still think you like Cap best." She gave Maya a big smile.

Sophie leaned in to give Maya a hug. "You can like whoever you want. But make sure you add Alex to that list, okay?"

Maya sighed. "Already done."

Kiera, the newly-in-love one of the bunch, beamed at that. "Yes, have fun," she said. "Definitely."

Maya narrowed her eyes. "This is kind of like when we insisted that Zach was the perfect one to keep an eye on you after your concussion, right?"

"If it is like that," Kiera said, "run, don't walk, to that guy."

Maya still couldn't get over the glow she saw in her

longtime friend when her boyfriend, hot EMT Zach, was around. Or on her mind, for that matter.

Maya felt a little flutter of butterflies in her stomach when she thought that Alex could maybe make her glow. That was crazy. She'd just met him, and maybe most of all, she didn't have butterflies. Ever. She had nerves of steel. Maybe she was just hungry.

But when she walked out of the locker room and saw Alex sitting on the bench at the end of the hallway, she felt that same little tickle. And when he looked up from his phone and gave her a big, slow grin, she suddenly knew exactly what butterflies felt like.

She didn't hate it. She didn't love it either. But it reminded her of the humming she got in her bones before an exhibition or competition. It helped her focus and made her anticipate what was coming next. That humming meant that what she was about to do was important and she was going to give it her all.

She took a breath, smiled back at Sophie and Kiera, and then headed for Alex. "Want a tour before the pizza gets here?"

"Sure."

That deep voice. She sucked in a breath and told herself the jumping in her nerve endings would go away.

He got to his feet, and she forced herself to watch his face rather than the stretch of his long legs or his torso unfolding in front of her. She loved that he was over six feet tall and had big hands and feet and was trim and hard, but she also loved his voice and his smile, and frankly, the dad thing was actually hot. Maybe not to all women, but it really worked for her.

She started down the hallway toward the classrooms.

Away from the front studio and all her friends. So if he wanted to push her up against the wall and . . .

Maya made herself stop that thought before it went too far. No pushing anyone up against anything.

"The kids also learn actual fighting? Like what you were demonstrating at the mall?"

She nodded. "Yes. But it's really more of a performance class, like a dance or gymnastics class."

"So the other person facing you knows what you're going to do at any moment."

"Right."

"So when you got hit in the shoulder—that wasn't planned?"

She smiled. "Um, no. I was . . . distracted, remember?"

His grin said he most definitely remembered.

"Stop looking smug," she told him.

"But I'm feeling smug."

She shook her head but couldn't stop smiling. "Are you hungry?"

"No."

"Then here." She crossed the room to the rack of bo staffs and took two down. She tossed one to Alex, who caught it easily. "Put your staff up like this."

He did, still grinning . . . and looking smug.

She put her hands up in the same position he had his in. "You learned the spins earlier, but I'm thinking we can advance you a little faster than the rest of the class."

"Special treatment?" he teased.

"Yep. Let's start with basic movements and footwork."

"Okay, Supergirl, show me your stuff."

"Just mimic my moves," she said. "Keep watching me."

"Not a problem."

She concentrated on the first two basic moves she wanted to show and began moving her hands, talking him through her footwork and what she was doing with the stick and how he needed to move to block her. He was an apt student, executing each move perfectly.

"Okay, good," she told him. "Now we'll add more body to it. Don't look away from my hands, but try to be aware of the rest of my body at the same time."

"Again, definitely not a problem."

She tried to fight the smile this time but didn't quite win. He might not want to be interested or to get more involved, but he was attracted.

Maya moved back, then forward, from side to side, and Alex followed, seemingly easily.

"You're a fast learner," she praised him a few minutes later.

"I'm raptly interested in the subject."

She didn't ask if he meant the staff moves or her moves. He was also very distracting. Still. She made him repeat the pattern again and again, acutely aware of his body, the heat and hardness there behind the cotton of his shirt as his muscles bunched and lengthened.

"It really is like dancing," he said.

She nodded. "It is." It certainly felt like it to her right now. It had all the sensuality of dancing with someone for the first time; being fully aware of his body and the way it moved with hers made her even more aware of her body—and the fact that she was warmer than she should be and her heart was beating faster than it should for such a simple routine. Their sticks were the only things actually touching, but she felt a connection zipping between them.

They continued to move for a few minutes. Then a few more. Maya hesitated to stop. Being this close to Alex, moving together, sharing this moment—she didn't want it to end. But she finally dropped her arms and shook them out.

Alex did the same and gave her a smile. He seemed to be having a good time.

That was good. She could never share a pizza with a guy who didn't think a bo was at least kind of cool.

# CHAPTER FOUR

Okay, so let's see how routine these moves are now," Maya said. "We're going to try having a conversation while doing the spins and blocks."

"Alright."

She raised her arms again and was proud that she didn't even grimace as her left shoulder protested. Alex mimicked the position, and they started the pattern over.

"So, what's one thing you want to know from me?" she asked as he blocked her first strike.

"What happened to your arm?"

She was surprised by the question only because she'd been expecting something more along the lines of "So what's the deal with Iron Man and the Hulk?" "My arm? I thought we were going to talk superheroes."

"I want to do that too, but you asked what I wanted to know and that was the first thing that came to mind," he said. "If you don't want to talk about it, I completely understand. It's none of my business."

"I don't mind talking about it," she said honestly. She talked about it a lot. To every class of kids she taught, if nothing else. She'd never made an effort to hide her scars. She'd earned every one of them.

"You're sure?" Alex asked with a slight frown.

"Completely. It's no secret."

"Okay, so what happened?"

She blocked his staff and stopped the routine. "Maybe we need pizza for this." And she needed to rest her arm. Dammit. She hated that. She didn't let it slow her down, but she also didn't love the bags of ice and ibuprofen tablets that were a nightly routine so she could sleep.

He regarded her seriously for a moment, then gave a nod. "Pizza it is," he agreed.

They put the staffs away and headed for the front. On the desk was a box of pizza that Maya knew her friends had left for her. They were all in the main studio, which was in a direct line of sight with the front desk area. But they were separated by about thirty yards of space, and Sophie and Rob were watching Kiera and Zach spar with swords.

Maya went to the minifridge behind the desk and pulled out two bottles of water. She handed one to Alex as she pushed the rolling desk chair toward him. She got up on the desk and sat with her legs crisscrossed, facing him. She put the pizza between them.

Alex grabbed a slice and sat back, crossing an ankle over his knee. "Okay, story time. And don't leave anything out. I have a strong stomach."

"I suppose that helps with the doctor thing, huh?"

"Most of the cases I see don't involve a lot of blood

and guts." He bit into his slice and chewed for a moment. "Tell me about your arm."

*Tenacious.* That definitely seemed like a good word to assign to Alex. He had moments when he let his grin loose or said something funny or flirtatious. But underlying all of that was a sense of... intensity. As if he was taking everything very seriously and was fully focused on every detail. Something about being the focus of his attention made her feel... something new she wasn't sure how to describe.

"Before I started Active Imagination, I was a cop," Maya told him.

"You said something about that at the mall."

She smiled and nodded. "I was a cop for five years after I got my criminal justice degree at Boston University."

"I'm even more turned on now."

Maya gave a surprised laugh. She really liked knowing he was turned on. But she tried not to show that she was melting on the inside. "Because of the handcuffs?"

He gave her a heart-stopping grin. "I'm more of a handcuffer than a handcuffee."

Oh boy. For some reason she could see that. He didn't come off as arrogant or domineering, but he gave the definite impression of someone who liked control. Never had that been appealing, even when she'd dated cops who were, no question, dominant types who knew their way around restraints.

But with Alex Nolan? After knowing him for a grand total of three and a half hours, including the time at the mall? She could get into that. Captain America would be hot with handcuffs. The thought flashed, unbidden, through her mind. Crap.

But it was the good-guy thing, just as Kiera had said. A good guy had to be really into a woman and know she trusted him to get to the handcuff point.

"It's the confidence that's so attractive," he went on, more seriously now. "The bravery and dedication. And the whole 'To Protect and To Serve' thing. You never know what's around the next corner, but you go anyway."

Oh, they were talking about her being a cop. Right. For a second there she'd gotten caught up in the idea of red-white-and-blue handcuffs and Alex kneeling over her in a tight blue shirt with a big white star on the chest.

Maya had to admit she was surprised, and impressed, by his assessment of a job she'd dreamed of doing and loved for far too short a time. "Thank you," she told him sincerely.

"So why did you leave the force?" he asked.

"My arm."

He still didn't change his casual posture, but she could see that he was completely into their conversation. "What happened?"

"My partner and I were called to the scene of a bad motor vehicle accident. Several cars. High speed. Lots of crumpled metal. Lots of injuries. One car, right in the middle of it all, had been hit front, back, and both sides. It looked like . . . I can't even describe it. It was barely recognizable as a car." Maya could see every detail, still, of that accident scene. The car she was talking about had been blue. The driver's shirt had been yellow. But the woman hadn't been behind the wheel—she had been lying next to it in a huge pool of blood. Maya swallowed. She'd had nightmares about that accident scene for months after.

"Maya."

The soft, deep voice pulled her back to the present. She looked up to see Alex watching her with concern.

She gave him what she was sure was a wobbly smile. "I'm sure there are things from medical school or residency or something that you just can't shake, that will always stick with you."

Again it took a moment for him to answer. He slowly nodded. "There are things almost weekly from my practice that I can't shake."

Pediatrics. She supposed it wasn't all cute cherub babies and little kids with tonsillitis. "Do you work in an outpatient office?" she asked.

He nodded. "I also have privileges at the hospitals."

"Do you do surgery?"

"No. I spend most of my time in research."

"What kind of research?"

"Genetics."

She thought about that. "Because you see kids with conditions that are genetic sometimes, right?"

"All the time."

The answer was simple, his voice a little tight. She looked closer at him. "All the time?"

"That's all I do," he said. "I work with children with genetic conditions."

There was something about the way he said it that made her pause. He didn't sound or seem proud or excited about his work, but he did seem...determined.

"That's amazing stuff," she said. "You help families through some really tough early stages, I bet. It must be really fulfilling."

"I don't get to fix anything," he said.

His mouth was a grim line, but his jaw and his eyes

definitely still had her thinking *determined. Staunch. Stoic.* He'd said something about not fixing his patients before and that being able to make things better for Charli was important to him.

"It's not like I get to see the kids get over their condition. It's not like the chicken pox," he went on.

No, she supposed it wasn't. "There must be a reason you do it, though." *Don't say money, please don't say money.*

"Someone needs to do it," he said after another of those pauses. "The kids and their families need and deserve the help and support. The more research I can participate in, the sooner we can get advances into the clinics. Into my clinic."

*Strong willed.* That was the term she'd been searching for.

She could see obstinacy in him—in the set of his jaw, in his dark eyes, in the way he held himself, in the way he measured his words. And the idea that his earnestness was being channeled toward making kids with chronic genetic conditions better made her feel everything she'd felt watching him with Ethan, times a thousand.

This wasn't the smiling, flirtatious guy she'd seen glimpses of, but there was something about this serious man that made other parts of her hum with awareness. Like her brain, which recognized the intellect he must have to work in such a challenging field. And her heart, which felt a kinship with him and his work.

So she wasn't saving the world from disease and genetic mutations. She was still helping kids, cheering for them, focusing her time and energy into making them better from the time they stepped into her studio to the time they left. Even if it was just from smiling bigger, laughing harder, or knowing someone cared, every kid left Active Imagination with more than they'd come in with. She was completely stubborn about that.

Maya took a long drink from her water bottle and set her slice of pizza to the side. She wiped her hands and then linked her fingers together in her lap.

"I was helping at the scene," she said, continuing her story. She'd told it a hundred times, but she always made herself really think about what she was saying. That accident had changed a lot of lives forever, and she never wanted to get to where it was just another story. "We helped rescue three people from their cars. All the survivors were loaded into ambulances and on their way to the hospital. They were towing the vehicles out of the way. It felt like things were getting taken care of. Then I suddenly heard a dog whining. I couldn't believe it when I realized it was coming from that car—the one that was in the middle of everything. When I got there, I couldn't see the dog at all, but I definitely heard it. There was too much damage to the car—metal twisted up, the roof smashed. The window had been broken out, which I guess is why I could hear him. It was so loud there, though. Sometimes I think back and I still can't believe I heard him over everything else. Anyway, I stuck my arm in there to see if I could find him. I finally felt him after I'd stretched as far as I could possibly go."

Maya looked up to find Alex watching her with rapt attention. She got that a lot when she talked about this.

"There was no way to get in to him. I knew that if I didn't get him out right away he was going to die. And then the car caught fire."

Alex didn't react other than by lifting both brows. Calm and cool. She could see it written all over him. She liked it. She liked calm and cool. And determined. Those were words she would use to describe herself.

Okay, that wasn't entirely true. She was determined. She could be calm and cool. In an emergency, when talking someone down, dealing with blood, or facing an opponent with a sword. But she wasn't calm and cool all the time. She'd seen lives cut short; she'd seen how everything someone knew could change in a heartbeat. Sometimes life just wasn't calm and cool.

"Anyway, what came next is a little bit of a blur. Everyone was busy, so I knew I had to do something myself. I broke out the window on the other side, and then I got in there as far as I could."

That seemed to snap Alex out of his calm interest and into alarm. "You got into the crumpled-up, burning car? Because of a dog?"

She knew that he was thinking she was crazy. A lot of people had told her that. But she enjoyed the rush of warmth Alex's concern gave her.

"I got halfway into a crumpled-up, burning car," she told him with a nod. "It was a tight fit, and I still couldn't see him, but I could reach him. I pulled him up to my chest with one arm but then had to twist sideways to get us both out of the opening. He was probably about ten pounds and was barking and wiggling—which I knew was a good sign that he wasn't too badly hurt," she said.

Alex gave a single nod, his gaze fixed on her.

Maya swallowed. Yeah, he was intense. She felt a strange urge to lean in closer while at the same time feeling as if she should pull back. Way back.

"I had to brace my other arm on the seat and push us out, and holding on to the wiggling dog caused me to shift funny, I guess. I felt something pop in my shoulder and the instant pain. A fireman saw me and tried to help. He took the dog, and I started to pull my arm out, but I realized I was stuck. My arm had gotten wedged in between two pieces of metal, and my shoulder was weak and painful and I couldn't get free. The fire was getting closer, the metal was hot, and there was jagged glass just underneath where my arm was jammed." She took a deep breath, the memories playing through her mind as if she'd prerecorded it all to watch over and over. "I tried to shift back. I tried to get someone's attention, something. Finally I just yanked my arm out as hard as I could."

She could still feel the sharp glass cutting into her flesh, the heat of the metal searing her skin. She could still see the black dots dancing in front of her eyes as her body strove to stay conscious through the pain.

"My God, Maya," Alex said gruffly.

The roughness of his voice made her skin prickle with awareness, and the images from the accident instantly evaporated. Instead she began cataloging all the things she really liked about Alex. His voice—especially when it went deep and gravelly. Also his mouth, his eyes, his hands. Oh yeah, those hands.

He was intelligent, devoted, funny, charming. But she was absolutely certain that she would have gone to bed with Alex just because of his smile.

She shrugged. "I got free. I ended up with a torn rotator cuff and labrum and a lot of cuts. I cut one of my nerves and some muscles as well. And there were a lot of burns."

"You've had surgery?" he asked.

She nodded. "Several. They repaired the rotator cuff, but with the burns and skin grafts, I couldn't really do much rehab, so it froze up and I had to have it manipulated. I'm still weaker on that side. The nerve, of course, also impacts that. The scarring from the burns limits my range of motion sometimes. But overall, I've got functional use of it, and I still work at it every day."

Alex's mouth thinned into a straight line. "It must hurt sometimes? Especially with some of the stuff you do here."

"Sure it does." She managed to stay away from the serious painkillers, but that meant that pain was a pretty normal part of her life now.

"You've had to give some things up, I imagine," he added.

She shook her head. "No. I mean, sure it hurts. There are times when an opponent gets a shot in because I can't swing fast enough on that side." And that always really pissed her off. "I've had some falls when my arm wouldn't catch me. But I still do everything I want to do."

Alex frowned. "That can't be good for it. You could retear the cuff, or you could hurt another part of your body, like your head or your other arm, if you take a blow or fall."

"Of course I could. And I could get hit by a bus tomorrow or choke on a banana muffin, but I'm not going to stop walking across the street and I'm definitely not going to stop eating muffins."

Alex's frown intensified. "The odds of you getting hit by a bus are far less than the odds of you injuring yourself because you aren't adjusting for your injury. This is something you can control. Why wouldn't you?"

She sat up straighter on the desk. She'd heard all of this from physicians, therapists, even coworkers and friends. Of course her arm put her at a disadvantage sometimes. But she didn't want to adjust. She wanted to do the things she loved doing. The pain was worth it.

"Someday this arm is going to be really bad," she said. "Someday I'm going to have raging arthritis in it, at least. Chances are, someday I'm going to have raging arthritis in other places too. But that's not right now. Right now I can still do all the things I like. And when I'm ninety-seven and sitting there with my raging arthritis, I want to be able to look back and remember all of these amazing things I did and all the fun I had."

Maya saw Alex's eyes narrow for a split second, but then he was back to calm and cool. He let out a breath and leaned back in the chair, the only major change in his completely collected demeanor.

"Have you ever been shot?"

She blinked at him. "Um, yes, actually."

"How many times?"

Should she be worried? "Three times."

Maya waited to see what he was going to do with that information. Because she had no idea what to do with this conversational turn.

"Ever broken a bone?" he asked a moment later.

"Yes."

"Stitches? Other than the obvious ones with your injury?" he asked.

She nodded. "Yes." She didn't know why it mattered.

"Would you say you were a tomboy growing up?"

Maya laughed. "I guess, kind of. I climbed trees and played sports, if that's what you mean."

"No dresses or dolls or tea parties, huh?" Alex asked with a small frown.

Maya got the impression she was somehow failing this test, but she had no idea where he was coming from. All she could do was be honest.

"I wore dresses and played with dolls, and yes, I probably even had a tea party or two."

The crease between his eyebrows deepened. "So not a tomboy?" he asked.

She leaned in, resting her elbows on her knees, intrigued by this man. "I don't know. I guess I was a pretty typical little girl. I liked lots of things. I had a mother who was very fashion conscious and loved to play with my hair. I had another mom who taught me to throw a ball and swim. But I saw them both in dresses from time to time. Both of them enjoyed watching football. I grew up thinking that I should pursue whatever I was interested in. So I did."

In spite of his penetrating gaze, Maya found herself distracted by the way he was running his thumb and forefinger up and down the side of his water bottle.

"Your mothers obviously raised a confident, strong, independent woman."

He seemed unfazed by the fact that she'd had two mothers. "Thank you."

Another pause. Maya took a long drink of water and watched him watch her. "You okay?" she finally asked.

"How hard did you try to get help?" he asked instead of answering. He seemed to have totally forgotten the pizza on the napkin resting on his thigh.

"What do you mean?"

"At the car accident with the dog. When you figured out he was in there and trapped, how hard did you try to get help?"

Strange question, but she answered anyway. "I looked around. Saw everyone else was busy and realized I had to do what I could."

"So not very hard," he said. "And you never considered just walking away?"

"I . . ." Maya shook her head. "I did what I had to do."

"You charged in and put yourself in danger."

Maya got the definite sense that the truth of that bothered him, and she felt warm again. "I was a cop, Alex. I put myself in danger every time I went out on patrol."

He pulled in a long breath through his nose, then let it out. He shifted forward in his chair, setting his pizza on the desk next to her hip. "So superheroes. I've been watching the movies. I've figured out who's who, their stories and how they all connect. I can learn all of that or look it up. What I'm looking for that I'm not getting is, why?"

The abrupt shift in topic made Maya shake her head and work to catch up for a moment. "Why?" she repeated. "Why what?"

"Why superheroes? Why the appeal? The obsession? You have an interest that doesn't always last into adulthood."

Right, okay. Superheroes. The reason he'd shown up in the first place. She was going to love this conversation. This wasn't a rundown of the Marvel world or Batman's gadgets. This was about the deeper stuff. This was about why she loved it.

"I think it's a little different for everyone," she said.

"There's actually a lot that can be taken from the characters and stories in comics."

"Okay." He pinned her with a direct look. "What is it about for you?"

She didn't have to think about that very hard at all. "Overcoming," she said. "The best superhcroes are flawed in some way. Typically something has happened to them—either a trauma or a freak accident or just good old destiny—and they either choose to rise above or they let it bring them down. We love them because they made the choice to rise above.

"Yet they still struggle, and that's what makes them relatable. A lot of them are human, but they have some power, acquired or born, that makes them larger than life. And we all have those fantasies—of being stronger or faster or smarter than we are. Able to fly or bend steel or see through things. They are flawed humans, who are given a power to use for good or evil. And they choose good."

He was staring at her.

She would have thought she had tomato sauce dripping down her chin, but she hadn't taken a bite of pizza. "What?"

"Wow."

"Wow?"

"Do you get that excited when you teach all your classes?"

She blushed but met his eyes. "Yes."

"You're very…that's all very…appealing."

She liked that he seemed to be having trouble finding the right words. "Knowing about superheroes?" she asked.

"Watching you get excited."

Wow indeed.

She realized she was staring at his mouth after she'd been doing it for a good five seconds. And doing nothing else.

She had never been this wrapped up in how a guy looked. It was as if she couldn't stop looking at him. And thinking dirty thoughts. Was this what it was like to be shallow? She didn't mind it as much as she would have thought.

"Did that…um…" She stopped and licked her lips. Because she was staring at his mouth, she saw when his lips parted. Her gaze flew to his and she saw a heat there that made everything from her belly button to her knees feel warmer. "Did any of that help?" she finally managed to ask.

He cleared his throat and shifted in his chair, and Maya felt a rush of satisfaction. She'd managed to affect his calm and cool. Hey, if she was going to be all worked up and squirmy, then it was only fair that he feel a little stirred up too.

"Yes, it did. Makes a lot of sense, actually," he said. "I've had plenty of times when I wanted to be more than I am."

Maya's breath caught in her throat. He was hot, he was a dad, he was a doctor. And he was human. And knew it.

She gave him a nod. "That's what we work on with the kids—empowering them with the things they admire in their heroes."

"The ability to fly?"

She smiled. "Interestingly, if you really get to talking with them, you find out—and they find out—that it's not about flying. Or bending steel. Or being invisible. It's about being able to do the right thing and be brave and help people."

"Or be funny," he said.

She nodded, remembering Ethan's superpower. "Right."

Alex was watching her with an unreadable expression.

Maya made herself take a breath. She could talk about this all night.

"Don't forget that the good guy always gets the girl," Alex added.

She laughed lightly. "They usually do, yeah. But those relationships aren't easy."

"The whole saving-the-world-versus-being-home-at-night-for-dinner thing?" Alex asked.

"Yep." She looked at him closely. "Kind of like doctors. The long hours and dedication it takes can make relationships hard, I would guess."

He looked mildly amused. "You're comparing me to a superhero?"

Actually, she'd been fishing for information about his relationships. "Of course. You've dedicated yourself to the greater good, faced obstacles and challenges, persevered even when things don't go perfectly, and make people's lives better."

"Stop," he said quietly.

"What?"

"That's all very nice, but no. I'm doing a job. A job that makes me feel like I'm helping. But just a job, like you are when you teach your classes."

She gave him a smile as she shook her head. "Actually, I think I am a little bit of a superhero," she joked. "I'm super cool, I love when good triumphs over evil, and I can rock tight leather."

Alex's eyes flared hot, and he gave her a slow nod. "I can't argue with that."

Her stomach flipped. Or her ovaries swooned. Or both. "So if you *were* a superhero, what powers would you want to have?" she asked.

He didn't hesitate. "Invincibility."

Maya felt an eyebrow go up. "Really? Don't you kind of already have that, being a doctor and all?"

His jaw tensed. "No. Definitely not. Being a doctor makes me even more aware of how vulnerable we all are."

Oh, she wanted to dig deeper into all of that. Alex was a fascinating man. Who she wanted to lick from head to toe.

"What power would you choose?" he asked.

She'd been asked this question by the kids about a thousand times. "Healing."

That seemed to surprise him. "Really?"

She nodded. "Really. You're not the only one who wants to make people better."

"You do some healing in your studio, don't you?" he asked. "You make the kids stronger physically. And emotionally."

That right there made it official. She had a big crush on him. "I really try," she finally said. "Thanks for saying that."

Then her stomach growled.

Alex handed her the unfinished slice of pizza, then picked up his own again.

They ate, but their topics of conversation were lighter. Alex wanted to know who her favorite superhero was and why. She went with Spider-Man, then, on a whim, challenged Alex to watch the movies and try to figure out why he was her favorite.

"Really? That's all I'm going to get?" he asked.

She laughed. Then she did something she was really good at—she took the plunge. "You can meet me here again tomorrow night, and we'll discuss. I'll be done around eight. We can have Chinese food."

Something flickered in his eyes. Temptation. She was sure of it. But it was followed by an obvious hesitation. "I have dinner with Charli and her mom every night. Tonight was an exception, but I can't make it a habit."

He couldn't make her a habit. Maya heard the message between the words clearly.

She was curious about what type of woman Alex usually dated. And then she wondered about his daughter's mom, even though she didn't want to. Rachel. Yep, the fact that Maya had remembered the other woman's name meant she was curious about her.

"You're going to keep coming to class, aren't you?" she asked.

He nodded. "But I think I need to go to the Internet about these other things."

She did not want him learning about superheroes and *Galactic Renegades* from any other source. "Let me tell you—"

"Maya." Alex got to his feet, which meant his long lean body stretching up from the chair right in front of her, an inch of air, at most, separating them.

But Maya didn't feel a single urge to move back.

"I can't spend a bunch of time alone with you," Alex said, looking down at her.

"It's all been innocent."

"I don't want it to be innocent." He sighed. "I want to come back tomorrow night. And stay longer. And then do the same thing the next night. And the next."

Maya's heart raced. "I'm free," she said with a smile.

"I'm not. At least, I shouldn't be. I need to be with Charli. Evenings are the only time I see her."

Dammit.

Finally Maya nodded, admitting defeat. "Fine. Just... read my blog. I'll do a blog post about the *GR* stuff we didn't get to, for sure. And whatever else you want to know." She couldn't just leave it alone. She couldn't not help him.

"Maya, I—"

She stopped him. "Alex, it's okay. Around here we believe that everyone makes their own choices and the rest of us respect those choices."

"I was wondering—" He grimaced slightly before continuing. "More than a blog... Could I pay you a consultation fee and maybe, I don't know, e-mail you questions? Or call?"

Maya almost laughed. Would she let him pay to e-mail her questions about superheroes? The same questions she probably talked to seven- and eight-year-olds about twice a week right here in the studio? Still, the guy was trying. For his daughter. "Yes, you can e-mail me." She wasn't sure about the phone calls. She really liked his voice. It almost seemed cruel for him to talk to her in the low, sexy tone but not say the things she really wanted to hear. Like "Do you like that, Maya?" and "That's so good" and "You're amazing."

"Thanks. You're amazing."

She stared up at him. "I don't know about that," she said with a forced laugh. "I just think it's going to make Charli really happy that you're showing such an interest."

Charli. His little girl. Maya could focus on her too. The greater good here. The touching-a-child's-life-in-a-positive-way thing.

Alex gave her a big, relieved smile. And Maya realized that no matter how great this was for Charli and how great that made Maya feel, it was not at all the same thing that Alex Nolan made her feel.

And now she needed to let him escape. Or maybe she needed to escape. Whatever. She slid to the floor, brushed past him, and moved around the desk to start for the front door. To say good-bye to him.

Alex followed, and Maya refused to categorize his mood as reluctant.

"Thanks for tonight," he said, stopping at the door that she'd unlocked so he could leave.

"Sure." *And thanks for helping me develop a huge, unrequited crush that's going to keep me up at night.*

"Now I have some beginning ember lance moves to impress Charli with."

She nodded. "There are some definite similarities with bo," she said. "But ember lances are really a combination of bo and sword fighting."

He blinked at her. "Yeah?"

"The first movie was more influenced by Japanese-style sword fighting—Scott Josh, the writer and director, is a big fan of samurai movies. But the director of the fights in the next two movies was more into the European style. And really, you have to also consider that ember lances aren't like swords in a number of ways. For one, the lance is essentially made of fire and can slice from any direction, while swords have a blade that's either single edged or double, and—"

She was cut off by Alex covering her mouth with his.

It took a lot to surprise Maya, but Alex Nolan suddenly kissing her in the midst of her elaborating on important points about wielding an ember lance definitely took her off guard.

So did how completely amazing the kiss was. He cupped the back of her head, his fingers diving into her hair. He slanted his mouth so that there wasn't one millimeter of his lips not touching hers. And while the kiss was hot and sweet and sexy and shot pleasure through every single cell of her body, it didn't even involve tongue.

It was easily three full minutes before Alex lifted his head.

She blinked up at him, her head spinning and her ovaries definitely doing something. "What was that for?"

"To stop you," he admitted. "I mean, besides really, really wanting to do that since I first saw you. But I will never need to know how the Japanese sword-fighting style influenced the ember lance battles."

"Charli could become a true aficionado—"

He cut her off again, this time with a finger on her lips. "Yes. She could. And given even five minutes in your presence, I have no doubt she would fall more deeply in love with the whole thing than she already is."

Maya pressed her lips together, and he slowly removed his finger. She was going to take that as a compliment. And not ask if that's how he'd meant it. She cleared her throat. "So then, I'll write up that blog post, but not worry about so many specific ember lance battle details."

"I'll read and study whatever you write."

"For Charli?"

"Yes. And because it's the safest way to be close to you."

Maya stepped back and crossed her arms. "That doesn't make it easier to think about you not staying after class again," she told him honestly.

He nodded, with that look of unhappiness flashing through his eyes again. "Maybe I don't want it to be easy for you to think about me not staying after class again."

She sighed. "And I thought you were a nice guy."

He shook his head. "Nope. Definitely no superhero."

Then he walked out the door of Active Imagination without a look back.

# CHAPTER FIVE

$\mathcal{D}$id you talk to the lady about the Piper costume?" Charli asked from across Rachel's dining room table the next night.

Damn. The costume. Alex shook his head. "I haven't had a chance." He thought he'd seen Maya's friend who did the costumes at the studio last night, but he hadn't even thought about talking to anyone but Maya. Which meant his decision to not stay after class anymore had been a good one. He'd skipped dinner with Charli last night because he'd been completely caught up in Maya. That was not good. "But I will," he said, focusing fully on Charli. "You'll still have to wait until your birthday, though."

"But I need that costume," Charli said. "I've been waiting so long."

Rachel rolled her eyes. Alex had to hide a smile.

"You'll have to make do until then," Rachel told her. "You need to practice your patience. And your gratitude."

"I'm grateful," Charli muttered. "Grateful that I won't have to wear that dumb red scarf anymore."

Rachel started to respond, but Alex spoke first. "I like the red scarf. It makes you a little different from Piper."

"I know," Charli told him. "I don't want to be different from Piper."

"But you don't want to be exactly like Piper," Alex said, scooping up a bite of meatloaf and mashed potatoes.

Charli turned big eyes on him. "I don't?" Her tone suggested that was easily the stupidest thing she had ever heard in her whole almost-ten years of life.

He shook his head. "No way. There's already one Piper. The galaxy needs more than one awesome, heroic girl out there kicking butt and saving people. You need to decide what you like best about her and make those part of your own character. And you need to realize there are amazing things about you that Piper doesn't have."

He was pretending to be totally nonchalant about the conversation, but the whole time he chewed he thought that Maya would have been pretty impressed.

Or really impressed. She would have given him one of those huge grins, and her eyes would have sparkled, and...

"Like what?"

He looked at Charli. The girl who should have his full focus. "You mean what amazing things do you have?" he asked.

Charli nodded. She was giving him more focused attention at that moment than she ever had, and Alex suddenly felt a little panic. *Don't screw this up, Nolan.* He'd seen the *GR* movies, though. And he'd been a part of one of Maya Goodwin's classes. He could do this.

"I think Piper is fighting for herself. She's all alone. But I think what you have is stronger—family, love, friends, people you would do anything for. I think that would make you tougher. I know there are things I would do for the people I love that go beyond things I would do for myself."

Alex was almost holding his breath waiting for a reaction. He glanced up at Rachel to find her staring at him. When she met his eyes, she gave him a big smile. And he knew he'd done okay.

"So maybe wearing red is a symbol of love," Rachel said. "You wear red. Piper wears black. But you're both fighters."

Charli scooped up a clump of potatoes and ate it, seemingly lost in thought. Finally she said, "Okay, let's ask the lady to make the scarf red. And maybe the hat too."

Alex nodded, trying not to look overly relieved. "Great idea."

"Charli, tell your dad about the painting class we're going to."

Alex listened while Charli told him that Rachel had signed them up for a weekly painting class with some other girls her age and their moms. The group got together for pizza beforehand, and Rachel thought it would be a great way for Charli to meet some new friends.

"It's every Friday," Charli told him.

"It will be fun," Rachel insisted. She looked over at Alex. "So no dinner those nights. Is that okay?"

"Sure. Of course. The class sounds great."

"It's *painting*," Charli told him, as if painting were the dumbest way to spend time ever invented.

He laughed. "I can't wait to see what you make."

Charli sighed. She was clearly much less enthusiastic about it than Rachel was.

Alex felt a surge of affection for his daughter. She was an active kid. Maybe overactive in some ways. She liked to move. She was fidgeting even as she sat at the dinner table. Painting didn't really seem like her kind of thing. Which made him even happier to be learning about bo staffs and swords. He couldn't wait to show her what he was learning. Which, of course, sent his mind right back to Maya.

As did the realization that there would be one night a week when Rachel and Charli would be busy for dinner. Fridays. It wasn't a night that the Super You class met, but maybe he could go to the studio anyway . . .

No. He shouldn't. Because it wasn't just about time away from Charli. It was about how much of his focus and attention he had to give. And that the more he gave to Maya, the more he would want to give.

All day today he'd felt guilty about the time he'd spent last night with Maya. Or maybe he'd felt guilty about how much he'd enjoyed the time. He'd texted Rachel to tell her he wouldn't make it for dinner while he'd been waiting for Maya to change clothes. She'd said it was fine, of course. But he'd felt bad anyway.

At least until Maya had walked out of the locker room in fitted blue jeans. Part of him had wanted to spend every night eating and talking with her. Which was his cue to stay away.

They finished eating, and then Rachel agreed to let Charli have ice cream in the living room. Alex settled into his usual spot on the couch with his own bowl and let the sense of family wash over him.

But it didn't come. Not the way it usually did. He was still happy to be there. He was still enthralled watching Charli—her constant motion, the way she could do seven things at once, the way she chattered on about whatever was on her mind.

But tonight was less…comfortable…than all the other nights over the past couple of months, because Charli's vibrancy reminded him of Maya. The way she talked in long, run-on sentences reminded him of Maya. And he was really trying not to be reminded of Maya. And he couldn't help comparing Maya and Rachel. He hated that the most. It wasn't fair to Rachel. Or Maya either, really. But he couldn't seem to help it. Just as he couldn't seem to help wondering what Maya was doing tonight.

"So, Charli, is Piper your favorite superhero?" he asked, trying to focus on the two girls who were with him right now. And hell, if he was going to take Maya's class and feel bad about it the whole time, at least he could try to apply some of the things he'd learned and use them to bond with Charli as planned.

Charli looked up from where she was drawing at the coffee table. "Piper's not a superhero," she said.

"No? How come?"

"She doesn't have superpowers. She's just brave and tough. And can fight. And fly spaceships. And fix robots," Charli said. "But she's learned all of that."

"Superheroes don't learn the stuff they do?" he asked.

"I guess they have to learn to fly and shoot their webs and stuff," Charli acknowledged. "But most of their powers are just natural."

Alex wondered about that and then wondered what

Maya would say about the topic. And then wondered if it was actually possible for him to stop thinking about her.

"If Piper's not a superhero, who is your favorite superhero?" he asked.

Charli's face lit up. "I like Supergirl," Charli said.

He made a mental note to make an actual note in his phone to look more up about Supergirl.

He was about to ask why when Charli asked him, "Who's your favorite?"

*Oh crap.* He so wanted to have a back-and-forth conversation with Charli. And he'd been right thinking superhero talk was the way to her heart. But he hadn't studied enough yet. Why had he brought this up?

He thought fast, but only one name came to mind. "Peter Parker," he told her. "Spider-Man."

Charli put down her colored pencil. "Really? Why?"

*Damn, damn, damn.* He'd planned to watch those movies this weekend. Or talk to Maya. No, watch this weekend.

"He's had to overcome a lot," he said, remembering Maya's words about how most superheroes were humans who had experienced trauma or tragedy. He hoped, since he was her favorite, that was true for Spider-Man. Or that Charli wouldn't know if it wasn't.

He cringed inwardly. He did not want this to be a fake conversation where he was barely getting by on bits and pieces and hoping his daughter didn't know any better. He definitely needed to do some homework.

"Like what?" Charli asked.

Alex relaxed slightly. Maybe she didn't know much about Spider-Man.

"Well, he's human," Alex said, "but bad things have

happened to him. But instead of being mad or letting that make him a bad person, he's chosen to do good things."

He might have a lot of studying ahead of him, he maybe hadn't binge-watched the right movies for this particular conversation yet, but he sure as hell had hung on every one of Maya's words from the night before.

Charli nodded. "So that kind of makes him even better—that the bad things couldn't make him bad. He's stronger than that."

Alex nodded, feeling an intense gratitude toward Maya Goodwin and her inability not to go on and on about the things she loved. The gratitude was so intense that Alex really wanted to go straight over to her studio and tell her himself.

Sure. Gratitude. That was all it was.

Rachel smiled at her and then at Alex. "It is even better," Rachel agreed.

Alex felt his chest tighten slightly as he and Rachel shared a silent moment. They were definitely on the path to being great friends. At least. Maybe this could all work out.

If he could just keep his thoughts off a spunky brunette who rocked purple leather.

"Night," Charli told him when her show was over. "I'll see you tomorrow."

"You got it, kiddo," he said. He looked at Rachel. "How about you guys come to my place for a change? I'll do dinner."

Rachel nodded. "That would be nice. What do you think, Charli?"

"Okay. Can I swim in your pool?"

She'd been to his condo a couple of times, but only for a few minutes each time. She'd seen the pool on the rooftop of his building when he'd given them a tour, but they hadn't gotten in. Alex loved swimming, and it was the perfect workout for a hemophiliac. He'd love to get Charli involved, maybe even on a swim team eventually if she wanted a competitive sport.

"Absolutely," he told her. "And how about homemade piz—spaghetti? I make amazing garlic bread." He wasn't sure he was going to be able to eat pizza and keep his thoughts where they needed to be. Which was off of Maya.

"I love spaghetti," Charli told him with a smile that seemed almost shy. "It was fun talking about everything tonight."

His heart clenched so hard he had to swallow twice before saying, "It was the most fun I've had in a long time."

And if his mind said, "What about last night?" he stubbornly ignored it. Tonight with Charli had been fun. It was something he'd happily do every night, forever.

"I'll be back down in a few minutes if you want to stick around," Rachel said, getting to her feet.

Alex looked up at her. There was something new in her eyes. Something that made him think, *Uh-oh*. But he shook off that reaction. This was Rachel. There was no uh-oh with Rachel. Or there shouldn't be, anyway.

"Okay," he agreed. "Wine?"

"That would be awesome," she said over her shoulder, following Charli out of the room. "There's some Riesling in the fridge."

Riesling and Rachel. That was what he should want.

Alex headed for the kitchen. But as he pulled the

bottle out and poured two glasses, he couldn't keep his mind off everything he and Charli had talked about tonight...because of Maya.

He pulled his phone out and brought up Maya's blog. He was just wondering...

Yes. She'd blogged about *Galactic Renegades*, just as she'd promised.

Fifteen minutes later, he was leaning against the counter, one glass of wine empty, thumbing through her blog, when Rachel came into the kitchen.

She noticed his empty glass. "Sorry, that took a little bit."

"No problem at all."

Rachel tipped the bottle to fill up his glass. "Should we go back into the living room?"

Should they?

Alex had Maya's words dancing through his head. Her explanation of the Tri-Alliance Force in *GR* alone had made him smile. It was stuff that would be way over Charli's head and was in no way part of his daughter's love for the movies, but as he'd read he had been able to hear Maya's voice—the way she talked faster and faster and her voice got a little higher with her excitement. It had made him smile. And remember the way she'd gone on and on at the studio and that he'd kissed her to stop her. And it made him want to see her even more.

But none of that was strange.

What was strange was that he'd also appreciated her analysis of the Alliance. She'd made it interesting. He could probably have an intelligent several-minute-long conversation about it now. The post probably hadn't taken her long to write, considering, well, everything about her. But she hadn't had to do it at all, and the fact that she had made him feel as if ... maybe he could go to a Comic Con.

And if someone had told him three weeks ago that he'd even think that thought, not to mention appreciate an analysis of a sci-fi movie series, he would have laughed in their face.

While he'd waited for Rachel, he'd gone on to read Maya's posts about a couple of other superheroes and a thoughtful piece on a popular fantasy book series.

The woman worked full-time in her studio— something that clearly took a lot of passion and heart along with time—and obviously indulged in all kinds of movies, TV shows, and books—and still found time not just to write about them, but to write about them with intelligence and humor and amazing insight.

"Alex?"

He focused on Rachel.

Rachel. Shit.

Riesling and Rachel.

That was what he should want, he reminded himself again.

But what he really wanted was to get home and e-mail Maya. He had a few questions.

Actually, he wanted to call her. Or go over to her studio. He had a sudden urge to twirl a bo staff, and that wasn't even a euphemism for anything. Of course, the studio would no doubt be closed at this hour. Or he could go over to her house—though he didn't know where she lived.

But he would make himself only e-mail her. And he

would stay on the topic of *Galactic Renegades* and Peter Parker. And maybe Supergirl.

Sure, he could look stuff up, but he'd rather hear it all from Maya.

"I should get going," he said, pushing away from the counter. "I know I said I'd stay, but I have some work to do yet tonight that I forgot about."

Rachel nodded. "Okay. Maybe tomorrow night."

Yeah. If he hadn't heard from Maya. Because if he had, he'd no doubt be distracted, and that wasn't fair to Rachel.

He wasn't sure any of this was fair to Rachel.

He moved to her and spontaneously pulled her into a hug. She was clearly surprised for a second, but she wrapped her arms around him too. Her hair smelled amazing. And he noticed for the first time that she'd changed clothes while she'd been upstairs. Instead of the jeans and button-down shirt she'd had on before, she now wore shorts and a tank top. A soft cotton tank that left her arms bare.

And while he appreciated the softness of her skin and the way her breasts felt against his chest—because they were, after all, breasts—Alex didn't feel the urge to lean in and kiss her.

Instead he flashed back to the kiss he'd spontaneously planted on Maya last night.

Maybe he needed to stop being spontaneous around the women in his life. And the ones he'd just met.

He pulled back. "I'll see you tomorrow night for dinner at my place. I'm cooking, so don't bring anything."

She gave him a smile, though he could see she was

slightly disappointed. "*I'm cooking* are two of the sexiest words a guy can say," she told him lightly.

He stepped back and decided it was best not to comment on what was sexy and what wasn't right now. "Good night."

"Night."

He let himself out and jogged to where he'd left his car, halfway down the block. One thing homes in Boston rarely came with was parking.

By the time he got home, he had narrowed his e-mail down to two topics. He went straight to his desk and fired up his computer. He tapped his fingers restlessly as he waited for it to boot up and open his e-mail application.

The moment the mail program was up he typed in Maya's address and then the subject—"Super Dad...or at least a good start." He smiled the entire time he typed the message telling her about his conversation with Charli and thanking her for what she'd shared with him and how it had helped Charli open up.

He had already sent it before he realized he hadn't asked her anything about Supergirl. So he typed another message asking for some key insights.

He sent that one before he realized that he hadn't asked her about Peter Parker. So he sent another asking which of the movies he should start with, the ones from the early two thousands or the more recent ones.

Then he made himself shut his computer down before he made an even bigger ass out of himself.

And he checked back only twice before he went to bed to see if she'd replied.

* * *

"He sent me three e-mails. In the space of, like, five minutes," Maya told Kiera and Sophie the next morning over coffee and muffins.

"That's cute," Sophie said. "It sounds like he was so excited he kept hitting send before he finished."

Maya hid her smile behind her cup. It was cute. And *cute* was not a word she used lightly. Nor was it a word that Alex Nolan had likely heard applied to him very often in his life.

His first message was especially cute. He'd called himself Super Dad. She wasn't the type of girl to go *aww* easily. But that had done it.

Up until the kiss—and the three e-mails late last night—she had been ready to let it go, to have Alex Nolan as a student in her class and nothing more. But that kiss was not something she wanted to let go. Then the three e-mails had come zinging into her in-box. He'd been thinking about her. That had made her smile, and tingle just a little, and had also relieved her. Because she'd certainly been thinking about him.

"So you're really going to loan him your personal copies of those books?" Kiera asked as they all cleaned up the kitchen and got ready to head out for the day.

Maya shrugged. "He asked for book recommendations."

"Yes, and he also said that he didn't think you two should spend any more time alone."

"I'm just going to take them to his office. It's not like we'll be alone."

"You weren't alone two nights ago either," Sophie said. "But it sounds like things got tempting and complicated anyway."

Complicated. Yeah, maybe. But at the same time, Maya wasn't sure anything had ever seemed so simple before. She liked him. He liked her. He wanted to be a good dad, and she wanted to help him with that.

"Look, I could just recommend he buy these books," Maya said. "But I have important things highlighted and underlined. I have notes in the margins and on sticky notes. This will be so much more helpful."

"Uh-huh." Kiera put her cup and plate in the dishwasher. "But hey, for the record, I like seeing you smile like this. I'm totally behind you going for it."

Maya gave her a quick hug. "Thanks."

Two hours later Maya strode toward the entrance to Boston's Children Hospital, her arms full of books. She wore capris and sandals, a red T, black jacket, and her favorite Kate Spade rain bucket hat. She was full of confidence and excitement about seeing Alex.

But as she approached the building, even distracted by thoughts of seeing Doc Wonderful, she couldn't help but take in the sights. The stone columns in front, the flags hanging over the entrance, even the glass doors leading into the lobby were all brightly colored. There were purples and reds and teals and yellows. It was bright and lively and welcoming.

Maya picked up her pace as she approached the doors and entered the lobby. The multicolored theme continued here, from the walls to the floors to the furniture. And they had a life-size 3-D giraffe head peeking over the wall behind the reception desk. Maya was grinning as she turned a full circle in the lobby. It was all so cheerful. But it also had a feel to it. It felt...hopeful.

Then she took in the people around her. There were the

ones who clearly worked for the hospital. They all wore smiles. Then there were the people who were obviously here for help. Families. Parents. Kids. Not as many smiles there.

Maya felt her heart clench a little. This was a children's hospital. The kids didn't come through those doors to dress up like superheroes and learn stage fighting and how to swing a plastic sword. These kids were sick.

But while they were probably scared, they knew that coming through those doors was the first step toward healing. They knew that the people inside these walls were here for one reason—to help them.

Alex was one of those people. He was someone these people needed. They were eager to see him too, not because they wanted to talk superheroes and *Galactic Renegades* but because he could offer them hope and healing.

That was damned sexy. It was a strange reaction, but she found the idea that Alex was here, in this colorful place, because he was someone these families were looking to for saving, very sexy. He was a hero.

Maya's perspective shifted abruptly. She loved what she did for a living with the studio and she believed it was important, but she wasn't doing anything like what Alex did. She suddenly felt silly for coming. He couldn't stop and gab about fictional characters and made-up worlds in the midst of all of this...reality.

She looked around, the books in her arms feeling heavier now than they had five minutes ago. She should just go home and e-mail him. That's what he'd said he wanted. His job took up a lot of not just time, but heart and energy too. He had a daughter he was trying to get to know. He had other people and their children depending on him. He couldn't hang out at Active Imagination every night and eat pizza and talk about comic books.

But she'd lugged the books all the way down here. And she did think some of them would be interesting to him and helpful with Charli.

Maya spotted the lobby gift shop and headed straight for it. She bought a "Thinking of You" card that was blank inside and borrowed a pen from the clerk to write a quick note to Alex. Then she slid it into the bright-green envelope and tucked it inside the first book, letting it peek out the top so he would see it.

She approached the front desk with a smile a minute later. "Hi, I'm here to drop these off for Dr. Alex Nolan. Can I just leave them here?"

The man behind the desk shook his head. "You can take those up to his office and leave them with his assistant," he told her. He typed something into the computer quickly. "Eighth floor. Suite twelve."

Right. His office. His assistant.

She wondered if Alex would be embarrassed to be delivered books about superheroes, and again contemplated just going home. But she headed back into the gift shop for a gift bag.

By the time she got to the eighth floor, suite twelve, Maya was fairly certain this was the dumbest thing she'd ever done. But she was going to do it anyway. She never let nerves get in the way of doing things she wanted to, and she didn't really believe in being embarrassed about the things she loved. If Alex e-mailed her to tell her to never darken his door again, so be it.

She shifted the paper bag to her hip and pushed open

the frosted glass door that had four doctors' names on it. Alex's was the second down, and even reading his name etched on that door made her heart flip.

That was the damnedest thing of all—all the heart flipping. She never felt this way about guys. But she liked it.

The inner office was a typical waiting room. There was a front desk made of oak, and several leather chairs surrounding a coffee table. No one else waited, and there was no sound except for some strangely familiar music coming from the receptionist's computer. It was a song from the soundtrack to *Galactic Renegades*—the first movie, if Maya wasn't mistaken.

The receptionist looked up with a smile. "Hi, can I help you?"

The nameplate in front of her on the desk read "Samantha Higgins, Administrative Assistant."

"I'm actually just dropping something off for Ale—Dr. Nolan," Maya said, hoisting the gift bag onto the countertop, careful to hold on to the bottom. Those books were going to fall right through that bag any second.

"Oh." Samantha seemed surprised. It was probably the gift bag with teddy bears and balloons on it that said, "Get Well Soon."

"Sorry, I didn't have anything else to put them in."

Samantha reached for the bag. "It's fine. I'll set it on his desk. He's out today, but he'll be in tomorrow morning."

"Oh, he's out today?" Maya repeated, eyeing the bag as the woman grabbed the handles. Maybe she shouldn't just leave it. Maybe this was a sign that this was a bad idea. Not that she believed in signs. But she hadn't really believed in developing a huge crush on a pediatrician who knew nothing about bo staffs or Arietis IV either. And that had sure happened.

"Yes, but he'll be back—"

Samantha lifted the bag, and Maya heard the tearing paper a second before the books thudded to the floor behind the desk.

Well, crap.

"Sorry." Maya grimaced as she peered over the counter.

Samantha reached for the book on top of the small pile, lifted it, and read the front. Her wide eyes went to Maya. "Wait, you're the superhero girl?"

Maya felt her eyebrows rise. "Um."

"You're the woman he met the other day. The one with the martial arts studio, right?" Samantha asked, her face suddenly bright. She was looking at Maya as if Maya had told her she was a lottery winner.

"I am," Maya admitted. She frowned. "He told you about me?"

"Yes. When he gave me this." Samantha handed her a piece of paper.

Maya read "Supergirl, Piper costumes, Peter Parker/ Spider-Man—why? Spider-Man's uncle."

"What is this?" Maya asked, looking up.

"Research he asked me to do today."

"Research? He has you looking up this stuff? Why?"

Samantha laughed. "That's my job. I'm his assistant."

"But doesn't that mean with medical stuff?" Maya asked, looking over the list again and noticing that she even thought his handwriting was sexy. That was definitely a new one.

"Well, usually it means medical stuff, yes. But I like

Alex and I've worked with him for a long time. I told him that I was happy to help with anything he needed with his transition with Charli."

"Oh... that's really nice," Maya told her, torn for a second between being thankful Alex had a friend who could help him out with the new-dad thing and a flash of jealousy. This woman knew Alex well. Maya realized she wanted to know him well.

"I've been looking up everything from what nine-year-old girls are into to anything I can find about *Galactic Renegades*," Samantha said. "I thought I'd become a *GR* expert. But then he came in yesterday and told me that the one website about Piper was all wrong, and I should read through this blog." Samantha smiled. "Your blog."

"You've read my blog?" Maya asked. That was... strange. And wonderful in a way.

Samantha nodded. "And he was right. The site I'd been on that was talking about Piper's appeal to young women and girls was way too simplistic. You did a great job of discussing it, in my opinion."

"Well—thank you." Maya had honestly never had a person tell her in real life, face-to-face, that they'd read and appreciated one of her blog posts. She often got comments on the posts themselves, but she'd never discussed the topics out loud with anyone but Kiera and Sophie and sometimes Ben.

"So these books," Samantha said, holding up the one with the bright-red cover that said *Superheroes: The People Who Love Them, the People Who Want to Be Them*. "He's probably going to have me read these and give him a book report."

Maya shook her head. "You're kidding. He doesn't do any of his own research?"

Samantha smiled. "Well, here's the thing. There are about a hundred things that need to be taken care of in his life every day. About eighty of those, someone else can do. The twenty things left? He's the only one who can do those. So I'm happy to help out with the other eighty. Because I'm not brilliant enough, driven enough, or well-known enough to do the other twenty."

Maya really liked Samantha. She saw that Alex was brilliant and was willing to help him out however she could. And it didn't seem as if Samantha was in love with him. She clearly admired him and liked him, but there was nothing about her that seemed swoony about his abilities.

Whereas Maya was swooning a little just hearing someone else say he was brilliant and driven.

"Well-known enough?" she asked. That was the only one she didn't understand. "How does that help him help the kids?"

"Alex is the leading expert on hemophilia in the country," Samantha said. "He lectures to the National Institutes of Health and lobbies in Washington, D.C., to get policy makers to help fund research and treatment. Alex can get stuff done that no one else in the country can get done."

*Yep*, Maya thought, that was a heart flip she felt for sure. She found that surprisingly hot. And she didn't even know what hemophilia was.

"So, I guess I should leave the books for you?" Maya asked. She felt a small stab of disappointment.

"I have to tell you, when he first brought this all to

me, I was rolling my eyes. But," Samantha said, "I've now watched two of the *Galactic Renegades* movies, and I'm getting into it." She leaned in as if about to impart a big secret. "And I get that Piper is who all the younger girls are into—and she's completely kick-ass—but I'm completely watching to see if Arith and Jase get together."

Maya laughed. There was indeed a romance between Arith and the human Jase. The screenwriters knew that a romantic subplot was always a good idea.

"But anyway, I think you should still take the books to Alex," Samantha said, leaning down to gather the three paperbacks and two hardcovers from the floor. "He'll bring me what he wants me to look at, but he should get these from you."

Maya took the stack as Samantha handed it across the counter. "Are you sure?"

"Absolutely. He would love to see you, and maybe he can ask you some of this stuff about Peter Parker. I haven't even started on all of that." Samantha tossed the torn gift bag into her trash can.

"But I don't know where he lives," Maya said, pushing the books back toward Samantha.

"Well, that's easy." Samantha scribbled an address on a blue sticky note and stuck it on top of *The Fandom: An Intimate Look at the Fans and the Freaks*, then pushed them all back to Maya. This time she left her hand on them, though, preventing Maya from sliding them back again.

"I can't just show up there," Maya protested.

"Why not? You're the one he needs."

Heart flip and tingles. Dang.

"You think so?" Maya asked.

"Well, you are the expert in all of these things, right?" Samantha asked.

Yeah, she was. He needed stuff only Maya could give him. Well, actually, it was knowledge that could be summed up in *What's Super about Superheroes?* Still, that was clearly not something anyone else in his life could easily help him with.

Maya felt an undeniable thrill at that.

Maya looked at the address Samantha had given her. It would take her only about ten minutes to get there. She pulled the stack of books into her arms. "Should I call and tell him I'm coming over?"

Samantha got a sly look in her eyes. "I'll take care of it. You just head on over."

Well, Samantha knew Alex and how he liked things. If she thought Maya showing up like this was okay, then it probably was. And Maya wasn't really that worried about it. He could tell her to leave if he didn't want to see her.

She wasn't too worried that he'd tell her that either.

And that made her heart flip hardest of all.

# CHAPTER SIX

$\mathcal{T}$wenty minutes later, because of typical Boston traffic that could make a ten-minute drive into an hour-long commute with no warning, Maya pulled into the parking garage of the luxury apartment complex on Boylston Street. She'd never been in this building, but she knew buildings like this cost some serious cash.

Pediatricians who specialized in hemo-something did pretty well.

With that thought Maya pulled out her phone and brought up the Internet. She typed "genetic, hemo, kids" into the search bar, then added "Dr. Alex Nolan."

A moment later a page full of information and articles and photos of Alex popped up. Including the word *hemophilia*. That was it.

Maya was so tempted to scroll through it all. But she was sitting outside his apartment building. He was, purportedly, inside. And as much as she wanted to know about his work, she wanted to see him more. So she book-marked the webpage and got out of the car.

She grabbed the stack of books from the passenger seat, then headed toward the lobby. The doorman asked her name and said that Dr. Nolan was expecting her. The butterflies kicked up in her stomach as she got into the elevator and pushed the button for the top floor.

But it wasn't Alex who answered the door when she knocked. Instead a good-looking guy in a T-shirt and gym shorts pulled the door open with a smile.

"Hi. You must be Maya."

She blinked at him. "Um, yeah."

"I'm Austin, I'm Alex's cousin. Come on in." He stepped back, opening the door wide.

Maya stepped into the massive entryway and worked on keeping her eyes in her head. But holy crap, the place was huge. And gorgeous. The ceiling rose easily fourteen feet above them, with a big skylight that let the sunshine pour down onto the cream-colored marble floor under her. The oak woodwork, gold accents on the wall sconces, and framed artwork made the area warm and welcoming. A sharp contrast to the bright primary colors of the hospital, which had been equally warm and welcoming.

"Nice to meet you, Austin," she said.

"Oh, you too," he said in a tone that indicated he was sincere, if slightly amused.

"You knew I was coming?"

"Sam called me."

"Samantha? From Alex's office?" Maya clarified.

He grinned. "Yeah, sorry. Samantha."

Suddenly Maya was nervous. It was the strangest

feeling. Not only did she not get nervous often, but this had come on all at once. She swallowed. "Then you know that I just stopped by to drop off some books for Alex."

"Yeah, Sam—Samantha—said you had a stack. That's awesome. Please tell me there's something in there about Supergirl. I've been going crazy reading about her."

Maya's eyes widened. "You've been reading about Supergirl?"

"Yeah. Did you see that list of stuff Alex gave Sam? She couldn't get through it all, so he asked me to help out." Austin gave her a wink. "And I don't mind a reason to get on Samantha's good side either."

Maya could see the resemblance between the men for sure, and guessed Austin to be about five years younger than Alex. But where Alex had seemed so focused and serious, even in the middle of some of their flirtation, Austin had a more carefree air about him.

"So what have you learned?" she couldn't help but ask.

"That Supergirl's real name is Kara, and she's Superman's cousin."

Maya waited but Austin didn't go on. "Anything else?"

He shrugged. "She's basically Superman as a teenage girl."

Yeah, Alex needed her.

"Can I leave these with you?" she asked Austin before she launched into a long-winded recitation of Supergirl's origin story.

Austin shook his head. "You should give them to Alex."

Her heart thudded. She did want to see him. "Is he here?"

"Yeah, upstairs. Come on."

There was an upstairs? Maya followed him back out the door of the apartment and to the elevators.

"What's upstairs?" she asked as Austin pressed the button for the roof.

"The pool."

"There's a pool?"

Austin nodded. "That was the main reason Alex bought a place in this building. He's a champion swimmer, and it's obviously the best way for him to stay in shape."

He was a swimmer. Maya wasn't sure what was obvious about that, but she could acknowledge that Alex had the build of a swimmer, now that she thought about it. He was long and lean, toned, but not with bulging muscles from lifting weights. His shoulders were more defined than a runner's or biker's, though.

And clearly she'd spent too much time thinking about his body.

They stepped off the elevator into a gorgeous rooftop garden. There were potted trees, flowers, and even patches of grass. There was an area with thickly upholstered outdoor chairs, a barbecue, a fireplace, and twinkle lights overhead. And then there was the pool.

Maya assumed the pool had water in it and was...well, a pool. But she really had no idea, because as she turned to face it, Alex was just getting out.

He wore red swim trunks. And nothing else. It was kind of ironic, really, that her mouth went entirely dry, because there seemed to be a lot of water sliding off the contours and planes of his hard, lean body as he walked toward her.

He ran his hands through his hair, then down over his face, but he didn't reach for a towel. Or a shirt. He came to stand right in front of her.

"Maya."

She simply nodded. What with her tongue being stuck to the roof of her mouth and all.

"What are you doing here?" Alex shifted his gaze to his cousin. "What's going on?"

"Maya came by to drop off some books," Austin said. "Right, Maya?"

*Maya.* Hmm. That word sounded familiar. But she couldn't really focus on that right now. She was busy watching the water drops chase each other over his hard pecs and down the ridges of his abs.

She felt someone bump her from behind, and, startled, she looked up. Into the green eyes that were watching her with a mixture of confusion and amusement.

"You brought me books?"

Then there was that deep, rumbling voice. And that smile. She felt her own mouth curl up. "Um, yeah."

*What was the question again?*

"Hey, Austin, you don't have to stay," Alex said, his eyes never leaving Maya's.

"Oh no, I'm fine. Totally good right here."

"Austin. Leave."

Alex's voice had gotten more commanding, and Maya felt a tingle low and deep.

Oh yes. She loved tingling low and deep. That hadn't happened in far too long.

"Alright," Austin said with a chuckle. "But now that your Supergirl is here, I'm shutting down the computer research."

Maya didn't turn to see if he was gone. There was water still clinging to Alex's naked skin—and she didn't blame it. Why would she possibly look anywhere else?

"You brought me books?" Alex asked again.

He was standing really close. Not close enough that she could lean forward slightly and lap up that one drop of water right in the middle of his chest, but close enough that she was able to see the light stubble on his jaw and the way his wet eyelashes clung to one another.

"I did... bring you... books," Maya said, as the words slowly came back to her.

"Books about what?"

"Superheroes." But if she did lean in and lick him, what would he do?

Alex ran a hand over his bare chest, wiping away some of the water, then ran his hand through his hair again.

For the life of her, Maya could not remember ever thinking the area under a man's arm and down the side of his torso was sexy. But she did now.

"Thought we were going to e-mail," he said, his voice gruff.

Maya started to wet her lips but froze at the flare of heat in Alex's eyes as he focused on her mouth. Oh boy. She finished the motion slowly, fascinated by the way he watched the tip of her tongue.

"We were going to e-mail," she agreed. "But you had so many questions, I thought maybe this would be better."

"There's only one problem with that theory," he said. "Now that you're here, talking about superheroes is not even in the top three things I want to do."

Lust flashed through her. She really wanted to take her jacket off before she overheated, but her arms were full of books. Books about a topic that was not in Alex's top three at the moment. She definitely wanted to hear that top three.

She glanced around and noticed a small glass-topped table. She moved to set the books down and then pulled off her hat and jacket, tossing them onto the chaise longue next to it. She fluffed her hat hair as she faced Alex again.

"Let's talk about that top three," she said.

"You don't know what they are?"

"I'm hoping that at least two of them match up with my top three."

"You have a top three for what you want to do right now?"

She shook her head and went to stand right in front of him again. "More like a top ten."

Alex sucked in a breath, then blew it out slowly. "Maya—"

"Oh no you don't," she told him quickly. "You can't suddenly play the we-can't-be-alone card. You said top three first."

"I know…Dammit. It's like I lose my mind when you're around."

He combed his fingers through his hair again, all those pec and shoulder and arm muscles bunching and flexing, and Maya gave a little sigh.

"I'm doing a few things around you I'm not used to too," she told him.

"Oh?"

"Yeah, like having tingles where I haven't tingled in a long time."

His eyes darkened.

"And having dirty dreams at night about playing doctor. And finding giant plastic giraffe heads sexy. And realizing that swimming is a really wonderful sport."

Alex just stared at her for three heartbeats. Then he shook his head. "I followed the tingling and the dirty dreams."

She grinned. "The giraffe head in the lobby at Children's."

"You went to the hospital?"

She nodded. "To find you. And okay, so it wasn't the giraffe that was sexy, but it was the realization of what you do every day, that people are bringing you their children and putting their trust and hope in you..." She trailed off and took a step forward. "That's really sexy. I never realized that before."

Without thinking too hard about it—or maybe thinking about it much at all—she lifted her hand and traced a fingertip over one of the few water drops the air hadn't yet dried from his chest. "And I've always thought that I was more into contact sports, but swimming has just jumped to the top of my favorite spectator sports."

Very much as on the night he'd come to the studio, Alex took her finger and pressed her whole hand against his chest, covering it with his. She could feel his heart hammering under her palm and realized immediately that skin to skin was exactly how she wanted to be with Alex Nolan.

"You've got to stop thinking I'm some kind of hero," he said gruffly.

She shrugged. "You are. Super Dad in the making, remember?"

"Thanks to you."

"Well, some of the best superheroes have someone in the background giving them advice and cheering them on," she said. "Batman has Alfred, Tony Stark has Pepper, my favorite is Felicity for the Arrow." She wrinkled her nose. "Interesting that two of those three are women—"

Alex cut her off by sealing his lips over hers. Again.

\* \* \*

Alex felt heat and desire rip through him as Maya melted into him and opened her lips with a soft sigh.

The first time he'd kissed her had been spontaneous. And it had been enough to haunt his dreams afterward. It had given him just enough of a taste to make him a complete addict.

But it was nothing like this.

Maya seemed to recover from her surprise much quicker this time. Which was a problem. Because the moment she got over that surprise was the moment she started touching him. And the moment she started touching him, Alex was done for.

Not only did she slide both hands up over his chest and shoulders to link her fingers behind his neck, but she did it slowly and sensually, as if she was taking in every sensation. Not to mention that it was skin to skin.

Alex had never wanted to feel a woman's hands on him as much as he wanted Maya's. She seemed to feel the same way. Her fingers stayed linked behind his neck for all of five seconds, then she ran them up into his hair, then down his back, then around to his sides, sliding up and down over his ribs.

Every single stroke seemed to wind him tighter and tighter and finally he simply admitted that resisting her would take superhuman strength, and he was very human.

With a low near growl, he grasped her hips and brought her closer. She arched into him with the sexiest moan he'd ever heard, and Alex worked on memorizing the feel and taste of every millimeter of her mouth even as he calculated the risk of laying her down in the nearest lounge chair and simply following every male instinct he had.

A moment later it seemed that Maya had the same idea. She began walking backward, bringing him with her, the sides of his swim trunks bunched in her fists. However, she seemed unaware that at some point in trying to get as close as they possibly could, they'd turned and she was walking toward the edge of the pool.

Alex tore his mouth from hers as he stopped her progress. He had to take a couple of panting breaths before he could speak, however. When was the last time a kiss had been that hot and all-consuming?

Had a kiss ever been like this one?

"If you're going to keep doing that every time I start to ramble, I should warn you, I have a lot of ramblings where those came from." She was also breathless.

"I do keep doing that, don't I?"

"To shut me up, right?"

"Truthfully?" Alex wasn't sure he should tell her this, or even admit it to himself, but he found himself saying, "It's not so much to stop you as it is that there comes a point in your explanations where I stop being able to follow and I kind of zone out and then I have nothing keeping me from thinking about how much I want to kiss you."

"Oh." She seemed pleasantly surprised. Her smile grew. "Still not a reason to stop rambling."

He laughed but shook his head at the same time. When Maya was around, he wanted to do stupid shit like battle with bo staffs and binge-watch *The Flash* and find out what kind of popcorn she liked. She struck him as a Cajun-spiced popcorn kind of girl. Talk about things that didn't matter.

"You were about to fall into the pool," he told her, focusing on the water behind her.

She glanced back, then smiled at him. "Oops. Guess you're still distracting."

Distracting. God, he liked that. Losing his mind was one thing, but at least she was having a similar reaction. He did everything so carefully in his life. He considered everything, always had. Even the night he'd gotten Rachel pregnant, he'd been careful about taking a cab and using a condom. That was probably what made him the craziest about her getting pregnant in the first place. He was never reckless. But damn, throwing caution to the wind in those few moments with Maya had felt so good.

Of course, it wasn't something he could sustain. There were very good reasons he was careful, and if his need to consider every potential physical threat carried over into the rest of his life, it wasn't as if that were a bad thing. "Wouldn't want you to get wet," he said.

Her smile instantly died, and she stepped forward. "I don't mind getting wet."

If her words hadn't been enough to make his cock

jump up with a "How you doin'?" then her hand on his chest again primed him so hard and fast that it was a wonder he was able to stay upright.

Everything about her screamed, "Take a chance, work hard play hard, you only live once." Those were practically his antimantras.

But the mischief in her eyes, the teasing smile, the go-big-or-go-home that seemed to seep from her pores called to him. For better or worse.

He swallowed hard. "You're not dressed for swimming." Yeah, swimming. That's what she'd meant by her comment.

Maya looked down. "Huh, look at that. You're right."

Then she kicked off her sandals, pulled her T-shirt over her head, and shed her pants, all before enough blood made its way to Alex's head for him to even begin to form a thought of stopping her.

"There, that's better."

She had on a cherry-red bra-and-panty set that made Alex so damned grateful that he was a heterosexual man and that he was standing in this very spot at this very moment.

She wasn't overly endowed, but her breasts filled the bright-red cups perfectly. She was trim and toned, and Alex's palms itched with the urge to touch.

She stood grinning at what he was sure was a completely stupid look on his face. But he was, literally, struck dumb.

Then she did exactly what he would have expected even after only having known her for a few days. She jumped right into the deep end without a second thought.

What a perfect metaphor.

Maya came up a moment later, her dark hair slicked back, treading water as she smiled at him. "Come in with me. You know you want to."

Yep, a perfect metaphor indeed. Maya Goodwin inviting him to jump into the deep end with her. And him wanting to. He was so fucked.

Three seconds later he dove in. Headfirst.

When he surfaced, he swam to her. "I can't believe you're here, swimming with me in your underwear."

"I could take them off if you'd rather."

Oh yes, he definitely would rather. "If this was my private pool, I'd be all over that."

She swam a little closer and looked him directly in the eye. "Would you?"

He frowned. "Why would you question if I would take the chance to get you naked?"

As soon as he said it out loud, he knew where this was going.

"You don't have time for things like that."

Yep. That was where it was going. He sighed. "It's true."

"And I'm guessing that you feel a little out of your element with me."

He laughed. "You think?" With her he was completely out of his comfort zone in every way. With the exception of the fact that she was a woman wearing only her underwear. "Though I do know what to do with a woman once she gets down to her bra and panties, thank you very much."

Maya laughed. "See? This was just my attempt to make you feel more comfortable."

Knowing he shouldn't, but drawn like a sailor to the

sirens, Alex moved in close enough that their chests were practically brushing. "I don't feel more comfortable with you in your underwear, Maya."

"More in control, then?" she asked.

"Definitely not that."

She looked up at him, studying his eyes. "And you hate that? You hate these feelings?"

He didn't answer right away. Instead he took her hand and swam toward the shallow water, tugging her with him. When they could both touch the bottom, he let go of her and faced her.

"Yes," he said honestly. "I hate feeling distracted and thrown off. I kind of hate that you can make me do things like go after some punk teenagers at the mall or buy a bo staff or jump into a pool after you." He took a deep breath. "I hate that you've been shot, burned, and scarred. You don't even hesitate to charge in, even if you might get hurt."

She didn't flinch away from his words. In fact, she moved an inch closer and nodded. "Our bodies are made to do things," she said. "For me, sitting around and not doing things that need to be done would hurt more."

He couldn't help it any longer. Alex lifted his hand to her cheek and confessed. "And even while I'm hating all of that, I also love that you're willing to reach into a burning car to save a dog's life and that you've been a cop and now dress up as a superhero to help kids figure themselves out. I love that you didn't hesitate to step in when you saw a teenage girl getting harassed. And I love that you're here, bringing me books to help me out even after I tried not to see you again." He leaned in and put his forehead against hers. "And I especially love that you have the answers to everything I'm wondering about right now. It isn't very often that I get to have all the answers. Because of you, I can for Charli."

He trailed his hand down the side of her neck, over the bumps of one scar, across her shoulder and down her arm. Every bit of the puckered, tight, ravaged skin made his heart turn over. This woman was a problem. She was unpredictable. She was fun and tempting, and fearless. But she was also clearly willing to dive—literally at times—into situations before thinking through the possible consequences. He wasn't that guy. He couldn't keep up with that.

Maya linked her fingers behind his neck. But this time it was so he could continue to explore her scar. Alex lifted his head, watching as his fingers trailed along the underside of her arm over the jagged lines and remnants of bad burns. He couldn't imagine the pain and, maybe more, the frustration the injuries and healing time had caused her.

"God, Maya," he breathed.

"It doesn't hurt," she said softly. "I like your hands on me."

He liked it too. Too much. "And you don't even let this stop you," he said. "Even facing a permanent disability that took you out of the field, you still found a way to do things you love and make a difference."

She pulled back a little. "Thank you. But it's not permanent, Alex. Don't worry. I'll be back in the field soon."

He frowned slightly, running his hands over the tightness that kept her from lifting her arm fully over her head. "Back in the field?" There was no way she was going back in the field with this injury.

She nodded. "Eventually. I'm working on it. It's gotten a lot better."

The scars were the perfect symbol of her daring...and her recklessness. He wanted to kiss every one of them. "I'm glad it's getting better," he said.

Maya smiled. "Me too. I love the studio. But I want to get back."

"You think that's going to happen?" Alex asked.

Maya nodded. "Of course. If I want it bad enough. I can overcome a few tight muscles and scars. Attitude is everything."

No, it wasn't. Alex wanted to tell her about how no matter how great Charli's attitude was, no matter how hard she worked, no matter how much she wanted something, her hemophilia would always be a consideration and would always hold her back.

And Maya's arm wasn't that different. Pushing past her restrictions wouldn't kill her, but it could do permanent damage. There was a limit to how much she could expect an arm with muscle and nerve damage to do. Not everything got better with hard work and a positive outlook.

But Maya was in denial. He got that. He saw it in parents sitting across his desk from him every day.

Alex moved his hand up her arm to her neck and cupped the back of her head. "Why do you need to go back? What you do at the studio is so important."

Her smile dimmed. "It is," she agreed. "But..." She chewed on her bottom lip.

"What is it?" he asked.

She sighed. "Okay, honestly?"

"Please."

"I really like kids. Like really. But—"

"You like real weapons more than pretend ones?" He let the corner of his mouth curl up.

She tipped her head. "Yes, there is that. But I also like chasing real bad guys." As she said it, it was clear she couldn't fight the big grin that stretched her lips.

He chuckled lightly even as his gut churned with the truth—that was Maya. "You prefer real danger, putting your life on the line every day going after bad people who do bad things, to working in a safe studio, with little kids in capes who love everything you say and do?"

She shrugged her uninjured shoulder. "I would love to do both."

"But you really like the danger?"

A tiny frown wrinkled the space between her eyebrows. "No. The danger is just part of it. It's the doing good that I love."

"You do good at the studio." For some reason he really wanted her to just keep working at the studio.

But then he realized that she would have reached in for that dog even if she hadn't been in uniform. Just as she'd gone after those troublemakers at the mall. She would always plunge in where she thought she could help. And he really liked that about her. Even while he acknowledged that it was what made her the wrong woman for him. And his daughter.

"What came first? Your love for chasing bad guys or superheroes?" he asked, feeling a thickness in his throat. Regret. He knew very well that the emotion had a physical feel to it.

"Superheroes." She hadn't even had to think about it.

"And so being a cop was the best way for you to be

a superhero?" he asked, envisioning Maya as a little girl with a blanket tied around her neck as a cape.

She shrugged. "I'm not sure. I was always fascinated by the good-versus-bad thing. Those were my favorite bedtime stories, my favorite movies even as a kid. My moms were always fighting for their rights as gay women. They were always talking about how important it is to stand up for what you believe in and for what's good and right, even if it's not popular. And sometimes because it's not popular. I'm sure I got it from them."

They were talking about her childhood and super-heroes, but Alex wasn't sure he'd ever been as turned on by a woman as he was by Maya. Her skin glistened with water, the red silk clung to her, her nipples were hard points pressing into his chest, and her body was hot and soft under his hands, seemingly offered up for him to appreciate and explore. Just the ease with which she exposed her body, her injury, even her stories, drew him in. She didn't try to hide anything. She was open and honest, and he couldn't have stopped touching her for anything.

Alex moved his leg in the water, sliding his knee be-tween hers. He leaned in, pressing more of his body against hers. His mouth hovered over hers.

"Alex," she said, almost in a whisper.

He couldn't resist. He kissed her, more slowly this time, savoring her mouth as he ran his hands over her body. He stroked his palms down her back, and she arched closer. He filled his hands with the curve of her ass, the wet silk doing nothing to disguise the smooth skin and firm muscles that his fingers explored thoroughly.

Maya pressed her hips forward, and Alex slid his

hands up to cup her breasts, teasing her nipples as she moved restlessly against him.

"More, Alex, please," she panted.

With a groan he tugged one cup of her bra down, baring her gorgeous breast. He thumbed her nipple, making her gasp. He rolled it between his thumb and finger, watching her face. Her lips parted as she breathed raggedly. Maya's hands moved over him too, stroking his shoulders, his chest, down his sides and around to his ass. She brought him forward, more firmly against her, and he knew she could feel every inch of how much he wanted her.

But that wasn't enough, apparently. She reached between them and traced over his hard cock with her open palm. Her hand was hot against him even in the cool water, and Alex knew he was about ten seconds from losing his mind.

The pool was for the building only and very few tenants really used it, especially at this time of day, but there was no guarantee they wouldn't be interrupted. And that was the only thing that kept him from stripping her bare and taking her right there and then.

"Maya, we can't," he said roughly.

"I know." Her voice was breathless. "Just let me touch you. Just keep touching me. A little more."

She was not the type of woman to back off. He needed to remember that. She was a risk taker. But Alex couldn't quite make himself take his hands off her just yet.

She whimpered as he peeled the other bra cup away from her skin. He felt desire pulse through him as he took both breasts in his hands, and he groaned again as her grip on him tightened when he tugged on her nipples.

"More. Skin," she said, moving her hand to slide it into the front of his swim trunks.

The feel of her hand on him with nothing between them, the way she wrapped her fingers around him and stroked him perfectly, made Alex do something he hadn't done in a long time—he threw caution to the wind.

He walked her backward to the edge of the pool farthest from the door. He pulled her hand from his cock—reluctantly—and turned her to face the cement wall. If she kept stroking him, he was going to embarrass himself in his building's community pool. But he wasn't done with her just yet.

"Hands on the side," he told her huskily in her ear. He noticed the little shiver that went through her and couldn't help but smile. He ran his hands up her arms and then around to cup her breasts again. He played with her nipples until she was squirming against him. Then he slid one hand down over her stomach and into the front of her panties.

She was hot and wet—not swimming-pool wet—and, most of all, willing. Hell, it wouldn't surprise him if Maya loved the whole we-could-get-caught thing and took risks like this all the time. Her fingers gripped the edge of the pool, and her head fell forward as she gave a heartfelt, "Yes, Alex."

He ran his middle finger over her clit while pinching one nipple and felt her buck against his hand. "What is it about you?" he asked against her neck before kissing her there. "You're under my skin. We just met."

She ground her ass against his cock. "I know. Me too. You too."

Alex prayed for a few more minutes of privacy as

he moved his hand lower, sliding two fingers deep. The hot tightness nearly buckled his knees, and he couldn't help but immediately start moving, stroking, circling his thumb over her clit.

"Alex." She moved a hand to grip his wrist, holding him against her as she rode his hand, and it didn't even take minutes to get her there. It was one, maybe two, before she tightened around his fingers and cried out.

Hard and fast. That didn't surprise him a bit.

Alex breathed deeply, kissed her neck, then eased back and moved the straps of her bra up to her shoulders before turning her around. He kissed her with all the confusion and passion and happiness that were coursing through him.

But when he pulled back and looked at her, she didn't give him the big satisfied grin or even the smug smile he'd expected. She looked...dazed.

"You okay?" he brushed a strand of hair back from her cheek.

She swallowed. "So, that was...wow."

He couldn't agree more. "Maya—"

Suddenly a high-pitched chirping reached them. Alex recognized it immediately. It was the alarm on his phone. He'd set it to remind himself to get ready in time for Charli and Rachel to arrive for dinner. Here.

Dammit. He'd completely forgotten everything for a few minutes there with Maya. But Charli and Rachel were coming here for dinner. Soon. His first thought after that was that he needed to get rid of Maya. Not because of Rachel, but because of Charli. His heart sank.

The very scars that he wanted to kiss one by one were the reasons Maya wasn't good for Charli. If only Maya weren't so physically daring. If she didn't go all out in everything she did. She was amazing. She was just the type of person he should want Charli to look up to—smart, confident, big hearted, funny. But she didn't believe in physical limitations. And Charli had to believe in them.

"I'm sorry. That's my alarm to remind me to get ready for dinner." But he didn't move to exit the pool. Alex ran his hand over Maya's arm again. He felt her tremble slightly. "Your sense of touch is intact in this area."

She smiled up at him. "I think I could lose every nerve ending in my whole body and still feel you touching me."

Damn. Alex couldn't remember having wanted a woman the way he did Maya Goodwin.

"Okay. So . . ." She took a deep breath. "I should go so you can get ready," she said.

He grudgingly let her pull out of his arms. She seemed similarly reluctant.

"Oh," she said, as she made her way to the four steps that led up out of the pool, "I also wanted to tell you that I've been thinking more about Charli, and there are lots of modifications we can make in class. If you do want to bring her."

That pulled his attention from the clingy wet red silk and the inches and inches of gorgeous bare skin that were emerging from the water.

"What kinds of modifications?" he asked. Not that they would make him take Charli to class, but maybe they were measures he could implement at home.

"Well, anything, really. I've had asthmatics and a girl with epilepsy and a couple of kids in wheelchairs in class. It just depends on her needs."

Alex's mind spun to find something that was similar

to hemophilia but that didn't require him to say *hemo-philia*. It was crazy, he knew. He said and read and wrote and thought the word every day, hundreds of times. It was what he did—almost his entire practice and research agenda. But it was such a habit to deflect when talking about himself and now, apparently, his daughter in relation to the condition.

Alex carefully, purposefully kept his life in compart-ments. His hemophilia was in its own box. Always. When he was growing up, the hemophilia had governed every part of his life. He'd gotten so exhausted thinking about it, talking about it, adjusting for it, that at some point when he was out from under his parents' constant care, he'd stopped telling anyone he had it. And he didn't talk about it now. It had been his motivation for choosing his field, but no one at work knew that he shared the condi-tion with his patients. His patients certainly didn't know. None of his girlfriends had known. Charli didn't know. Rachel did, but they'd spoken about it minimally. Rachel had picked up on the obvious signs that he didn't like to discuss it and had never pushed for more conversation than was necessary.

He kept his professional life separate from his personal life, but after only a couple of months, Charli had already started mixing up his boxes. Alex had his assistant look-ing things up for him, and he'd asked Austin for help too. He talked about Charli with his coworkers and friends. He couldn't not talk about her. He was proud of her, and she was taking over so much of his...everything. But he didn't talk about her hemophilia with anyone but Rachel.

And now there was Maya. Her friends were also her coworkers, her hobbies were also how she made a living.

She spoke candidly about her injury. Everything in Maya's life seemed to blend together.

"Charli has a bleeding disorder," he finally said after he realized Maya had been standing on the steps just watching him. And waiting. "Her blood doesn't clot normally. Which means she has more risk of bleeding badly from relatively minor injuries." This was important stuff for people working with Charli to know, and Alex realized he owed his mother an apology. She'd gone overboard, for sure, but as a father he now understood that he needed to discuss his child's condition and what considerations and modifications were needed to keep her safe. "Obviously cuts and scrapes are an issue, but blows and falls are especially dangerous because they can cause internal injuries that are harder to see, and treat."

Maya's eyes were wide, and Alex prepared for either a barrage of questions or a stuttered apology and agreement that her class was not a good place for Charli.

But this was Maya Goodwin. She'd been surprising him since he'd met her.

"That's so not a problem," she said.

He quickly realized her eyes had widened in excitement rather than shock.

"We can make her some armor," Maya said, clearly thinking out loud. "We'll pad it really well. We can make it thick, but light. The kids don't swing their swords that hard anyway, but with the added protection, she would be okay. And we can totally make the swords out of foam board or something."

Maya was standing on the steps of the pool in only her bra and panties, her skin glimmering with water, talking about weapons and armor as if it were the most natural thing in the world. As if he hadn't just had his hands all over her body, making her come, a few minutes ago in a semipublic pool. She'd been fully caught up in those moments with him, and she'd sucked him in too, making him ignore the thoughts that told him that they should be more careful, that they'd just met, that touching her like that would be the start of a serious addiction.

And now she was fully caught up in this moment and the possibilities for Charli. And damn if Alex didn't feel himself getting pulled into this idea too.

"You can just make armor and swords?" Alex asked. But of course she could. He was starting to wonder if there was anything Maya couldn't do. Or at least anything she didn't think she could do.

"Oh, definitely."

Her enthusiasm drew him to her. Literally. He walked through the water until he stood at the base of the steps.

"We do it all the time. We do costumes and props for Sophie's theater and for the studio and for our cosplay. I'm awesome at making weapons. I win awards at Comic Con every year."

Alex blinked at her several times. He was completely turned on by a woman who had just said the terms *cosplay* and *Comic Con* to him. "So you could show me how to do it? For Charli?" Had he really just asked to be taught to make weapons out of foam board—whatever that was?

Maya gave him a smile. "Of course."

Every warning system in his head was going off. The more time he spent with her, the more he was going to be drawn in and attracted. But he still said, "Great."

"You can bring Charli to our house this week."

"Just me," he said. "Charli...lives with her mom. We get together for dinner but we haven't spent a lot of time alone." That was all true. They hadn't gotten to the one-on-one point yet.

Maya nodded. "Okay." Then she tipped her head, studying him. "And you want to be the cool one, right?"

Alex stepped up next to her. "What do you mean?"

"I mean, you want to learn the bo staff and sword moves, you want to learn about the superheroes, and you want to make armor and weapons with me, and then you want to do it all at home with Charli so you're the cool one."

Well...yeah. That was definitely part of it. "I could use some cool points with my daughter," he admitted.

Maya's smile—part delight and part affection—hit him directly in the chest. "I can totally help you with cool points."

Yeah, he knew she could. It was the heat she produced in him that was the problem.

"Great."

"But you should also come to the studio Monday night. We need to fast-track your bo staff and sword routines."

Damn. He really wanted to go. And it was for Charli, after all. Maya knew where he stood. This would be fine. "I can come over after dinner with Charli. Okay if it's late?"

"Anytime."

He wondered what she'd do if he showed up on her doorstep in the middle of the night. But he knew—she'd let him in and rock his world. So he promptly stopped thinking about that.

Maya climbed the rest of the way out of the pool, and Alex followed, never taking his eyes off her.

He did need to get ready for Charli and Rachel. They had done most of the family dinners at Rachel's new place or had gone to restaurants. This was the first time they'd been to Alex's for dinner. He had a bo staff ready with a big red bow on it for Charli, and he was excited—and anxious—about the evening ahead.

But he still didn't want Maya to go. And it wasn't even about the clingy red silk.

In fact, part of him said it was stupid to have her leave. She should absolutely stay for dinner. Maya was the perfect person to make sure the evening was a success. Giving Charli a bo staff and introducing her to someone who could show her everything about it, all while talking about Charli's favorite things, would get him huge cool points. So many points that he could probably screw a whole bunch of things up afterward and still be in Charli's good graces for a long, long time. That would be really nice. He was sure screwing things up was going to happen.

But he couldn't have Maya stay. Maya would dazzle Charli, no doubt about it, and there were several things wrong with that. Alex would never out-cool Maya, for one thing. And then there was Rachel. He didn't know how Rachel would feel about Maya—or vice versa—but he did know that putting the women side by side for an evening wouldn't help him figure out any feelings. He wanted to try to have something with Rachel. Maybe they would only be best friends raising a daughter together, but Maya was already a huge distraction.

Yeah, he couldn't have her here.

He handed Maya his towel first. She ran it over her face and then handed it back.

"Here, hold it for a second."

He did. As he watched, dumbfounded, Maya unhooked her wet bra and tossed it on the chair. Then she slid her wet panties off and tossed them too.

She was bare-assed naked in front him. Beside the pool. The not-exactly-public-but-definitely-not-private pool.

She took the towel back from him and ran it over her body. Her nipples were hard, and Alex had no idea if it was because she was cold or because she was still as turned on as he was. But he didn't care. She was completely gorgeous, and her nipples were only the beginning.

When she was dry, she handed the towel back, seemingly unconcerned about being naked in semipublic and oblivious to Alex's reaction. She pulled her shirt and pants back on, then plopped her hat on her head.

"You can bring those back to me when they're dry," she said, gesturing toward her bra and panties.

She came close, rose on tiptoe, and put her lips to his cheek. She whispered, "You can blink now, Doc." Then she kissed his cheek, turned, and headed out the door.

Alex watched her go, not blinking, until the door bumped shut behind her.

Then he shook his head. She might have been unconcerned but she had definitely not been oblivious. That was also very Maya.

His alarm sounded for a second time, snapping him back to the moment. He quickly dried off, not unaware that the towel was damp because of Maya's body and not unaffected by that. He also picked up her bra and panties.

Yeah, definitely not unaffected. He quickly wrapped the wet silk in his towel to get it out of sight and hopefully out of mind. Eventually. At least until he closed his eyes at the end of the day and replayed the entire thing from the moment he'd seen Maya standing by the pool to the moment the door had closed behind her.

# CHAPTER SEVEN

ey."

Maya looked up from her laptop as Sophie came into the kitchen. "Hey."

Sophie crossed to the stove and grabbed the teakettle, but she was watching Maya. "You okay?"

Maya thought about that. Was she okay? She really wasn't sure. It had been only a few hours since she'd been at Alex's, but she missed him.

"Alex's daughter has hemophilia," she said. She'd been sitting at the kitchen table for over an hour reading about the condition.

"What's that mean?" Sophie asked as she filled the kettle.

"Her blood doesn't clot like a normal person's, so when she bleeds, it can be really serious."

Sophie turned the burner on and joined Maya at the table. "Alex told you about this today?"

Maya nodded, her eyes going back to the webpage in

front of her. It was one thing to hear that bleeding could be dangerous for Charli, but it was another to really read about hemophilia and the risks. "He doesn't want her to take the class with me because of it. If she gets hit or falls or something, it could be really dangerous."

"But the kids in your class don't hit each other or fall, do they?" Sophie asked.

"Well, at first I didn't think so. But as I'm thinking about things, yeah, I mean sometimes. It's always accidental, and it's minor—but minor to a regular kid isn't minor to Charli."

Sophie nodded. "So she doesn't take the class."

Maya sighed.

Sophie smiled. "But you really want her to take the class."

"I do. The kid loves everything we do in that class. She's a dream student."

"And you have a thing for her dad."

Maya didn't even bother to deny it. "Yep. A big thing. But you know what? It's not even about getting into his pants."

Sophie snorted and gave her a look.

Maya grinned. "Okay, it's not just to get into his pants. He's so . . . and he doesn't even realize it."

Sophie lifted an eyebrow. "He's so . . . ?" she asked. "It's a weird day when you run out of words."

"He wants to be her hero," Maya said. "How can I not get all hot and bothered about that? But he's so focused on what he doesn't know and what he can't do for her that he's not realizing what he's already doing."

Sophie's expression softened, and she propped her chin on her hand. "What's he already doing?"

"Being there. Dinner every night with her. Binge-watching movies so he can talk to her about what she loves. Coming to my studio—the last place in the world he belongs—to find out how to relate to her." Maya sighed. And she never sighed over guys. "He's so far out of his comfort zone, and it's all for her."

"Sounds like Dawn."

Maya smiled as she thought of her mother. "It does."

"No wonder you like him."

Dawn was the less maternal of Maya's two moms. She had been the one who had been happy being only a couple rather than a family, but who had agreed to adopt a baby when Kristine, Maya's other mother, wanted to. Dawn had loved Maya, supported her, cheered her on, but she'd never been the warm, cuddly, expressive type that Kristine was. However, she had sat and played dolls and had done Maya's hair and had made four dozen cookies at midnight one night when Maya had forgotten she had to bring them for the bake sale the next day. The braids and cookies had been terrible, but Maya had understood that it was all done out of love.

"I do like him," Maya said, thinking about that as she said it. "I want to lick him from head to toe and beg him to do me in that pool he's got at his building, but I also really like him."

Sophie seemed to think that was hilarious. "You do realize," she asked, after she'd stopped laughing, "that liking him and wanting to lick him are a pretty great combination?"

"I do," Maya said, nodding. She totally did. She couldn't remember the last time it had happened, actually. She liked a lot of guys, and she'd had sex with a few of

them, and it had been fine. Maybe even good in a couple of instances. But wanting to lick someone? That was
a rarity. "And besides all of that great dad stuff, he's also
this guy who works with kids on some of the most complicated stuff there is. They have genetic conditions that
won't get better, that he can't fix. And that frustrates him.
But he does it anyway."

"What does he treat?" Sophie asked.

"Kids with hemophilia. Like Charli," she sighed.
Again. "I mean, he chose his life's work because of her."
That was amazing in and of itself.

Sophie frowned. "I thought you told us that he'd just
met her."

"Right. She's nine. I think it's been only a few
months."

"So he couldn't be a genetic specialist because of
Charli," Sophie said.

*Oh.* Maya thought about that. That was true. *Right.
Huh.* "That's...interesting," Maya agreed.

What were the chances that Alex had a daughter with
the same condition he specialized in, without knowing it?

"Well, it's genetic, right?" Sophie said. "That means
Charli got it from one of her parents, right?"

That was exactly what it meant. How had Maya not
thought of that? She quickly opened a search and typed
in, "how do kids get hemophilia?" She opened the link to
the World Federation of Hemophilia's website, her heart
pounding. It had a short, easy-to-understand explanation
and a diagram explaining how inheritance occurred.

"Well?" Sophie asked. "What's it say?"

"The gene for hemophilia is carried on the X chro-
mosome." Maya lifted her head and looked at Sophie.

"The only ways for a female to have hemophilia is if her mother is a carrier or her father has it. A daughter of a man with hemophilia becomes a carrier, actually, but sometimes carriers can have symptoms just like a true hemophiliac."

Sophie's eyes widened. "Oh."

Maya nodded. "Yeah."

"Maybe her mom is a carrier," Sophie said.

Maybe. But somehow Maya knew that wasn't how Charli had inherited her hemophilia. Alex had it. She was sure of it. "It does say that thirty percent of people with hemophilia don't get it from their parents. Something in their genes changes and causes it."

"But that's a pretty big coincidence considering Alex has made his whole career about it. Even before he knew Charli," Sophie said, echoing Maya's thoughts exactly.

The teakettle whistled, and Sophie got up to make her tea.

Maya quickly typed "Dr. Alex Nolan" into the search. She opened page after page, reading his bio over and over, but nowhere did it mention that he was a hemophiliac. Only that he was a respected expert in the field and had contributed greatly to the knowledge base.

"I don't think he talks about it," Maya said softly.

"Why do you think that?" Sophie asked, pushing a cup of tea toward Maya.

"It's not anywhere on any of the websites or in any of the articles about him or the interviews he's done."

"And he didn't tell you," Sophie said.

Maya knew it sounded ridiculous that she would even expect that. But...yeah. "We talked all about my arm. How it happened, how I'm working to get back on the force, everything. And he told me about Charli. He knows that I know what he does for a living. Why not tell me?"

"Maybe he will. Maybe he didn't think it was time."

"Not time?" Maya asked. What the hell was he waiting for?

Sophie laughed. "Not everyone is as open and honest about everything as you are, Maya."

Well, that was for sure. Kiera had only really come around to sharing emotionally with her roommates since meeting Zach. And Sophie, for all her sweetness and friendliness, didn't talk about her past or her family much. Maya knew that her mom hadn't been around and her dad had been a con man, even spending time in jail, but Maya didn't know where he was now. As far as she knew, Sophie didn't have anything to do with him, and she definitely didn't talk about him other than the one night when the margaritas had loosened her tongue enough for her to share about his arrest record.

Okay, so not everyone was the open book Maya was. Still, she felt very left out thinking that Alex had a major health condition that he hadn't told her about.

Then again, he'd made it pretty clear that he had intended only to take her class. Not to get to know her. Not to spend time alone with her.

She couldn't say why, but it really bothered her that there was something huge about Alex she hadn't known until she'd stumbled upon it accidentally.

She'd known the guy for days. Not even weeks. Why did she think that she should know something—anything, really—about him? She couldn't explain it. But it did bother her.

And suddenly she was worried too.

"Oh my God, Soph," she said, opening the search page yet again. "He has a bleeding disorder."

Sophie's wide eyes told Maya that she didn't understand Maya's sudden urgency.

She typed in "what happens when a hemophiliac gets injured." She read with her heart in her throat.

"Maya, what is it?" Sophie finally asked after a few minutes.

Maya shook her head. "He could have been really hurt at the mall that first day. In fact, I think he was hurt. That asshole kid kicked Alex in the knee. This says that a hemophiliac can easily bleed into a joint or muscle and cause a lot of damage. They have to take a clotting factor to help stop the bleeding." She looked up at her friend. "He never should have gotten into that whole situation with me."

Sophie rolled her eyes. "Sure, a guy like Alex isn't going to step in."

"But he shouldn't," Maya said. "He could get really hurt. This is serious!"

Sophie reached out and laid her hand on Maya's. "I know. And I'm very sure Alex knows. You don't have to worry about him."

Maya chewed on her lip. Maybe she didn't have to. But suddenly she did.

"He looks at me like I'm crazy when I talk about pushing my arm," she said, thinking back on their conversations. She shivered as she remembered him touching her scars, running his hand over her so gently. She'd never wanted a man more than she had in that moment. "God, Soph, an injury like mine could have killed him." She shivered again but for a whole different reason. "I bled like crazy. They had to give me a couple of units at the hospital." She sat back in the kitchen chair and pulled her leg up, propping her foot on the seat and wrapping her arms around her leg. "The things I do would be suicide for him. The falls and blows I take, the way we twist our shoulders and knees and ankles, the cuts—even the sai the other night. I mean that was minor, but it would have been something he'd have to worry more about."

Sophie nodded. "I guess you're right. I don't think of all of those things as dangerous, really. But in his case, yeah." She leaned back in her chair too. "But you don't do that hardcore stuff with the kids. You don't even do that stuff in most of your adult classes. Those are your own workouts and when you spar with Ben and stuff."

Maya shrugged. "I guess I had visions of teaching Alex and doing some sparring with him."

Sophie grinned at her and wiggled her eyebrows. "Well, you can still spar with him—you'll just have to be gentle."

Maya smiled. She knew Sophie was just joking around. But she couldn't shake the idea that hanging out with her and doing the things she loved could be incredibly dangerous for Alex. At least there wasn't anything they could do sexually that would be a risk to him. Was there?

She sat up and immediately started searching that as well. She needed to know. Because, even if she did have to be gentle, she was going to get into Alex Nolan's pants.

"Your class should be okay for Charli, though, right?" Sophie asked, sipping her tea.

Maya pulled her eyes from the screen even as her mind

yelled, "Well, can you ride Alex like a bucking bronco or not?"

She cleared her throat and focused on Sophie. "I started looking all of this up because I told Alex we can make some modifications for Charli so she can do sword and bo staff work. He was really interested, but he wants to keep it at home. I suppose so he can monitor her and modify things more specifically." *And get her treatment faster if something goes wrong.* Maya's stomach knotted.

As she'd told Alex, she'd had kids with medical issues in class before. Asthma was common. She'd had a couple of diabetics. She'd had a kid with a prosthetic leg and several autistic kids. She wasn't completely clueless about modifications and watching for signs of trouble. But hemophilia was a new one. Something like four hundred babies in the entire United States were born with the condition each year. A girl having it was even rarer.

Sophie sat up, excitement in her eyes. "Were you talking about armor?" she asked.

Maya grinned in spite of her troubling thoughts. Of course Sophie would guess Maya had been talking about armor.

"Who's talking about armor? Armor for what?" Kiera asked, coming into the kitchen. Zach was right behind her.

"Are we making armor?" Zach asked. "Is it a new play?"

Sophie was most often the reason they all needed to get together for costuming. Her little theater barely made ends meet, so her friends pitched in however they could for costumes, props, backdrops, and more. Besides, it was fun and completely up all of their alleys. Even not-a-geek-at-all Zach. Since he'd been with Kiera, he'd been won over by their geeky ways.

"No, we're making armor for Maya's boyfriend's daughter," Sophie said.

Zach leaned back against the counter. "The doctor who's taking your class? The one that knows nothing about superheroes?"

"Well, he's not my boyfriend exactly," Maya said. "But yes, the doctor who knows nothing about superheroes."

Kiera plopped down at the table while Zach opened the fridge. "So what kind of armor and what for?"

Maya sighed happily. This was why these people were her best friends.

She explained the situation. By the time she was done, Zach had joined them with a sandwich and a can of beer.

"Sounds like a great idea," Zach said. "Something hard on the outside but light and really padded underneath. Fiberglass, probably? I don't think foam would be hard enough." He lifted his beer and took a swallow. Then looked around the table. "What?" he asked when he saw they were all smiling at him.

Maya pretended to wipe a tear from her eye. "I'm just so proud. You've come so far."

Zach rolled his eyes. "I'd have to be an idiot to not have picked up some of this stuff by now."

Kiera laughed. "I vote fiberglass too."

By the time they were done with their tea and beer, Kiera had sketched an idea for the armor, and Sophie was planning to take inventory of their supplies in the other room.

For a moment Maya was choked up. They were going to make armor for Charli. Actually, for Maya. Sure, they loved doing it, and it would be a good time—dorky as that sounded. But they were doing it because she had asked them to. Even though it was a little ridiculous.

"When's Charli coming to class?" Kiera asked, putting some finishing touches on her sketch.

Maya sighed. She really wanted Charli in class, and yet she really didn't. She'd be worried the entire time. "She's not. I'm going to have Alex give this to her." She smiled softly. "He wants to be the expert she turns to for all of this." Which was wonderful.

"But she'd have such fun in the class," Kiera said. "Couldn't he give it to her and then bring her to class?"

Maya shook her head. "I don't think that's a good idea. I don't want her to get hurt."

Kiera looked a little concerned as she set her pencil down. "Do you really think you need to worry about that?" she asked. "I mean, the armor and stuff will help, and you'll watch her. Plus she's nine. She must know a few things about how to keep herself safe. She doesn't live in a plastic bubble."

Maya frowned. "No. But this is serious stuff. And I don't know what her severity is. There's a range to how badly people with hemophilia bleed. If she has a severe case, she could just spontaneously bleed, not to mention having trouble if she gets hit or falls."

Kiera looked surprised. "I didn't know that. But kids do fall down sometimes. What do they do when that happens?"

Maya pressed her lips together and shook her head, suddenly overwhelmed by it. She'd wanted Alex to spar with her. Hell, at this point she might have trouble even kissing him aggressively next time.

"What's the headshake mean?" Kiera asked. "You don't know how they treat it?"

"Clotting factor," Maya managed. "Something they inject when they have a bleed."

"Okay," Kiera said soothingly. "That sounds good. There's something they can do about it."

"Maya," Sophie said, clearly reading her distress, "Alex isn't just a thirtysomething-year-old hemophiliac who's been living with this for all his life, he's also a doctor. A doctor who specializes in this. I'm sure he knows what he should do and shouldn't do."

Maya shrugged again, feeling suddenly depressed. "Yeah. And he tried not to see me again."

"That's not true," Sophie admonished.

"It is true. He wanted to exchange information via e-mail. I was the one that showed up there without an invitation."

"And he kissed you senseless," Sophie reminded her. "It didn't sound to me like he minded you showing up."

"No, but he hasn't told me about his condition."

"Maybe because he doesn't think it's an issue," Sophie said.

"Or maybe he doesn't intend to ever do anything strenuous with me," Maya said. Then a thought occurred to her. "Oh my God," she muttered.

"What?" both women said at once.

"Maybe he's scared of me."

They both looked startled.

"What?" Sophie asked.

Maya nodded. "He might be scared of me. He's concerned about how hard I push and that I'll go into a burning car after a dog and after some teenage assholes at the mall. He jumped into the pool after me today but he said he hated that I could make him do stuff like that." He'd also said he loved that stuff, but Maya understood— he was attracted, but he knew he needed to fight it. "He's afraid of what I'm going to get him into."

Sophie's eyes were wide. "Do you really think that?"

Maya did. She really did. "I'm a little…aggressive sometimes."

"You're brave, and you do the right thing," Sophie said loyally.

But Kiera was nodding. "Yeah, you can be aggressive."

Maya looked at her. "I can, right? I come on strong."

"You do."

"Kiera," Sophie said with a frown, "Maya is wonderful just how she is. If Alex can't keep up with her, then maybe he's not the right guy."

Maya didn't like that. She wanted Alex to be the right guy. That was strange, of course. A guy who had to be careful about everything he did physically? But yeah, she wanted Alex.

"I'm not saying she's not wonderful," Kiera said. "I'm just saying our go-all-in-hard-as-you-can girl here might be a little much." She looked at Maya. "I love you. You're awesome and kick-ass."

Maya patted her friend's arm. "I know you do. And yes, I am." That wasn't conceit. That was a fact. She liked being kick-ass. She worked at it. It fit her personality, of course. She'd been raised to confront things head-on by two very strong, independent women. And she loved to be physical—to use her body, to work up a sweat, to breathe hard. So yeah, she was kick-ass.

And she could be bad for Alex. Dammit.

"Okay," she decided with a deep breath. "I can tone it down."

Kiera frowned hard. "No. You should not have to change for him."

Maya knew exactly where Kiera was coming from. She'd had an ex-boyfriend who'd wanted to change everything about her, and he'd crushed her heart and soul when she'd refused. But this wasn't the same thing. "I'm not changing for him," she said. "He's not asking me to, for one thing. And I'll still be me. I can make adjustments like I do with you," she told Sophie with an affectionate smile. "You don't like to sweat, and you prefer long sword work to the up-close hand-to-hand stuff. So that's what we do. And that's fine."

Kiera seemed to be thinking that over. "Okay," she finally said. "You make adjustments, but you keep doing what you're doing."

"Well, I can do what I've been doing with all of you," Maya said. "I can spar with you guys and Ben and Rob and everyone else. But there are some things I want to do with Alex that I'm not doing with any of you."

She gave them all a grin, and they laughed.

Maya felt a lot better as they shut the kitchen lights off. But she definitely kept her laptop tucked under her arm. She had some articles to read before she saw Alex next time. Because she had also been known to be a little aggressive in the bedroom. Not whips and leather, but she loved it hard and fast, just like everything else in her life.

But she was totally up for learning some new techniques.

\* \* \*

"For me? Really?" Charli turned to Alex with wide eyes.

He nodded. "One for each of us. I know they're not ember lances, but I haven't been able to make a trip to Arietis IV to pick those up."

Alex actually felt as if he were holding his breath. With his luck, they didn't have ember lances on Piper's home planet. They were probably made somewhere else. And with his luck, Charli would know that. He resisted the urge to pull out his phone and e-mail Maya. She definitely would know.

He was trying too hard. He recognized that. But he couldn't pull it back. Dinner had gone well. Then they'd gone swimming and Charli had shown some real natural talent. She'd even said she would be interested in a swim team the next summer. Rachel had given him a grateful hug on her way back into the house afterward. At least he told himself it had been grateful. He wasn't sure he was up to dealing with it being more than that.

"This is still really awesome," Charli told him, taking the bo staff from where he'd propped it against the wall in his den.

"I can show you some spins if you want," he said, taking the other staff.

He really hoped she wanted to, but he was trying to play it cool. He didn't want to come on too strong. This was a relationship, it would take time to build, time for them to get to know one another. He knew that. But this was his kid. He should have been getting to know her from the first day she took a breath. She should know him and be completely comfortable with him. But instead of feeling as if they were a father and daughter, in many ways Alex felt as if he were an awkward teenage boy with his first crush. She was this amazing creature he didn't understand and who thought he was nice but a little weird. He wanted to do anything to make her happy, he wanted to keep her safe, he wanted to make sure she knew how special she was, and even a tiny smile from her made his heart leap.

"You know how to use these?" The question came from Rachel, though.

He nodded. "I do." He didn't have to admit that his entire knowledge of the subject was only a few days old and that it had come from a woman he wanted more than he'd ever wanted anyone.

"Wow, so maybe this is genetic," Rachel said with a smile.

Alex forced one too, but damn, that hit him right in the gut. One, this was most definitely not genetic. He basically shared no known interests with his daughter at all. His interest in the bo staff had come from wanting to have a conversation with a nine-year-old and from a new addiction to purple leather and sassy tough girls who wore it. Period.

But Charli did have something she'd gotten from him. And it was the thing that was going to keep her away from many of the things she apparently loved. Fuck.

Alex spun the bo staff. "Want to learn a spin or two?" he asked Charli.

She nodded enthusiastically, and he concentrated on the task, the moment, and just making her smile.

They went over the spins for about twenty minutes, then Charli asked, "What else can you teach me?"

"Well, there's more with the staff, of course," Alex said, assuming that was true. "And then there's sword work. If you're interested. The ember lance is really more like a sword. Josh Scott was into swords, mostly Japanese, and he put that into the movies when he wrote them." Alex had the niggling thought that he should send Maya flowers. He was basically plagiarizing everything she'd told him the other night.

"You mean Scott Josh?" Charli asked. "The director of *GR*?"

Well, of course his nine-year-old would know the director. "Sorry, yeah." He frowned. "How do you know that?"

"He has a vlog."

Of course he did. "Do you follow a lot of vlogs?" Alex asked.

"Yeah. And blogs too," Charli said. "The fandom of *GR* is amazing."

Right. And he almost hated to ask the next question. "Who are some of your favorite bloggers?" If Charli followed Maya, he was toast.

"Lots of different ones." She shrugged. "Some are about just *GR*, some are about a whole bunch of geeky stuff."

"Geeky?" Alex lifted a brow. "Is that an okay word to use?"

Charli grinned at him. "Us geeks know we're geeks," she said. "We're proud of it."

Terrific. Charli was basically a mini-Maya already. And she would love Maya's blog. Alex could only pray that the World Wide Web really was wide and that Charli wouldn't find Maya while he needed her for instruction.

Maybe after he knew everything there was to know . . .

He couldn't finish that thought. If he got to that point,

he wouldn't have an excuse to see Maya anymore. Or e-mail her. Or hope that she stopped by his apartment unannounced. He'd gone to her studio for a specific purpose, but eventually he'd be caught up. He was an intelligent guy. He just needed a little help. And the *GR* universe was only so big.

And maybe Charli would eventually move on to something he knew about. Maybe she'd really love swimming, or she'd enjoy geometry, or she'd want to learn to golf.

Or maybe she'd move on to a new geeky fandom that he'd need to learn all about from Maya. He could only hope.

"I think it sounds like someone could spend less time on her computer and more time on her English homework," Rachel said, interrupting Alex's crazy train of thought.

"Having trouble in English?" Alex asked Charli.

She shook her head and frowned at her mother. "No. It's fine."

"The teacher said you were rushing through your work so you don't have to bring any home," Rachel said.

"Yeah, because I want to get it done at school," Charli said. "I hate homework."

"Because you love computer time at home," Rachel said.

"So?"

"So, you need to take more time on your schoolwork, even if it means homework and less computer time," Rachel said.

Charli's frown grew. "You moved us to Boston. I don't have friends here. So I have to be online to talk to them."

"The people who write blogs and the people who comment on them are not friends," Rachel said.

"They are too," Charli told her. "You don't understand. These are my people."

Rachel sighed. It was clear they'd had this conversation before. More than once.

Alex knew that, if he was going to be fully involved as Charli's dad, he was going to have to lay down some rules for more than just her hemophilia. He was really not looking forward to that.

"Do you want to take some of those Italian cookies home?" Alex asked Charli, choosing diversion over confrontation for the moment.

"Sure," she said, still pouting over what her mother had said.

"There are plastic bags in the bottom drawer by the dishwasher," he told her.

"Okay." Charli started to return the bo staff to its position on the wall.

"You can take it with you and practice. Then I'll teach you something new next time."

"Tomorrow night?" she asked, brightening.

Could he see Maya and learn something new by tomorrow night? Alex didn't mind the idea. The thought of showing up on her doorstep went through his mind. But he wondered if they'd get to any bo staff routines. He couldn't get his mind off kissing her or off the bright-red underwear that was hanging on the towel rack in his master bath drying out. He did need to return that, though.

"We have tickets for *Into the Woods* tomorrow night, remember?" Rachel asked.

Alex had completely forgotten about the musical.

Rachel had asked him to go with them almost a month ago. A lot had happened in the past month.

"Oh." Charli looked crestfallen.

"We'll do the musical tomorrow night," Alex said. "But I promise we'll do more with the staff, okay?"

"And swords," Charli said.

"Definitely." Maya was right about the fast-tracking. He was going to need to see her more often. He was trying to be a good guy here, to keep his priorities straight, but this was all making it damned difficult.

Charli took the staff with her when she ran from the room.

Rachel turned to him. "You bought her a bo staff and are letting her take it home?"

"I know it seems like a bad idea, but if I teach her and we made some modifications, she'll be okay."

"I brought her here so that you could help me keep her safe." Rachel wrapped her arms around herself, looking worried. "I thought maybe she'd get excited about swimming again when she found out that you swim and saw your medals and stuff. And tonight she said she'd try it. It was all going well. And then you brought out that staff."

Alex had a case full of medals and trophies. He'd been a state champion swimmer in high school and a national champ in college. His coach had pushed for him to try out for the Olympic team, but Alex had wanted to go to medical school without the time off he would have needed to train and compete.

"I'd love for her to swim," Alex said honestly, "but we have to go slow. She's just getting to know me."

"And you don't want to tell her no," Rachel said.

They'd had this conversation too. Alex knew Rachel

needed help in setting boundaries with Charli and helping her understand the reasons for the boundaries. But he wanted time to get to know her first. And no, he did not want to tell her no.

"I don't want to tell her no," he admitted. "Ever. But I get it. I have to. I know. But let's let her like me before she hates me."

"Parenting isn't about being liked, Alex," Rachel said. "It's about protecting her. The right thing isn't always the easy thing."

Alex had said those words—or similar ones—to many parents over the years. But today, when Rachel said them to him, he flashed to entirely different things. Maya sticking her arm through the window of a burning car to save a dog. Maya protecting a teenage girl she didn't even know from harassers. Maya trying to get back on the police force to take down bad guys in spite of the pain and frustration her injury caused.

He admired her. And he wanted her with an ache that was becoming impossible to ignore. He was in so much trouble.

"You're right," he said to Rachel. She was. "I'm hoping that this bo staff and sword stuff will teach Charli that she can do the things she loves if she considers her condition and makes modifications."

Rachel took a deep breath. Finally she nodded. "Fine. I know your intentions are good."

Alex worked on not wincing at that. He wasn't doing this completely for Charli. He knew some of it was so he could keep seeing Maya.

"Thank you," he told her sincerely. "I promise you, Charli is my first priority."

That was true. But seeing Maya might be his second. Right where helping Rachel should have been.

Rachel crossed the carpet to him. She had to tip her head to look up at him, and Alex compared her height to Maya's before he could stop himself. Rachel was smaller, more slender where Maya was tight and toned. Alex made himself stop thinking right there. Before he got to breasts and asses.

"I'm sorry," Rachel said.

Since he was the one who should have been apologizing, even though she didn't know where his thoughts had gone, he shook his head. "You don't have to say that."

"I do. I should have told you about Charli a long time ago. I should have brought her to Boston before now."

Alex swallowed before replying. Rachel had never apologized for that. "I wish you had," he said honestly. "I've missed a lot." But she hadn't known how to find him. "But I don't blame you."

"This wasn't supposed to happen," she said softly. "It was supposed to be just one night. We weren't supposed to see each other again."

She was right. All of that was true. But now, picturing Charli in his mind, feeling how his heart had expanded, how his life had expanded, he knew that it—he and Rachel, Charli, all of it—had been meant to happen.

He reached out and folded Rachel into a hug. "That's not true," he told her, resting his chin on her head. "This is all happening exactly the way it was supposed to. For whatever reason."

Rachel wrapped her arms around him too, her cheek against his chest. He admired this woman. He loved her for loving and raising Charli, and for finally bringing her to him.

"Well, I'm sorry for me then," Rachel said against his shirt. "I sure could have used you a long time ago."

Alex ran a hand up and down her back. He couldn't imagine how hard the single-mom thing had been, especially with a child with a serious, chronic medical condition. And he realized that he hadn't really thought about that with his patients either.

When he faced the parents across his desk, he was the expert, with knowledge they needed, and it was his job to be sure they got that knowledge as thoroughly and quickly as they could so that their child's risk was mitigated. But he was so focused on the facts, the test results, the treatment options, that he didn't really think about them. The parents who were dealing with not just an overwhelming amount of information and a number of decisions but also the fact that their child, their Charli, was facing a lifetime of risk.

He felt a thickness in his throat as he held the woman who had carried that burden by herself for his child. "Rach," he said gruffly. "Thank you."

She pulled back to look up at him. "For what?"

"For being Charli's mom."

Rachel looked surprised for a moment, but then her expression softened with understanding. She put a hand against his cheek. "It's been my pleasure."

"And thank you for bringing her to Boston." She hadn't had to do that. There were other specialists. If she'd chosen to keep Alex out of her life, there had been other options for Charli's care.

Rachel stroked his jaw, not saying anything to that.

Then her hand slid around to the back of his head and she pulled him toward her.

Alex knew exactly where this was going, and he had a split second to make the decision—kiss her or not.

Maya's face flashed through his mind. Then the memory of Rachel at his door telling him about Charli. Then the memory of Charli walking into the restaurant where they were meeting for the first time. The love that had washed over him the moment he met his daughter's eyes for the first time rushed through him now, and he met Rachel's lips.

The kiss was brief and sweet. Until Rachel opened her mouth.

*Do this.* That was all he could think. He remembered butterscotch schnapps and Rachel's laugh and the way she'd climbed into his lap in the cab back to his apartment eleven years ago. It had all been great. But...

"Oh, gross!"

And Charli was back.

Alex and Rachel pulled apart. Rachel gave him a small smile as she ran a hand through her hair and faced their daughter. Their daughter. It was thoughts like that that made Alex think that kissing her was absolutely the right thing to do.

And as he walked them to the door and hailed a cab and said good night, making Rachel promise to text him when they got home safely, he knew that not e-mailing Maya to tell her how great the bo staff had gone over with Charli was also the right thing to do.

But that didn't mean he didn't want to.

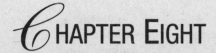

# CHAPTER EIGHT

Alex couldn't believe how much he'd been looking forward to tonight. It was ridiculous, really. He shouldn't be seeing Maya in the first place and certainly shouldn't be anticipating it like a kid looking forward to a trip to the amusement park.

And he definitely shouldn't be thinking of Maya as an amusement park.

But as he entered the Active Imagination studio and turned the corner to the big main room, that was exactly how he felt.

Charli and Rachel had been invited to dinner by a mom and daughter they'd met in the art class they were taking. That meant that Alex could get to Active Imagination earlier than usual tonight. So far, balancing weapons class and his nightly dinners with Charli and Rachel had been working. He went over to Rachel's straight from the hospital and then met Maya at the studio for private instruction after hours. But tonight he and Maya could get a longer workout in, and he'd have more to show Charli the next time she came to his house. His excitement was all about learning something new for Charli. Or so he told himself.

But the moment he saw Maya, he knew he was completely full of shit.

Well, maybe 60 percent.

Still, he couldn't deny that the majority of why he was here was the woman at the front of the class. Maya was barefoot and had a plain black headband holding her hair back, but those were the only neutrally colored things about her. She had on bright-blue tights, a yellow tank over a purple tee, and a hot pink belt sitting low on her hips that had a sparkly silver sword swinging from it. The other outfits in the room were just as loud and mismatched. There were masks, there were capes, there were tights, there were shields and swords and helmets. Clearly the kids had finished developing their superhero characters, and the costumes were complete.

Along with all the color, there was also a lot of chatter and laughter. At the moment the kids were broken up in pairs, and Maya and a couple of other adults were weaving through the room, adjusting stances, coaching swings, and giving lots of praise, while parents sat along the perimeter watching.

The greatest surprise, however, was that the whole thing struck Alex as oddly familiar. He wasn't used to costumes or swords, but he was accustomed to seeing children playing.

At Children's there were multiple playrooms with toys, books, and craft supplies. They were impossible to avoid as he strode through the hallways. Not that he wanted to avoid them. They were happy places, and he knew he smiled whenever he passed one. He might specialize in a serious condition and have to deliver serious news, and he might have gone into his specialty because of his own experiences and loathing for the genetic mutations that caused conditions like his and those of his young patients, but he was a pediatrician. He'd chosen part-time patient care over full-time research because he loved kids. It was hard, in his opinion, not to love kids. And he had always figured he wouldn't have any of his own, so he enjoyed being around them. Especially when they were just being kids.

So Alex propped a shoulder against one side of the huge doorway and watched.

It was true that the kids here were more able-bodied than the ones in the hospital. These kids weren't taking a breather from needle sticks and beeping machines and a parade of healthcare workers. These kids could look over at their parents and see bright, happy smiles rather than worry and sadness and fear.

But the similarities were more striking than the differences. There was a light feeling in the air. The kids moved in the slightly clumsy but carefree way that kids moved. They made sounds that only kids could make— whooshing sounds when they swung their swords or executed a turn, along with growls and gasps and battle cries. The place was filled with color and silliness and a palpable sense of fun.

The kids here weren't burdened or worried. Nor should any kid be. And Alex thought maybe he fell a little in love with Maya for having created all of this. It was one thing to be a healthcare provider. To be called to make the obvious physical things better and to understand laughter and play as part of the healing process. It was another to create a place that provided confidence and fun, happiness and play, just because you wanted other people to have what you did.

Alex pushed away from the wall with that thought. Wow, that was deep and...uncharacteristically whimsical of him.

But Maya seemed to be having a strange effect on him. He was relating to his daughter with more confidence and a lot less fudging. It had been only a few days of knowing Maya and already he felt as if he was doing better with the dad thing.

If only things weren't complicated in the relating-to-his-daughter's-mom area.

The kiss with Rachel had been on his mind too. They'd gone to the musical, they'd had dinner every night, they'd taken Charli shopping for new shoes and out for ice cream on Saturday. Very normal family stuff. But he and Rachel hadn't kissed again.

Because Alex was holding back. He sensed that Rachel wanted more. Or to at least try for more. But his heart wasn't in it. It wasn't fair to her to kiss her with another woman on his mind.

The only problem was he wasn't so sure the other woman would ever not be on his mind.

He felt happier just watching Maya. He tried to tell himself that it was just about her tight pants. And he did wonder what color her panties were today and if they matched her bra. He also thought about how she'd tasted and sounded when he'd kissed her and how she'd trembled in his arms. But then he thought about her scars and how touching them had moved him and how her determination to get back on the force had frustrated him while also making him want to hug her. And that's when he knew that this wasn't about her tight pants. Or her panties—of any color.

He watched as Maya put her arms around one of the kids, covering his hands with hers and moving the sword in the pattern they were practicing. She did it with smiles and praise and an affectionate touch that Alex was sure sunk in deep to each of these kids.

"Okay, so role reversal," she called out to the room. "Trolls, you're now the treasure keepers, and treasure keepers, you're trolls."

Several kids let out *yay*s as they resumed their practice battles. It was only then that he noticed a big wooden wheel off to one side. It looked like the wheels people spun on TV game shows or at the fair for prizes. There was a bright-red needle, and the pie pieces on the circle said things like "Prince/Princess," "Old Hag," "Elf," "Wishmaster," "Dungeon Dweller," "Star Captain," and, yes, "Treasure Keeper" and "Troll." Clearly they spun the wheel to decide what parts they played in their mock duels.

Alex shook his head, unable to keep from smiling.

He never got to be a part of playing with his patients. He encouraged it, he understood the importance, but that wasn't his role. He didn't relax and laugh with the people who came to him.

Maybe he should.

The thought seemed to come from out of the blue, but as Alex watched Maya gather the class back together and then demonstrate the next part of the routine, he envied her. She not only understood the idea of fun and play, she not only provided a safe place for that, she was right in the middle of it. And the way she was glowing right now, looking out over her class, made him want her even more than he had when she'd been wearing nothing but red underwear.

"Arms up!" she said, standing in the front of the room and facing the students. "The next move is a block for a downward swing. Your partner will go like this—" She demonstrated. "And you'll go like this." She showed them by herself three more times, then Ben stepped forward and they demonstrated together.

Alex also envied Ben. Ben was clearly Maya's go-to partner, and whether their relationship was boss-employee or friend-friend, Ben got to do things with Maya that Alex didn't. But maybe he could. There were modifications for Charli. Surely there could be some for him as well.

"Okay, everyone got it?" Maya asked the room.

The kids all shouted, "Yes!" in unison.

"Then go grab your grown-up partner and let's practice," Maya said.

The kids scattered to the edges of the rooms, each pulling an adult to their feet. Maya, Ben, and a couple of other staff members partnered with the kids who didn't have an adult with them, and they all went through the moves slowly and carefully before increasing the speed. There were still happy noises—laughter and whooshing sounds—but it was quieter and there were the added voices of the adults coaching their younger partners. After about ten minutes of practice, she again had the kids pair up and practice together.

"Okay, partner one—you are doing the attack routine.

Partner two—you are defending," Maya told them. "Ready? And go!"

The sound in the room changed. Now it was happiness—amplified. So were the motions. The kids swung with more enthusiasm and wider arcs, there were sinister laughs and shouted *got you*s.

Alex smiled, taking it all in. Kids played differently with other kids. Of course they did. And for a moment he had a niggling doubt about keeping Charli out of the class. It was one thing for him to get to know everything about *GR* and everything else she loved. It was great for him to practice the bo staff stuff at home with her. But she needed other kids. She couldn't just hang out with them online. She needed...

"Hi. I didn't expect to see you before class was over."

He looked to the side to see that Maya had come up beside him while he'd been engrossed in the class.

"Hi. Yeah, got done early." That wasn't entirely true. He'd left a huge stack of paperwork on his desk to be here.

"Well, I'm glad to see you," Maya said, with a big smile.

That smile made him feel completely full of himself. "Ditto."

The softness in her eyes made him want to kiss her. In fact, he almost leaned in.

She must have read something in his face because she laughed softly. "We'll have the place to ourselves in a little bit."

Damn, that sounded good.

"I like how you get the parents involved," he commented as he watched the class.

She looked up at him. "That's new. You gave me the idea."

A shot of surprise and pleasure went through him. "Really?"

She nodded. "It's a great way to make sure that the kids are careful as they learn their first moves. It also keeps the parents engaged. Otherwise a lot of them pull their phones out and don't notice what's going on at all."

Fully engaged. Right. Like not daydreaming about a feisty brunette with swords while having dinner with his daughter and her mother.

Alex sighed. This was getting complicated.

Oh, who was he kidding? This had been complicated from the moment he saw Maya up onstage at the mall.

"The kids do it differently with one another than with their parents," he commented.

Maya nodded. "No matter how much we try, no matter how creative or imaginative we might be, adults just don't pretend like kids."

He agreed. "That's because adults are pretending. To the kids, it's real in that moment."

She gave him a bright smile. "Exactly. Very good."

"I paid attention to most of my classes in med school."

She laughed. "Glad to hear that."

Her eyes, and most of her attention, was back on her class, so Alex stayed quiet.

"So no dinner with Charli tonight?" she asked after a moment.

He cleared his throat, really trying not to feel guilty. "She and her mom are having a girls' night."

"Everyone needs those sometimes."

"Yeah, but they had almost ten years of girls' nights, you know?" He wasn't sure why he'd said that.

"Well, hopefully they'll be having girls' nights together for the rest of their lives. I don't think there's a limit on those."

Alex nodded. He knew she was right.

"Oh, you're jealous," Maya said, studying his face.

He was, but he hadn't realized she would know that. "You think?"

"You're jealous that Rachel had all this time with Charli that you didn't," Maya said. "And you're wishing for a dad-daughter date."

Alex was stunned. "You remember Rachel's name?" He had said it to her once. Once.

Maya shrugged. "Of course."

"Of course?"

"It was a pretty important piece of information," she told him. "I try to remember those."

That didn't surprise him a bit. "I realize it's ridiculous to be jealous of Charli's mother spending time with her," he said. "But I am a little. Because Charli's not to the place where we can spend time just the two of us yet. And I want that. But I can't push it."

Maya rewarded him with a bright smile. "That's all really normal, Alex. And really nice. And . . ." She trailed off, biting her bottom lip.

"And what?"

"Nothing."

"Maya, and what?"

She sighed. "I was just going to say that sometimes pushing is okay. It means you care about something. It shows the other person you really want . . . whatever."

He thought about that. She wasn't wrong. Her pushing to spend time with him, to give him private classes, had definitely made him feel good.

"But you'll get there," she said. "With Charli. In time."

They would get there. In part because of the woman in front of him. "I'm also feeling happy about the night off and feeling guilty about that," he admitted. "I wanted to be here. A lot. And I feel bad about that."

"But you're here for Charli," Maya said, her voice a little lower now.

He looked into her eyes and nodded. "Yeah. Partly." But Charli was definitely not the whole reason, and... yeah, guilt.

Maya wet her lips and took a deep breath. "Okay, hold that thought for"—her gaze flickered to the clock over the front desk—"twelve more minutes."

"And then what?" He didn't know what he wanted her to say. Did he want her to tell him it was fine to be so distracted by their chemistry? And that she was too? Or maybe he just wanted to be distracted—totally, completely, thoroughly wrapped up in everything that was Maya.

Her gaze dropped to his lips and she said, "I'm either going to make this lesson worth the guilt, or..."

"Or?" he asked, his heart thumping hard.

She looked back into his eyes. "Or I'm going to make you feel even guiltier."

Alex watched her walk back into the room to finish her class. And wondered if he'd ever get used to being speechless at times around her.

Fifteen minutes later she was saying good-bye to her students at the door. She hugged the ones who wanted that, she high-fived or touched the shoulders of the ones who didn't. She smiled and laughed and looked each kid in the eye, looking genuinely pleased to have each one there. It was clear that this was what she was meant to do. Alex was sure she'd been an amazing cop—fearless and caring. But this, this was where she needed to be.

Three instructors, including Ben, came over after the last kid was through the door.

"You ready?" Ben asked Maya, shooting a questioning look in Alex's direction.

"Actually, I've got some stuff for Alex. Can we do it later?" she asked.

Alex knew it was juvenile even in the moment before he said it, but he said it anyway. "This might take a while."

Maya looked at him with surprise. And a smile.

Ben's smile was even bigger. "Well, I won't wait up, but you know where to find me."

He gave Maya a wink that Alex thought was maybe for her benefit and then smacked her on the ass—which Alex was sure had been for his benefit when he caught Ben's smirk.

"Want us to lock up on our way out?" the female instructor asked.

"That would be great," Maya told her.

They headed for the front as Maya turned to Alex. "You ready?"

He was. And he didn't even know what she had in mind. That had to be a first—he was always prepared and knew what to expect.

"Come on then." She led him down the hall to the second classroom. "I have everything in here."

"So you go to Ben's house a lot?" Alex asked. Definitely still juvenile.

Maya stepped into the classroom and flipped on the light.

"It's almost like we live together," she said.

Alex couldn't remember the last time he'd been jealous. Of Rachel's relationship with Charli. That was all he could come up with. And Charli could have—was meant to have—a relationship with Alex and Rachel at the same time. He wanted Maya all to himself. And certainly didn't want to share her with another man.

"So you and Ben work out together a lot?"

"Ben's my best sparring partner because he loves it as much as I do, knows as much as I do, and doesn't take it easy on me," she said.

"So teach me," Alex said. "I'll work out with you."

Maya's eyes widened. "No. That's okay. I can find him later."

Alex approached her and stopped toe to toe with her. "I don't want you to find him later. I want to do it."

"You can't," she said quickly.

Alex frowned. "Why not?"

"I work out four times a week with weapons."

"I'd love to see you four times a week. Maybe we'll up our workouts to six times a week." He hadn't been expecting to say that. But he didn't regret it once he had. Later he might. But seeing Charli earlier in the evening and then spending time with Maya seemed like the best of both worlds. Six times a week seemed like the best idea he'd had in a long time.

Alex wondered briefly if Maya's imagination flickered

to other types of workouts they could do. But no, probably not. She was serious about this. He was the one
with the hormones of a fourteen-year-old boy here.
Apparently.

"It's high level," she said, crossing her arms. "You're
not there."

"I'm exceptionally intelligent, enjoy hard work, and
am very motivated. I'll get there."

"You're—" She broke off and pulled her bottom lip
between her teeth.

Alex cocked a brow.

"I'm teaching you stuff for Charli, not for me," she
finally said.

Alex had a feeling that was not what she'd been about
to say. "Are you and Ben sleeping together?"

Maya blew out a breath. "That's not the only reason I
like to spend time with people."

That wasn't a no.

Alex knew he shouldn't prod. He had Rachel. They
weren't sleeping together, but she was another woman in
his life, who was making this thing with Maya complicated. It wasn't fair of him to demand to know about other
men in Maya's life. Still, he asked, "And?"

"No," she said.

"You tried it, and it didn't work?"

"Ben and I have never tried *it*."

"Why not?"

She shrugged. "No spark there."

"You sure?"

"We have enough common interests and have seen
each other in pretty skimpy clothing and have gotten
pretty physical in our workouts," she said, obviously a

little exasperated. "If something was going to spark, it would have."

Alex had to admit she had a point. "You've thought about it, though."

"To the extent that he's funny, good-looking, and is the only person I know who can actually take me down one out of three times? Yes. But we're friends, and while I wouldn't cover my eyes if he was naked in front of me, that's all we are." She put both hands on her hips. "So are we good on that topic?"

"He knows *GR* as well as you do?" Alex asked.

"No one knows *GR* as well as I do. But he's close."

"That's important to you?"

"To share interests with the guy I'm sleeping with?" she asked. "A month ago, I would have said yes, very."

Alex gave her a slow smile and reached up to tuck her hair behind her ear. "And now?"

"Well, strangely, I've found that being able to name the planets of the sixth quarter is not a prerequisite after all."

Sixth quarter. Alex felt his smile stretch. "Arietis IV, Jeuter, and Loeturn."

Her face brightened. "Wow."

"That's only three."

"Three of five," she agreed.

"So not great."

"It's three more than you knew six months ago," she told him. "So yeah, it's great."

"There's hope?" he asked, loving that his memorizing three random fictional names could make her so happy and deciding he was going to memorize the entire *Galactic Renegades* encyclopedia. He knew all the bones, nerves, vessels, and muscles of the body. How hard could learning every single detail about a fictional galaxy be?

"Hope for you and your membership in the *GR* fandom? Yes," she said with a grin.

"Hope for sleeping with you."

Her grin turned sexy. "Dr. Nolan, I think you could talk about clotting factor all night and I'd still want to sleep with you."

Two words that he thought—and said—a hundred times a day, probably, but from her they stopped him. "Clotting factor?"

She nodded.

"How do you know about clotting factor?"

"I've been reading," she said. "Ever since you told me about Charli's hemophilia."

Did she emphasize "Charli's"? Alex couldn't be sure. He was too distracted by the fact that Maya knew about clotting factor. Because she'd been reading about hemophilia.

"That's really—" He broke off, not sure what it was. It was sweet. She'd taken enough interest to study hemophilia. But it felt strange for some reason. Maybe because she didn't know he was a hemophiliac too.

But damn. He didn't like talking about his condition on the best day with strangers. He did not want the woman in front of him to know about it.

"Here." Suddenly she spun away from him and crossed the room. She grabbed a huge white cardboard box off the table near the door and came back to him.

"What's this?" he asked as she handed it to him.

"It's for Charli," she said.

She'd gotten his daughter, someone she'd never met, a present?

"Open it."

He pulled the lid off. Inside were two swords.

He picked one up, setting the box to one side. It wasn't a real sword. It was light and made of—something not metal.

"Fake swords?" he asked.

"Safe swords. For Charli and you. You can teach her swordplay with these with less risk."

Alex wasn't sure what to say. "Are they plastic?" He swung it through the air. It was light but had the length and width of a real sword from the Middle Ages. Except that it was painted black with multiple colored buttons and the blade was painted to look like a lance of fire. The detail on the mock ember lance was amazing.

"Foam board," Maya told him, her eyes sparkling.

He wasn't used to sparkling eyes. But he'd seen them more and more lately. From Charli.

Lord, he loved that look.

Alex lifted the sword and looked at it closely. The details were extraordinary. It wasn't just paint. There were metal rivets and raised areas that looked like actual electronics.

"And there's this."

Maya held up something that was shaped like the breastplate of a suit of armor, but it was painted to look like the front of the black leather vest Piper wore in *GR*. And a helmet that looked like Piper's.

Maya had a smile on her face that made him want to kiss her for days.

"Armor?"

She nodded. "The swords are soft but they could still cause bruising technically. This is extra protection. It looks really cool, right?"

Alex was stunned.

"We can do real leather," Maya said. "We can pad it really well. And it would work with the foam board. But this is harder." She knocked on it. "It's fiberglass."

Alex swallowed. "No, this is great. It's perfect." He looked down at the sword. He couldn't believe Maya had done this. "How much do I owe you?"

Maya laughed. "Nothing. We already had everything."

"You had all of this?" he asked. "For the classes at the studio?"

"At home." She gave a little shrug.

"You had swords and armor at home?"

"We had all the supplies to make swords and armor at home."

"You had fiberglass, foam board, and paint?" He was sure they had used several other supplies that he had no idea about.

Maya nodded.

"You made this stuff?" He moved closer to the armor she was holding. He ran a hand over the painted-on laces that looked completely real from a distance.

"Yep. We do this all the time."

"But this is really amazing."

"I'm really good," she said, her eyes definitely sparkling. "I told you about the awards."

She had. Not that Alex had any idea what was involved in winning an award for making cosplay weapons. Or what was involved in making cosplay weapons at all.

"I can't believe you did this." It wasn't that he couldn't

believe she was able. It was that he couldn't believe she'd done it. For Charli. For him.

"Charli wants to have sword fights, she needs to have sword fights," Maya told him.

Alex reached out and grasped her arm, pulling her in. He covered her mouth with his, pouring his need and his gratitude and his admiration into the kiss. God, he loved kissing this woman. And he so loved kissing her intentionally. Not spontaneously as he had before, but with every intention of tasting her, affecting her, absorbing her.

Maya moved the armor out of the way so she could press closer, and Alex slid a hand into her hair, getting stopped by her headband. He gripped the band and pulled it loose, letting it drop to the floor, then combed his fingers through the silky strands of her hair.

Maya gripped the front of his shirt and moaned. It was soft but it shot through Alex as if he'd swallowed a mouthful of brandy.

When they finally separated, Alex caught a moment when her eyes were still closed and she pulled in a long, shaky breath. She was always beautiful, but she was gorgeous when she was overwhelmed by him.

Maya Goodwin wasn't vulnerable very often. She fought vulnerability and won. But in these moments she wasn't tough and kick-ass and driven to right wrongs. She was soft and sweet and open. With him. Because of him.

Damn, that got to him. "Thank you," he said huskily, tracing his thumb over her bottom lip.

She opened her eyes and seemed to need just a second to focus. "No problem," she finally said. "We love doing this stuff."

He ran his hand over her cheek. She was so soft. And the touch made her close her eyes again. He really loved that. He also really wanted to see what else he could do to get reactions from her.

"Charli's going to love it," he told her.

Suddenly she pulled back. "Oh, I have more."

"More?"

Maya pulled out of his arms and spun away. She went back to the table by the door and picked up an eight-by-ten envelope. She pulled papers from it as she walked back to him. She presented them to him with a huge smile.

"I'm going to teach you this tonight."

He looked at the pages. They were drawings. Or diagrams. Or, really, they looked like pages from a graphic novel or comic book.

It was a sword-fighting scene, drawn out move by move. But these weren't simple stick figures with arrows. These were drawings, black and white, but fully formed, of a man and a little girl.

"I don't know what Charli looks like, so—"

"You drew these?" He stared at her.

She laughed. "Oh God, no. That's Kiera. She's amazing, right?" Maya looked at the page he held. "She got a little carried away, but this is fun for her."

"You asked her to draw this?" He ran a finger over the man in the picture. It was a decent likeness of him.

"Well, I was sketching it out, and it pains Kiera to watch me draw, so she grabbed the paper and went at it," Maya told him.

"Did you meet at the police station?" he asked. "She could be a sketch artist."

"We've actually mentioned that to her," Maya said, amused. "But no. She's a graphic designer and works on the video game World of Leokin."

Alex raised a brow. Even he had heard of World of Leokin. Its advertising was everywhere. "But this idea and routine is all you?" Alex pressed. He knew it was, but he wanted her to admit it.

"Yes. I think Charli could do all these moves safely. You can learn them and then teach them easily, but it will feel like a true sword battle."

Alex studied the pages, knowing that he was going to have to settle for being just friends with Rachel. Because he was going to keep seeing Maya. Graphic novel sword fights and foam board swords or not.

"So come on," she said, clearly oblivious to his emotional turmoil. "Let's do this. I'll use Charli's sword."

She took the pages and started spreading them out on the floor.

As she bent to lay the fourth one down, Alex grasped her hips and pulled her up. He turned her and wrapped his arms around her, hugging her tightly.

"This is incredible," he said against her hair. He also knew he'd never get tired of the way she seemed to easily relax into him, molding her body to his.

"You're welcome."

It also did not escape his notice that hugging Maya felt every bit as natural as hugging Rachel did, but with the added heat that he wished were there with Rachel.

Shit.

"Charli and I started bo the other night," he said, pulling back and releasing her. "I was hoping to add on to that."

"I think the swords are better." Maya ducked her head and resumed laying the pages out. "It's more like *GR* and the ember lances."

"Right. Sure. But bo is cool too," he said. "And I told her I'd show her more next time she was at my place."

"The swords are lightweight. For a little girl, the bo might be too—"

Alex caught her wrist and turned her to look at him. "The swords are great. I want to learn all of this. But what's wrong with more bo? What's going on?"

Maya sighed. "I think the lightweight swords are safer according to my reading about hemophilia."

Because of her research, she now knew about some of Charli's limitations. That was probably a good thing. But if she'd read much about hemophilia, she'd likely come across his name.

"You're worried about her," he commented.

Maya frowned. "Well, yeah."

Maya didn't even know Charli, but she cared. In part because she had a big heart. But he knew it was in part because of him too. How long had she spent writing a routine and sketching this out so that he could bond with his daughter?

"It will be okay to do more bo," he assured her. "It's just her and me."

"But accidents happen all the time. Especially when both people are novices. I never realized how much, really, but in the past few days, I've noticed the kids really get into it and even if you tell them not to, they get caught up or they swing harder than they mean to and—"

Alex kissed her to stop the stream of words. When he

let her up for air several long seconds later, she was slow to open her eyes.

"It will be okay," he repeated, holding her face between his hands.

"You should stick with a sword too," she said softly. "Charli won't have control. The sword is safer."

"We'll be safe. I'll be sure of it."

She looked right back at him, a slight crease appearing between her brows, but finally she gave a single nod. "Fine."

"Bo?"

"Yes. For a little while."

"Okay," he agreed. He let her go.

She crossed the room to retrieve two staffs from the wall. "Show me what you remember," she said, tossing him one.

He demonstrated the spins from before. Maya nodded her approval. "Alright, next are offensive swings and defensive blocks."

"Great."

Maya took him slowly through three offensive moves. Then the three matching defensive ones. After a few practices, he moved to block one of her swings and her staff hit his knuckles.

"Ah." Alex shook his hand.

"Oh my God, are you okay?" She looked completely stricken.

Alex frowned and nodded. "Of course. Just glanced off my knuckles."

"I'll be more careful."

"I'm guessing this is a common thing with bo," he said.

"Well, yeah. That's what I'm saying," she told him. "You and Charli should stick with swords."

"Maya, it's not a problem."

"I'll slow down. It's like driving—it takes some time for those blocks to become second nature."

Of course it did. He knew that. "I'm fine," he insisted. But he had an idea why this was such an issue for her. "Let's do it again."

She took a deep breath but went through the pattern again. It was a lot slower, and she was swinging with virtually no power now.

Finally frustrated, Alex lowered his staff from the overhead position—just as Maya swung.

The staff hit him in the side of the face. She wasn't swinging hard enough for it to do anything but surprise him, but he dropped his staff as Maya lunged forward.

"Alex! Oh my God!" Her hand went to his face. "Dammit! I told you we shouldn't do this! Crap. Let me get you some ice." She started to turn toward the door, but he caught her elbow before she could get away.

"Whoa. I'm fine, Maya. You're overreacting."

Which was strange. She didn't seem the type. No, more than that. She was not the type.

"I'm just—" She looked up at him, worry clear in her eyes. "Are you sure?"

And the suspicion in the back of his mind grew.

Maya was an intelligent woman who had been reading about hemophilia. She had to have run across stats. Like how rare it was and how much more rare it was for a girl to have it. That could have easily led to information about the genetic situation that would have to be present for it to happen.

So Maya knew he was a hemophiliac. Fuck.

Clearly she was a little intimidated by it. Would she ask him about it? Want to know more? Or would she shy away? Try to pretend it was no big deal while letting it affect everything she thought about him and did with him?

"We're fine," Alex said firmly.

She gave a nod. "I also want to be sure that you love this and enjoy it and want to keep doing it."

"I already enjoy it," he told her. "And I want to keep doing it."

"You won't if it hurts you. Or her."

Yeah, she knew. She had to.

"Maybe if you told me more to keep you—Charli safe. Are the swords and armor enough? Should we make leg pieces too? That will make it harder to move but if it makes it better for her, we should do it."

Alex thought about kissing her again, but this wasn't rambling. This was true concern. And she was asking questions. She just wasn't directly addressing that the issue was his as well as Charli's.

"The swords and armor are a great compromise," he said. "And Charli working out with me is perfect because I'll know how to control the situation."

"Can we please just work with the swords?" she asked. "That would make me feel so much more secure."

She was truly worried. Alex appreciated that and recognized that it was part of her caring about him. But it also proved, once again, that once people knew about his condition, they acted differently toward him. Frustration rolled through his gut.

Yes, he wanted to keep Charli safe and was pleased Maya understood that and was trying to help. But this was

Maya. She didn't do things the safe way. She didn't hang out with people who did things the safe way.

That might not be entirely fair. He was sure they used precautions in their battles and sparring to keep everyone from any true injury. But she didn't hang back. She didn't worry and modify things before she went in.

He stared at Maya. He hadn't been riled up about his condition for a long time. Mostly he felt it was a huge waste of time. But Maya was making him face it. He didn't like it. He also didn't want Maya keeping him safe.

Of course that was ridiculous—that was what Maya did. She went out of her way to do it. Burning cars, malls, her studio—no matter where she was, she was taking care of others. Ironically, only a few days ago he'd decided she wasn't right for him because she was reckless and fearless and couldn't be intimidated.

He'd been wrong. She was a protector.

But he'd had eighteen years of being overprotected. He didn't need, or want, that anymore.

"More bo stuff," he said. "But not Charli stuff. Let's do some grown-up bo stuff."

"Grown-up bo stuff?"

He picked his staff up again and tossed it back and forth between his hands. "Yeah. Grown-up. Stuff you and Ben do."

Maya's eyes narrowed. "Ben's been working with bo for years."

"I'll catch up." He started to spin the staff.

"Alex—"

"Maya, show me the stuff you do with Ben."

She didn't need to be gentle with him, and he was going to prove that to her.

She was watching him with a contemplative look. Finally she nodded. "Okay. You know the blocks I just taught you. Let's see what you can do with those techniques and some instinct."

Alex positioned himself and focused. Maya swung, not slowly but not as fast as she could have. He blocked three swings and then her staff hit his shoulder.

She hesitated, biting her lip, but she didn't say anything.

"Again," he said, resuming the starting position.

Maya did too and started swinging and advancing again. He blocked five swings before she caught him in the side of his thigh. She was swinging slowly.

She frowned and opened her mouth.

"Again," he said. "And stop holding back."

"You're new at this," she snapped, clearly irritated.

"I'm a big boy, Maya. Do it again and swing."

"Fine." She repositioned, and Alex faced her.

She came at him faster this time but with the same pattern of swings. He blocked them all.

"Again. More," he said.

"Alex, are you—"

"Dammit, Maya, more. Change it up. I know you're coming."

Her jaw tightened. "Okay. Let's go."

This time she swung harder and faster, and Alex got only two blocks in before she altered the routine. She struck him in his ribs. Hard.

He stopped, breathing fast. "Again."

"No." She tossed her staff to the side and faced him, hands on her hips. She looked angry and possibly on the verge of tears. "I'm not doing that anymore."

"Fine." He tossed his staff away. "Why don't you tell me what's wrong?"

"What's wrong?" she asked. "There's nothing you want to tell me, is there?"

He met her gaze and held it. He took in a deep breath that made his side twinge. "You figured it out," he said simply.

"That you have hemophilia and don't talk about it?" she asked. "Even in a situation where it's very pertinent? Like this one?"

Yeah, she was worried. And mad.

"I don't like you treating me carefully," he said. "I don't want that from you."

"No, you want me to hurt you. Because you have something to prove. And I'm not going to do that, Alex, so you can forget it."

"I don't want or need you to take care of me, Maya," he said firmly.

"Really? You say that you hate how I just jump in. Well, I hate how you're not even telling me that you have a condition that makes my favorite things a huge risk to you. It's like you don't think I'm capable of reeling it in and understanding precautions."

She was. Obviously. "I don't want you to reel it in." He planted his hands on his hips. "That's not you. And I like you exactly as you are."

"I don't want you to get hurt."

"I know what I can handle and what I can't."

She wet her lips. "How severe is yours?"

She'd definitely done her reading if she knew there was a spectrum. "Moderate."

That was the first time he'd truly acknowledged

anything about his condition to anyone other than his doctor in years.

"So you will need treatment since I hit you?"

"Maya."

"Why don't you talk about it in any of your articles or interviews?" she asked. "You never give a perspective as a patient—only a physician."

"Maya—"

"I'm sure it helps Charli to know that you know what she's going through."

"If you don't stop talking, I'm going to kiss you to shut you up—and I'm not going to stop until you're naked this time."

That worked. Her eyes widened, but in the place of the worry was heat. That was so much better.

"I have a nice, big, soft bed at home," she said. "I'm sure I could ramble about something all the way there."

So the naked thing was on the table. But speaking of tables—

"A big, soft bed, you say?" he asked, moving in to tower over her intentionally. "You think I need a soft surface for this?"

She pressed her lips together as if hesitant to answer. But then she nodded. "You could strain something," she said quietly.

He wanted to laugh. He'd love to think that sex with her would be strain-worthy. But this was serious. Maya, who he suspected was a go-hard girl in the bedroom too, was worried about sex with him? Oh hell no.

Was it a stupid macho thing to want to prove her wrong? Of course.

But he was only human, and he definitely wanted the

woman he was with to be thinking of nothing except how fast she could get undressed and where she wanted his mouth first.

"Maya," he said, low and firm. "What have you been reading?"

"Websites."

"Clearly I'm not the only one who needs a lesson here tonight," he told her.

"You have nothing to prove to me," she said quickly.

"That's obviously not true."

He pulled his T-shirt over his head. He appreciated her tiny indrawn breath as she took in his naked torso. He took one of her hands and pressed it to his chest. "Feel that? Solid, strong. I'm not going to break or crumble."

She ran her hand over his pecs, brushing a nipple and making him bite back a groan. Her hand slid down and over the spot where she'd struck him in the side. "But inside..."

He growled. "Stop being gentle with me, Maya. I'm tempted to put you up against the wall to show you just how not-gentle this can all be."

She lifted her eyes to his. There was heat along with a flicker of amusement. "You could do that?"

Jesus, had he thought she was too reckless and didn't think things through? He now needed her to stop thinking. "Damn right, I could do that," he told her. Just before pulling her shirt over her head.

# *C*HAPTER NINE

*M*aya couldn't deny the thrill that shot through her. She wanted to have sex with Alex. No question. Probably had since seeing him in the crowd at the mall. She'd entertained some pretty great fantasies, especially since the pool. But after reading up on everything, she'd realized she was going to need to change her likes-and-dislikes-during-sex list. She liked hard, fast, hold-nothing-back sex.

Rather than writing the whole thing with Alex off, though, she'd found herself adjusting her fantasies. She'd imagined a big bed, silk sheets, candlelight. Slow, luxurious foreplay with lots of hands and tongues before an easy, sensuous pace in missionary. Or better yet, her on top. It wasn't as if she were opposed to any of those things.

But when Alex backed her up to the wall and pulled her sports bra over her head and stripped her workout pants off, taking her panties with them, her heart leaped. She really did love sex against the wall. And a fast, frenzied pace. *Frenzied* seemed a good word here.

Alex lifted her, cradling her butt in his big hands, and she wrapped her legs around his waist. He pressed her to the wall, kissing her hungrily. She opened her mouth, and he swept his tongue against hers as his fingers curled into her butt. Maya clutched at his shoulders, desperate to be closer to him, needing to press against all of him.

"Take your pants off," she said raggedly against his lips.

"Can't. Don't want to let go," he told her.

She had to admit that staying right exactly here sounded great to her. But there needed to be a lot less material.

She wiggled against him. "Need you, Alex. Skin to skin."

"Like that idea." He lifted a hand to her breast, cupping it and brushing his thumb over the nipple.

She moaned against his mouth. Okay, that was pretty good.

"But you're right." He ran his thumb over it again. "I can't really get at everything I need. This position will have to wait a bit."

He let her slide down until her feet touched the floor, but he didn't move back. He braced one hand on the wall next to her head and ran the other down her side from her breast to her hip. He tipped his head to look down as he touched her but gave her no room to do much more than glide her hands over his chest.

He stroked her outer thigh, then moved up to her stomach, his palm rubbing back and forth until he slid it lower to cup her. He lifted his gaze as he ran his middle finger over her clit.

Maya gasped and grabbed his forearm. She wanted so much more of that.

"You're gorgeous." His voice was rough and made the tingles from his finger increase.

She decided to finally give in to the temptation that had been tugging at her when she'd been at the pool with him. She leaned in and rested her forehead against his sternum, pulling in a long breath of his scent. Then she flicked her tongue against his skin where that drop of water had been.

There was a low rumble in his chest. She looked up at him with a smile. "You're looking delicious too." Then she dipped her head and licked his hard pec, unable to resist giving it a little nip in the process.

The rumble got louder. "Delicious, huh?" he asked gruffly. "Now that you mention it—"

He dropped to his knees in front of her.

Maya felt her mouth fall open, but when he gripped her butt with both hands and placed a kiss on her inner thigh, she let her head drop back against the wall behind her. She was a grab-the-moment kind of girl. And this was a moment she was happy to grab.

Alex wasted no time. He brought her forward, putting his mouth on the spot that needed him most. His lips and tongue, along with a few strokes of a finger, ratcheted her desire from a hot hum to a screaming need in minutes. The man knew what he was doing. She hadn't been with a man who knew what he was doing in that department for a while. Maya's fingers clutched the back of his head, and she wondered if she should be embarrassed by the way she arched against his mouth. But she wasn't. Not a bit. Not even when she heard herself begging, "Please, Alex, yes, please." He confirmed that he knew exactly what he was doing a moment later when he suddenly let her go just as she was on the verge of what had promised to be her favorite orgasm ever. He got to his feet, his eyes dark, almost dangerous, as he yanked open the front of his pants.

"Don't move," he told her firmly as he kicked off his shoes and shed his pants and underwear.

"I really do love swimming," she said softly as she took in the sight of him gloriously naked for the first time. He was hard and sculpted everywhere. His thighs and abs and ass and... everything. Yeah, the word *gentle* was nowhere in her vocabulary at the moment.

Alex said nothing. Instead he just watched her as he took the condom in his hand and rolled it on. That was a sight she could watch over and over. Then he stepped toward her.

Maya lifted her gaze to his just as he scooped her up and pressed her back into the wall again. The look on his face was that of a man focused and determined and just as on edge as she was.

"Hold on tight, Supergirl."

Maya barely had time to grip his shoulders before he thrust into her, sinking deep.

She gasped at the sensations that seemed to pour through her, and then he pulled out and thrust again, grinding perfectly to send her flying.

On the second stroke.

Maya didn't miss that fact. And it was the second time he'd made her come so quickly. Maybe he was a bit of a superhero. Granting hard and fast orgasms would be a hell of a superpower.

Alex held her tightly against the wall, the hardness behind her perfectly matching the hardness at her front. He continued moving, not giving her a chance to breathe or move or even really help with the giving-him-an-orgasm thing she was supposed to be doing. He was in total control of them both, the power in his body incredible. All she could really do was hold on.

He didn't seem to mind. He was moving slower now, but his strokes were deep and sure, his eyes locked on hers, as if he knew exactly what he was doing. Again.

"You feeling super?" he asked, with a sexy smile.

"I think you're in the running for Man of Steel," she told him, breathlessly.

He flexed his hips, and she moaned.

"I gotta say, I like you in kick-ass mode, but I'm loving this warm, boneless, soft side of you too." He thrust again.

"I gotta say," she said, mimicking him, "if you want to see more of this side of me, I'm all for it."

He leaned in and kissed her. The kiss was leisurely and deep as his hips moved in long, slow strokes as well.

Maya couldn't do much as far as leverage, but she flexed the one muscle she could. She tightened around him and felt Alex blow out a hard breath.

"Damn."

She did it again, just because she liked how that affected him.

"Keep that up and this is going to be over fast," he told her.

"If it's over fast, then we can get to round two sooner."

He squeezed her ass. "You already tired of this one?"

She laughed. "Hardly. I just kind of rushed ahead there and thought maybe you'd want to catch up."

He stilled—which was not at all what she'd been going for—and pulled back slightly. "Maya, there's something you should know about you and me and sex."

"Oh?"

He leaned in and put his mouth against her ear and said huskily, "This is just the beginning." Then he thrust deep and hard. "I can, and will, do anything and everything you'll let me do to this gorgeous body. As many times as you'll let me do it," he promised darkly.

She didn't think numbers actually went that high.

Then she forgot all about everything except the delicious way her thighs stretched as he moved between them, the way his fingers felt digging into her butt as he held her still for his thrusts, and the way her entire body seemed to liquefy. Boneless indeed.

But then everything started tightening and, even as she couldn't believe it was happening again, she felt herself reaching for another orgasm. It came crashing over her a moment later as Alex pumped into her a final time and shouted her name as he went over the peak behind her.

As the waves of pleasure slowly abated, Alex let her legs go and she reached for the floor with her tiptoes. Then she just kept sliding until she was sitting against the wall, still trying to catch her breath.

Alex collapsed as well, rolling onto his back with a huge sigh.

Maya wiped her hair back from her forehead and then crawled over to curl up next to him. Alex drew her against his side as his chest continued to rise and fall rapidly. Maya put her hand on his chest. "Man, if I hadn't been calling you Doc Wonderful before, that would have done it."

He grinned down at her. "I was pretty wonderful, wasn't I?"

She laughed. "And you did most of the work. I appreciate that. I've had a long day."

He ran his hand down her back to her butt and palmed one cheek. "I appreciate all the work you've done on this amazing body that I don't think I'll ever get enough of."

"I've never had better motivation to stay in shape."

A comfortable silence drifted over them, Alex stroking her back, her hand sliding down to rest on his stomach. She really did love his abs.

"It occurs to me that I was unfair to you earlier," he said after a few minutes.

Maya looked up at him. "We haven't known each other very long. It was unfair of me to expect you to tell me every personal detail."

He shifted to put his opposite hand behind his head, his other one firmly on her butt. "I'm very used to keeping it to myself so that people won't overreact to it."

"Does that happen?"

He lifted an eyebrow at her. "People read things on the Internet and get uneasy."

She had to nod. "Right."

"Most people don't need to know about it," he went on. "It doesn't affect ninety-five percent of my relationships."

"What about your relationships with your patients?"

she asked. "Wouldn't it help them to know that their doctor has personal knowledge of the condition and what it's like to live with it?"

"None of the other specialists that I work with have personally experienced the condition, yet they give excellent care and counseling."

"I'm sure," Maya agreed. "But I'm just saying that it would be even more reassuring to know that you know exactly what they're going through."

"No one needs to know," he said firmly.

A thought occurred to her. "Your staff doesn't know, do they?"

He shook his head.

"What about the other doctors you work with? Or the other specialists?"

Again he shook his head.

Maya sat up, bracing herself on one arm. "Really? You don't tell anyone?"

"It doesn't matter," he insisted.

Her wheels were turning now, and she had a gut feeling about the answer to her next question. But she had to be sure. "Does Charli know?"

He hesitated long enough that she knew the answer.

"Alex! How can you not tell her?"

"It's not that easy."

Maya got to her feet, suddenly aware that she was naked. She grabbed her clothes and pulled them on, not bothering with her panties or bra. She planted her hands on her hips. "How can you not want Charli to know that you've been through all of this too?"

Alex got to his feet with a heavy sigh and pulled his pants on too. "We haven't even talked about her condition yet. We're getting to know each other. It takes time to build trust."

"Keeping things from her isn't going to help with that."

He frowned. "I don't need advice, Maya. I counsel families and parents every day about this."

She knew that, and he certainly hadn't asked for her opinion, but this gave her a bad feeling. "I just want things to be good for both of you," she finally said.

"I appreciate that," he said. "I do. But you probably need to know that I don't do very well with people trying to protect me and advise me. I've had a hell of a lot of that in my life, and I'm definitely able to take care of myself."

Okay. Ow. Maya had to admit that hurt a little bit. She wanted to respect him and this situation, but...dammit, she cared. "Well, you probably need to know that I don't stay out of the business of the people I care about. And I'm also pretty protective of the people I love."

He faced her with an exasperated look that somehow managed to be hot at the same time.

"And," she said before he could respond, "I'm that way with everyone, so don't go getting all ruffled because you think I'm treating you differently or gently."

Her heart beat at least ten times before he finally said, "No more reading the Internet. If you want to know something, you ask me."

Her heart thudded. He wasn't telling her to stay the hell out of his life. "Deal."

"And no backing away from anything unless I say so. If I don't say stop, you go."

"Are we talking about the sword fighting or the sex?"

His eyes narrowed. "Both."

She lost the fight against her smile. "Got it. Full steam ahead. I'm not even tapping the brakes."

He rolled his eyes. "There's no happy medium with you, huh?"

"That's maybe something else about me you should know."

"Already knew it."

"And yet here you are."

"Here I am," he agreed.

Maya wasn't sure what exactly it was, but it felt as if something was hanging in the air between them.

"But I will answer your questions," Alex finally said. "As my martial arts and weapons instructor and the woman I'm dating, you're probably in the five percent of people who do need to know about my condition."

"Am I the woman you're dating?"

It was silly. They were grown-ups. She was perfectly capable of having a casual relationship. But Maya found herself holding her breath waiting for Alex's answer.

He crossed the few feet between them and looked down at her. "Please be the woman I'm dating."

She swallowed hard. Why did this seem like such a big deal? They could date and then end it anytime. This wasn't anything that had to be permanent or serious or life altering.

But it felt as if it was.

Because she tended to give everything 110 percent, and that meant this could be spectacularly good... or bad.

"You have to promise that you'll tell me about your treatment. I think if I'm going to be teaching you these fighting moves and screwing your brains out, I should know what to do in an emergency."

"Screwing my brains out, huh?" Alex asked. "Yeah, that could require some quick intervention."

"Promise you'll tell me about it," she said.

"Promise. But not tonight."

"Fine," she agreed. She studied him. "And you have to promise not to get annoyed if I don't hit you hard with my big stick."

"I will get annoyed if you don't give me all you've got," he said, "in everything we do."

Whoa. Heat arced through her, and she had to take a moment to gather her thoughts. "You'll get whatever you want from me," she finally said, realizing that her words sounded very serious. But this whole thing felt very serious suddenly.

He nodded. "Then we keep up with the tutoring."

"And the . . ." She slid her gaze to the wall he'd had her up against a little bit ago.

He didn't smile. His gaze grew even more intense. "I don't think there's any way I'm going to be able to keep my hands off of you now."

"Well," she said, trying to sound flippant but realizing the husky quality of her voice completely ruined it, "I am the woman you're dating. I guess you don't have to keep your hands off of me."

Alex drew a breath in through his nose. "That is a very good point."

Feeling light and warm in spite of the serious tone to the whole conversation, Maya went to where she'd laid out the ember lance routine earlier. "Tell you what. We'll work on this routine for a while, and if you do a good job, I'll take my clothes off for you again before you leave."

Alex headed straight for his ember lance and got into the first position.

* * *

"Do you have to swing so hard?" Maya asked as Sophie moved to block Ben's attack.

"Well, I am trying to kill her," Ben said drily. "She's convinced my fair maiden to defect to the South."

Maya frowned at his flippant answer. "Yeah, well, don't swing so hard."

She was watching the scene she'd helped choreograph for Sophie's upcoming play at her theater. It was a variety of short scenes for a kids' program she was doing on Saturday mornings. Sophie wrote the scripts, Kiera helped with the makeup and costumes, and Maya choreographed fight scenes, even dance numbers if needed.

It was hard to tell if it was more fun for the kids or for the adults involved. Ben was definitely getting into it. He loved playing the villain.

Maya realized she'd missed hanging out with her friends. Alex wasn't going to make it tonight because of something he needed to attend at Charli's school, and Maya had decided to throw herself into this rehearsal so she didn't miss him too much. Or think about how Alex's tendency to keep everything in his life very separate had started to influence her routine as well.

Over the past week, she'd seen Alex every night after she'd finished her classes and after he'd had dinner with Charli. They worked on the bo and sword routines. They talked and laughed. She'd learned more about his work, his family, and, of course, Charli. She'd told him about her friends, her moms, her time on the force, her business. But it was always at the studio and it was always just the two of them.

She loved every minute with him. Especially the minutes when their workout got cut short by their tearing each other's clothes off. In fact, when she was with him, she thought of very little but him. But she realized now, a week later, that her friends didn't really know him, and the only time they'd been together outside the studio had been at the mall the very first day they met and at his apartment when she'd just shown up, uninvited. She hadn't been invited back either...Maya shook that off. It didn't matter.

Tonight was a night for catching up with the other people in her life. And figuring out how to balance all of this. Alex might be a pro at keeping everything compartmentalized, but she wasn't. She didn't want to be. She loved everything all swirled together in her life. And she wanted Alex to be a part of that.

"Soph, let's try this." Maya moved to stand next to her friend. "When Ben swings down, you pivot this way." Maya stepped back and twisted away from where Ben's staff would come down.

Sophie shrugged. "Okay, so just dodge it?"

Maya nodded. "I think so. Then it's not so likely he'll actually hit you."

Sophie practiced the twist, and Maya added to it to get her out of Ben's way.

Ben stood watching with his hands on his hips. When they were finished, he asked, "Should we just fight with foam noodles or squirt guns instead?"

Maya gave him a frown. "Stop it."

"Well, I'm just thinking you're getting into Sophie being the damsel in distress. Thought we wanted strong, powerful women here."

Maya faced him squarely. "What's your problem? Just pull it back a little. That's all I'm saying."

"Sophie, you okay?" Ben asked, focusing over Maya's shoulder. "Did I hurt you?"

"Uh." Sophie looked between Maya and Ben, clearly not sure what was going on or how to answer. "No," she finally said.

"Exactly. I would never hurt you." He looked back to Maya. "So everything is good. I know how to control myself and how to gauge my opponent's skill level."

Maya gritted her teeth. She knew she was acting out of character. She never asked people to pull back. The problem was, Ben was like Maya. He always pushed, he always went a little too hard, he always gave it all he had.

"How about I play this part?" she asked. Then she wouldn't worry about what Ben would bring to the scene. "Maybe you just need to go up against someone who can handle you. Then you don't have to deal with figuring out how to dial it back."

Even as she heard her own words, Maya realized that, in a way, she was talking to herself. She wouldn't have to dial it back if she was sparring with Ben either.

Ben stepped closer. "I don't need to figure anything out. I'm good."

"Really? Because you seem surly." No, she seemed surly. She was projecting all her feelings and frustrations about her and Alex onto Ben.

"I'm surly?" Ben repeated. "All week you've been skipping our workouts, and this is the third time you've told me to tone it down. I'm sick of it."

He was right. She was pulling back in her workouts with Alex, whether he liked it or not. Though she had to admit that her arm had felt a lot better this past week. She'd still been using it, getting good workouts in, but she'd realized that she hadn't taken any ibuprofen in two days, hadn't iced in three, and was sleeping better than she had in a long time. At first she'd chalked all that up to the amazing orgasms she'd been having on a regular basis. But it hadn't taken long to admit that it was, at least in part, because her arm was better.

But she'd been on Ben's ass all week in class. She needed to back off. She couldn't piss him off or lose him. He was her best instructor.

"Okay, let's go," she said. She crossed to the rack of bo staffs and took one down. She tossed it to Ben. "Give me your best shots instead of everyone else."

Ben shrugged. "You got it."

They faced off and gave each other a little bow. Then they battled.

Maya felt the pleasure streaking through her muscles as she swung and thrust. She welcomed the vibration through her limbs as their staffs connected. She relished the feel of her lungs working and her heart pounding. She even smiled at the trickle of sweat she felt running between her breasts.

She'd certainly breathed hard and sweated in the past several days, and there had been definite thrusting. But there had been a lack of cracking wood and the whoosh of air around her as she swung and turned.

Until Alex, she hadn't realized how sexual hand-to-hand combat could be. Groaning, hearts racing, dominating and submitting. Though, on the mat, she liked to dominate. Not so much with Alex. She loved when he took over, braced her hands above her head, and reduced her to a quivering pile of goo while showing her just how much control he really had over her.

Maya forced herself to concentrate. She didn't want to be distracted. She wanted to kick Ben's ass.

This was a different type of release, and it was what she needed right now—to work off some of this physical energy. Or maybe it was mental energy. Either way, she needed this.

She swung harder on her next attack sequence, taking advantage of an old back injury that prevented Ben from twisting fully to the right. Ben blocked her and then shifted to attack when she was too late on her third swing. To block him she had to step back and bend left. Swinging up on her left worked fine with her shoulder, and she met his staff directly. But her swings down and across were weaker on that side. It was also difficult for her to block fully overhead. Which Ben knew well. He typically avoided making her do so. But not today. He moved to strike across her left side, and Maya forced her arm up to meet the blow.

The arm hurt, as usual, and it wasn't quite strong enough. Also as usual. Ben's swing met her staff directly, and then he pushed, forcing her left arm down. She saw the determination in his eyes, and she glared at him, pushing as hard as she could. She thrust upward with her legs, but Ben's height and strength and irritation all combined, and she knew she wasn't going to win this one.

She went to one knee, and Ben let up on the pressure. Maya lowered her left arm, wincing and sucking in a breath when pain shot up into her neck.

"That is how it goes when I go hard," Ben said, letting his arms drop. "You know the difference."

Maya got to her feet. He was right. And she didn't feel any less frustrated than she had before. Dammit. This was supposed to have worked things out.

"Okay, I'm—"

Her apology was cut off by someone taking her arm.

She looked up, surprised to see Alex had a hold of her. "Um, hey—" She scrambled to keep up with his long strides across the room. "Kind of being grabby," she said, trying to get him to at least look at her.

"Maya," he said, his jaw tight, "just walk."

What was he ticked off about? What was he even doing here?

Sophie and Kiera stepped out of Alex's way as he headed right between them and for the front hallway. Maya wondered if she should be glad or worried that they didn't feel inclined to stop him.

When they hit the corridor, Maya expected him to turn left to her office, but instead he took a right—and headed for the front door.

"Where are we going?"

"Somewhere I can get you naked. And yell at you. Not necessarily in that order."

Naked yelling. Well, okay. She didn't know what the yelling would be about, but naked yelling seemed preferable to clothed yelling. And she could tell by the look in his eyes that the yelling was inevitable.

"Why?" she asked as he stopped by his car.

He unlocked the passenger side and put her in the seat. "Because I'd rather yell at you than have Ben do it."

Alex slammed the door before she could respond to that. As he rounded the front of the car, she got distracted by the bobbleheads on the dash. One was Supergirl and one was Captain America.

"What are these?" She picked up Captain America as Alex got behind the wheel.

"For you," he said, putting the car into drive.

"You got me bobbleheads?" She stared down at Captain America.

"They had them in the gift shop at the hospital," he said. "They didn't have Spider-Man, but Charli said Captain America is better."

Maya felt as if her tongue were glued to the roof of her mouth. She simply nodded.

They didn't speak as they drove, and it was nearly thirty minutes before they pulled up in front of Maya's house.

"This okay?" he asked.

Alex at her house? Definitely okay. She wanted him here. In her space, in her life. "Of course."

"Is it creepy that I know your address?" he asked, turning off the car.

"I'm going to assume you found it so you could send me flowers." She opened the door and got out.

He followed her up the two steps to the porch of the house Kiera had inherited from her grandmother. As was typical in Boston, the big, old three-story home had been converted into side-by-side apartments. She lived on one side with Kiera and Sophie while Rob and Ben lived on the other.

Once inside, Maya turned toward Alex in the foyer. "Can we do the yelling thing?"

"You want the yelling first?"

"I want to not do the yelling at all," she said, with a shrug.

The foyer was dimly lit by the glow that filtered in from the porch light right outside the door. "That's not going to happen."

"Then let's do that so we can get to the naked part."

"I hate seeing you push yourself to the point of getting hurt," he said. "I know you're frustrated with your arm, but you need to accept the fact that you have limitations. And that those don't make you weak or less capable."

Maya cleared her throat. "How much did you see?"

"I saw you get on Ben about not swinging so hard at Sophie, and then I saw you challenge him. And I saw him take you down."

She hadn't noticed him. That was how wound up she was about everything.

"Ben doesn't know when to say when," she told him.

"Ben doesn't?" Alex asked, a knowing look in his eyes.

She sighed. "Fine. Watching Ben is like watching myself."

"And?"

"I've become aware lately that I might need to chill a little."

"Because of me?"

She nodded. "But I'm not being protective."

"Yes, you are."

Okay, she was. "Well, not just because of you. Sophie. The kids. Charli. I've just realized that going hard all the time isn't fun, or safe, for everyone. And when Ben and I do that, it can be a little intimidating."

Alex lifted a hand to the side of her head. "It's just you, Supergirl. You go all in. It's one of the best things about you. And the people around you want to be around you. We trust you. You might like to go hard, but you care about us even more, and you know when to push and when to pull back."

She wasn't so sure she did. Like now. She wanted to push. She wanted to say, "I want to meet Charli." She wanted to say, "I want you to get to know my friends." She wanted to say, "I want to eat food with you that's not in takeout containers." But she couldn't insist on being a bigger part of his life. She couldn't demand to meet his daughter. And eating takeout sub sandwiches at her desk at the studio while listening to him talk about his research was better than not seeing him at all.

This was a time that she needed to not push. This was probably a good lesson in self-control. Probably. She took a deep breath. "This doesn't feel like yelling," she said softly.

"That's still coming."

"Oh." Damn.

"Yeah. Let's talk about how you don't take care of you."

Maya frowned. "What?"

"You care about so many other people. You'll protect them no matter what. You'll go to bat for them. You'll risk yourself for them. You keep them safe. But you don't keep yourself safe. You push yourself. And your arm."

"I'm fine," she said quickly. Okay, yes, it was now

throbbing more after the workout with Ben than it had all week with Alex. But that wasn't exactly new.

"You were hurt, dammit," Alex said.

"I've been living with this arm for a long time," she told him. "It's...typical. I'm used to it."

"And I'm used to sometimes having to take clotting factor, but you still want to protect me."

*Well...* She nodded. "Yeah, I do."

"Exactly."

Maya pressed her lips together and waited.

"You have to accept that you're not invincible." He stepped forward and took her face in his hands. "You can't do everything you want to do, and that sucks. But it doesn't make you less. Don't you get that?" He pulled her close and rested his forehead against her. "The things you do in spite of and because of your injury make you even more amazing."

This still didn't feel like yelling, but she wasn't about to complain. Her throat felt tight, but she also felt warm and...protected.

"But," he said, letting her go and stepping back with a slight frown, "I don't like seeing you hurt because you can't accept that your shoulder isn't all you want it to be. My body isn't all I want it to be either. I know how you feel—maybe if you ignore it, things will be okay; maybe if you work harder, it will get better; maybe if you just look harder, you'll find an answer. But sometimes you have to face it. You have to figure out how to be okay with it." His voice gentled, and he touched her cheek again. "And Supergirl, there's a lot okay with you."

Maya swallowed hard. Lord, she liked him so much.

"You're good at this," she said. "The relating and pep

talk thing. It means more from you than even my friends. Because you really know."

He nodded. "I really know." Then he added, firmly, "So you're going to stop pushing yourself so damned hard. Starting right now."

Maya's eyes widened. This still wasn't yelling, but he was getting firm with her. That didn't happen. She took care of people, not the other way around. She was capable and strong and confident. No one ever really thought she needed anything. She rarely thought she needed anything. But having Alex scowling at her now because she wasn't taking care of herself— yeah, that felt okay. Better than okay.

"Okay," she agreed.

He looked surprised. Probably because she wasn't arguing. "Yeah?" he asked.

"Yeah." She stepped forward. "Are we to the naked part now? Because I'd really like to take my clothes off."

Alex's eyes heated, but he still looked ticked off "You're going to let up on yourself?"

"Yes. And Ben," she added, hoping that would speed up the part where they transitioned to naked and horizontal, but there was one more thing she wanted to say. "You know the part about being amazing in spite of my limitations and because of them?"

He nodded. "Yeah."

"Ditto." She pressed close and slid her arms around his waist. "A big, fat ditto."

She felt him sigh just before he wrapped his arms around her and hugged her tight.

"My bedroom is the second on the left," she told him. She was thrilled he was here. She wanted to show him the house, but she wanted more to show him how much she cared about him and how much she wanted him here.

They stripped on the way up the steps, kissing, their hands colliding as they tried to take their own clothes off and help with each other's at the same time. They each had an armful of clothing, a mix of his and hers, by the time they reached the second floor. They stumbled through Maya's bedroom door and tossed everything. Maya kicked the door shut, and they fell onto the bed, hands roaming everywhere, mouths following hands.

"This really is a nice, soft bed," Alex said when she rolled on top of him. His hands settled on her butt and pressed her against his already-hard erection.

"Yeah, now I don't have to go easy," she teased, reaching between them and taking him in her hand.

"There's no way the other night on your desk was easy," Alex said. "I don't think I knew I could strain a glute that way."

Maya frowned. "Did you—"

He flipped her to her back. "Don't you ever take it easy on me, Maya Goodwin," he warned in a low growl. "I want everything this beautiful body can do to me, got it?"

"I'm going to ask you this one time," she said. "And then I won't do it ever again."

He sighed. "Okay."

"Do you promise to tell me if there's ever something you can't do?"

"There is nothing—"

"Just say, 'Yes, Maya, I promise' and mean it, and I'll shut up."

"Yes, Maya, I promise."

She wrapped her arms and legs around him and arched into him. "I promise the same thing."

He chuckled. "Deal. And don't think I'm not intrigued by the idea of finding something you can't do."

"Well, it's more that there are some things I don't want to do."

"Oh? Still intrigued."

She laughed. She thought it was possible her list of don't-likes was shorter with Alex.

He slid his hands under her and lifted her hips against his. He kissed her neck, then moved his mouth to her ear. "How do you feel about being on all fours?"

She shivered. "One of my top three."

He flipped her over before she knew what was happening. He ran his hands up and down her back, and she felt the goose bumps all over her body. He massaged her muscles, spending a little extra time on her left shoulder and neck and melting her heart. He touched her gently there, but he didn't shy away at all, tracing the scars as if they still fascinated him.

Maya wiggled her butt, and his hands dropped to her cheeks, kneading them firmly. "So impatient."

She couldn't help it. Yes, she went hard and fast in all she did, but she also had this high-speed switch that seemed to flip on instantly when Alex touched her.

"I am," she breathed. "Need you."

Alex slid his hands to her hips and pulled her butt toward him, bringing her to her knees. He ran a hand between her legs. "Damn. What you do to me," he muttered.

He slid a finger into her and Maya moaned. "Yes. More."

But instead of a nice deep thrust, she felt his tongue.

"Alex!" she gasped, then moaned again as he licked and sucked.

She didn't mind having her first orgasm this way, but he moved just before she peaked, shifting so he could slide into her in one strong thrust that made her cry his name. Her name was on his lips as well as he stroked deep and hard, his hands gripping her hips. After only a few minutes, Maya felt her body clamp down on him just before he came with a shout.

They collapsed together, facedown on the bed, and Maya definitely noted the difference between her mattress and the floor mats at the studio.

"I feel like maybe not having the Spider-Man bobblehead was okay," Alex said after they'd caught their breath.

Maya didn't need to look to see what had inspired that comment. She had a Captain America framed poster on her wall. It was a movie poster. And a collector's item because it was signed by the director. It wasn't a completely geeky thing to have. But the Captain America throw pillow on her bed was.

Maya sighed. "I like Captain America more than Spider-Man," she confessed.

"Yeah?" Alex ran his hand up and down her back. "Why?"

He really wanted to know. She could tell. A gorgeous guy who saved lives, who was a great dad, who got her interests. Or at least really tried. It was almost too good to be true.

# CHAPTER TEN

*M*aking him a fan of *Galactic Renegades* had been impressive. Making him look cool with a bo staff had been a feat. But making him enjoy doing dishes was downright miraculous. Yet Maya Goodwin had made it happen.

Alex crowded close to her as he reached to put a glass back in the cupboard over her head. He loved this corner between the sink and the fridge. It was perfect for making out between the handfuls of dishes her roommates and friends kept bringing in from the backyard.

"Get a room," Rob groaned as he carried a stack of plates into the kitchen and found Alex's hands up Maya's shirt.

"Done," Maya told him. "But then you'll have to finish the dishes."

"You can't wash dishes and keep your hands off of him for ten minutes?" Rob asked.

"Trust me. You haven't seen his abs," Maya told him. "You wouldn't be able to stop touching them either."

Rob made a choking sound. "I'm very sure that would not be a problem." He looked at Alex. "And honestly, I don't care if you're offended by that."

Alex chuckled. "I understand."

He wished he had Maya to himself pretty much every minute of the time he spent with her. Yet he loved being around her friends. They were good people, and they were obviously very important to her. They made her happy. She smiled and laughed and teased and argued and rolled her eyes and practically glowed with it all when she was in their midst, and Alex loved watching her, listening to her, just being there and soaking up everything about her.

Over the week and a half since he'd brought her home from the studio and made love to her in her bed, everything had amped up between them. They'd fallen asleep, tangled up in her sheets. She'd made him grilled cheese in the middle of the night. And it was the best grilled cheese of his life. They'd had breakfast with her roommates the next morning—also the best French toast of his life—before he'd joined Maya in the shower. Then, as they'd been getting dressed, they'd ended up getting dirty again—in the best possible way—and had to repeat their showers. Separately, so they wouldn't be late for work.

Since then his routine had been work, dinner with Charli, workout at the studio with Maya, home with Maya, hot sex until they curled up to sleep, breakfast with Maya, then work again. He was getting everything done, spending time with everyone, being there for everyone. He'd found the perfect balance.

Being involved with Maya Goodwin was as consuming as he'd imagined it would be. She was on his mind constantly. They texted during the day and usually spoke at least once, and now it was Friday night. That meant Charli and Rachel were at their art class, and that meant he was at Maya's for a backyard barbecue with all her friends. She felt like his girlfriend now. And even if he was thirty-two years old, he loved it.

Maya ran her hand over his abs, and Rob set his stack of dishes down with a clatter. "I'm out."

Alex watched him disappear through the back door into the yard, where everyone was still sitting around talking with beers and margaritas. He looked down at Maya as the door shut. "Where was I?"

"About to unhook my bra, I believe."

That was exactly where he'd been. He was just reaching for the tiny hooks when the back door banged open again.

"I'll hose you down, I swear it," Ben said, as he came into the room with two serving platters and a bowl. "I know why you volunteered for dish duty, and I also know there's nothing clean going on in here."

Maya laughed. "We have the dishwasher completely loaded."

She and Ben continued to tease, and Alex just absorbed the moment. He felt completely included and comfortable with the group, and they all seemed to accept him and Maya as a couple without question. Which was good. The house—and Maya's life—was full, seemingly all the time. Sophie, Kiera, Zach, Rob, and, of course, Ben.

Alex didn't dislike the guy. Exactly. And since Alex

was the one next to her in bed, he wasn't worried about the other man. He still wished Ben slept more than fifty feet from Maya, wasn't quite as good-looking, and didn't handle weapons like a badass, but other than that he liked the guy. And damn, Ben made some kick-ass cheddar bacon burgers.

He'd done the grilling tonight, and they'd eaten around the picnic table in the backyard of the house they all shared. It wasn't a big yard—none of the ones in Cambridge, only blocks from the Harvard campus, were—but it was well kept, filled with flowers and surrounded by big, old trees.

Alex wondered what they did for meals in cold weather. Their dining room was not usable for dinner parties. The table was covered with fabric and sewing machines, the chairs and chandelier were draped with costumes, and the hutch was filled with helmets, hats, crowns, and other headpieces. The wall next to the window was his favorite part, though—it was covered with hooks that held a variety of weapons. It was clearly Maya's wall.

Alex readily acknowledged that six months ago he would have thought this was strange and a possible sign this was not the woman for him. Now it just made him smile. Maya made him happy, and it wasn't about her knowledge of comic books and movies or her skill with a bo staff or sword. It was just her.

"How do you feel about cats?" Alex asked Maya as Ben headed out the back door.

"Cats?" Maya took a plate from him and wiped it dry. "I like cats."

"Charli wants one, but Rachel's allergic."

Alex was happy that Charli had moved on to topics of conversation other than *GR* and bo staffs with him, but the last two nights at dinner all she'd wanted to talk about was cats. Alex had dutifully backed Rachel up on that one after Rachel explained how allergic she was and that doing day care made pet ownership difficult. He had, however, looked into his building's policy on pets. He could have a cat. But he wasn't sure he should.

"So you're going to get one at your place?" Maya asked.

"I'm thinking about it."

"How allergic is Rachel?"

Alex turned to face her, propping his hip against the counter next to him. "Pretty bad, I guess."

"Like red, puffy eyes and lots of snot?" she asked.

He narrowed his eyes but couldn't help but grin. "Probably."

"Then you should definitely get one," Maya said.

Alex watched her rigorously dry another plate. "You think?"

"Sure. It's Charli's only chance for one, right?"

"Right."

"Well then, there you go." She picked up a glass and rubbed it hard with the towel.

"And you're not allergic?" he asked.

She set the glass down with a thunk, and Alex was glad it was plastic.

"No, I'm not allergic."

"Because visiting a house where a cat lives is tough on Rachel. About thirty minutes in and she's sneezing and miserable."

Maya mimicked his stance, with her opposite hip against the counter. "Maybe you should get two cats."

Alex tried not to let his grin grow. Maya was extraordinarily great about him having dinner with another woman six nights a week, but there were moments when she showed tiny hints of jealousy, and—juvenile as it was—he liked it.

"For Charli," he added.

Maya nodded. "Totally what I meant."

He couldn't keep his grin contained. "I figured."

She narrowed her eyes. "But a cat would be no reason at all for me not to come over."

Alex wanted her in his house. He did. In his bed. But also in his kitchen doing dishes with him, on his couch eating popcorn, in his bathroom blow-drying her hair. But it was less complicated for him to go from his time with Charli to the studio to here and…not have them mingle.

Dammit. This was definitely easier. But it was still absolutely complicated.

"I wouldn't get a cat if you were allergic."

She looked at him for a few beats and started to reply but Zach and Kiera banged into the kitchen just then with Ben behind them. They carried more dishes and several bottles of condiments and were laughing and talking. Thankfully. He didn't know what to say to Maya about Charli. And his place. And their very complicated situation.

He had to consider Rachel when it came to getting a cat. And he definitely needed to consider her feelings and reactions to him bringing a girlfriend home. Didn't he? He didn't know. And he had exactly zero people to talk to about this.

Rob came through the door a moment later. "Hey, Alex, can we talk to you?" he asked.

Alex looked at him in surprise. "Me?" All of the men were watching him. Alex frowned. "What's up?"

"Do you play basketball?" Rob asked.

"Not really. I mean, I've played. I'm not very good." He'd shot hoops in his friend's driveway as a kid, but his mom would never have allowed him to play on an actual team.

"Uh, guys—" Maya started.

"We have a game Sunday night and need an extra guy," Ben said.

"We need two extra guys," Zach said. He looked at Ben. "You're not supposed to be playing football or basketball for a while."

"Why not?" Maya asked.

"It's nothing," Ben told her. "He didn't mean a Sunday-night league with a bunch of old guys."

"Hey, you're older than I am," Rob said.

"And you all play basketball like it's WWE," Maya said, crossing her arms. "What's going on?"

"Ben saw his doctor about his head, finally," Rob said. "Doc said his brain is practically mush, and he'd better let up or we're going to have to feed him and dress him."

"Oh Jesus," Ben snapped. "That is not what he said."

"What did he say?" Maya asked.

"He said I need to take it easy for a while," Ben said with a sigh. "But I can play a stupid game of basketball."

"He did not say that," Zach said. "He wants you out of all the aggressive, contact stuff."

"Seriously, don't be a dumbass," Rob told Ben. "Your

brain's gotten knocked around, but I know you're still a relatively smart guy."

"Concussions aren't something you should mess around with," Alex told him.

"Yeah, well, I don't—" Ben stopped abruptly and sighed.

Rob and Zach laughed.

"You don't what?" Alex asked.

"Typically, when we're telling him he should stop doing some stupid thing, he says he doesn't know where we got our medical degrees but he's sure his insurance won't pay us." Rob laughed at the look on Ben's face. "He can't say that to you."

Alex felt a corner of his mouth curve up. "Harvard," he said, unable to keep the humor out of his tone. "And I'm in network with all of the major plans."

"Yeah, yeah," Ben said.

Alex chuckled. "You got a concussion from basketball?"

"My last bando competition," Ben said.

"Bando?"

"Bando is a martial arts form," Maya filled in. "But his concussions first happened boxing."

Damn. Ben really was badass.

Maya moved toward Ben, concern on her face. "The doctor said you're done? With all of it?"

He sighed. "I can still teach. I can do bo competitions. But nothing more... aggressive. At least for now."

"For a long time," Rob interjected.

Alex took a deep breath. He knew what Ben was feeling. Regret, resentment maybe, a feeling of loss and unfairness. And maybe some fear. The idea that something was happening with his body that he couldn't control was hard to take, especially for a guy who liked to be in charge.

Maya shook her head. "But I—"

"Alex can fill in for me," Ben interrupted. "They can still play. And then I'll join them for beer afterward."

Maya shook her head, looking unhappy. "I don't like it. I think you should all grow up and—"

"I was a national champion swimmer," Alex said, stopping her before she pissed her friends off. The other guys didn't need to adjust for him. It was his issue, and he needed to handle it. "But no basketball, sorry."

"We play hard, but it's not exactly the NBA," Ben said. "I'm sure you can figure it out."

It wasn't that he couldn't figure it out. But he couldn't play basketball with these guys. Not if they went hard. And they shouldn't have to tone it down for him.

Alex felt a prickle of annoyance, but there was no one to be annoyed at except...No, there was no one. His condition was a fact. He couldn't change it. In that moment he felt every bit of Charli's frustration at wanting to do things her peers did and not being able to. It was a familiar feeling. He'd just gotten good at ignoring it.

But on the heels of his irritation was the realization that he could talk to Charli about this. He'd wanted to bond with her. He'd chosen comic books. But the real bond had been there between them all along. He just needed to be better about opening up about it. Now he could use this situation to illustrate that he understood what she was dealing with.

"How about you guys back off?" Maya asked, stepping forward.

Alex wasn't sure if she was consciously putting herself between him and the guys, but that's where she was. Literally.

"We're inviting your new boyfriend to play basketball," Ben said. "What's your problem?"

"Maybe not every guy has the insane need to knock a bunch of other guys around," she said. "Maybe Alex would rather hang out with me, or his kid, or maybe do anything other than get all sweaty with you guys."

Ben, Zach, and Rob all lifted their eyebrows in unison.

"What the hell's wrong with you?" Ben asked.

"I have a bleeding disorder," Alex said before Maya could answer. "I can't do WWE basketball. Sorry."

The men all focused on him. Alex thought he should be shocked that the words had come so easily. Or at all. But there they were. For better or worse.

"A bleeding disorder?" Zach repeated. "Hemophilia?"

Alex nodded. Zach was an EMT. He'd get it. "Moderate severity."

"What's that mean?" Rob asked.

"My blood doesn't clot normally. Contact sports set me up for the risk of bleeding, especially into a muscle or joint. I can treat it, take clotting factor, but as I'm trying to teach my daughter, I need to make good decisions about which risks I take."

Rob looked sincerely interested. Zach simply nodded.

Ben's gaze flickered between Maya and Alex. "Well," he said, "guess we've all got something then."

Maya gave Ben a soft smile that made Alex want to hug her.

"I don't have anything," Rob said.

"Dude, you couldn't make a free throw if there was a million dollars on the line," Ben told him.

"That's a physical limitation?" Rob asked.

"Are you saying it's mental?" Ben returned. "Because all I know is it's a limitation."

"What about Zach?" Rob asked, as everyone laughed. "He's our best player."

Ben rolled his eyes. "Yeah, unless he's nursing a burn on his hand from a hot glue gun."

"Or a cut from an X-Acto knife," Rob agreed. "Or a puncture wound from a staple gun."

"And every one of those was something he did for me," Kiera said, slipping an arm around his waist.

Zach gave Ben a wink as he pulled Kiera up against him. "I'll keep doing them too. Kiera kisses all of my injuries better. And then some."

Kiera blushed.

Ben laughed. "You might be good at basketball, but you kind of suck at some of the other stuff we do, and that impacts your playing too."

"Right. Thanks," Zach said with a nod.

Still grinning, Ben said, "So, guess we still need two guys for basketball."

And that was it. They accepted that Alex couldn't play basketball and moved on.

"Well, basketball might be out for both of us, but I could kick your ass in poker," Alex told Ben.

Ben looked as if he was considering that. "Poker, huh?"

"Yep. And any other card game you want to pull out. I can also humiliate you at chess or pool, for that matter."

"Damn, I haven't shot pool in forever," Zach said. "That could be fun."

"Until he takes all your money," Rob said, with a chuckle.

"You think you're that good?" Zach asked Alex, acting as if he was up for a challenge.

"As a hemophiliac with a very nervous, overprotective mother, I can assure you I spent a lot of time with quieter activities that required less exertion."

"I could play some chess," Rob decided with a nod. "And we could go shoot pool at the Good Life sometime."

"They have awesome wings," Zach agreed.

"They've got five-dollar pitchers on Thursdays," Rob said. "How about next week?"

Before he knew it, Alex had plans to hang out with the guys the following week and shoot pool. As if it were no big deal.

He glanced at Maya and thought maybe her eyes were a little sparkly. As if maybe she was tearing up a little.

"I'm going to go grab the rest of the dishes," she said, slipping around the guys and out the back door before he could say anything.

"I'll help." Kiera squeezed Zach and then followed her friend outside.

The guys watched them leave, then turned back to Alex.

"Damn. When you all came in to talk to me, I thought you were going to ask my intentions. Offer to kick my ass if I hurt Maya, that kind of stuff," Alex said.

"This is Maya." Ben gave a shrug. "If anyone needs their ass kicked, she generally takes care of it."

"And we kind of figured it was a given that we didn't

want you to hurt her," Zach said, giving Alex a narrow-eyed look. "These girls are special."

"Got it," Alex agreed. "And yeah, it's a given."

The guys all nodded. Well, that was easy. Maybe too easy. It was true that Maya was strong and bold and confident. But she deserved to have people protecting her. Or at least looking out for her.

Maya and Kiera came back in with the rest of the stuff from outside. Alex watched as Maya set her armful down and picked up the dishcloth from the sink. Making a quick decision, he took the cloth from her hand and handed it to Ben.

"Excuse us for a minute." He took her hand and started for the front of the house.

"Hey, what's going on?" Ben called after him.

But Alex didn't answer as he nudged Maya into the small powder room just off the foyer. He kicked the door shut behind them and lifted her onto the edge of the tiny vanity.

"What is going on?" she asked with a big smile, welcoming him with open arms as he stepped between her knees.

"You didn't tell your friends about my condition."

She caught her bottom lip between her teeth and shook her head, suddenly looking apprehensive.

He freed her lip with his thumb and stroked back and forth across the soft fullness. "Why?"

"After I realized that you don't talk about it with anyone, I didn't think it was my place," she said softly.

"You were protecting me again. You didn't want them to think I was weird."

She shook her head. "No. They wouldn't. They're

great. I just..." She sighed. "It was hard not telling them."

"You tell them everything."

"I tell them the things that matter to me," she said with a nod.

"And my condition matters to you?"

"Yes, of course. Well, I mean, not really. I mean...yes, because it's a part of who you are and you matter to me. But it's not like—"

"Maya." He could have stopped her by kissing her as usual, but once he started kissing her, he wasn't going to stop for a very long time.

"Yeah?" she asked.

"I really like mattering to you."

"Oh." The word escaped on a soft breath. "I'm glad."

"Charli and her hemophilia matter to me. If you feel even an ounce of that for me, then I feel...amazed."

"Amazed." She smiled. "That's a good way to feel."

He agreed wholeheartedly. "And thank you for not telling them," he said. "Telling them myself was...good. It was good for me."

She smiled, but her eyes were sparkling with tears again. "It was good," she agreed. "I'm glad you did. It helped Ben."

"Yeah?"

"You were protecting him," she said. "You were giving him a way to not feel so bad about not playing."

Alex shook his head. "Not protecting. Just relating."

"Wow," she said, looking into his eyes.

"What?"

"I really, really want to do dirty things to you right now."

Heat slid through him, but right on its heels was happiness so pure and full that he had to take a deep breath before saying, "That's funny. I was just thinking the same thing about you."

He cupped her head and leaned in to taste her. But when she lifted her hands to circle his neck, he caught them. He pressed them back onto the counter on either side of her hips. "Let me make you feel amazing," he said hotly against her lips.

"I do. You do," she said huskily.

But he shook his head. "Hands to yourself for a bit."

"Only for a bit," she said, curling her fingers over the edge of the countertop.

She was going to let him do this. Desire rocked through him. Not just the desire to plunge into her gorgeous, sweet body and claim her physically, but the desire to have all of her—heart, mind, and soul too. He wanted her time, her passion, her friendship.

Alex took a deep, shuddering breath and relaxed his grip on her hands. He slipped his fingers under the hem of her shirt and slid it up. Maya reached up to let him slide it over her head and toss it. Her eyes on his, she reached behind and unhooked her bra, letting it fall to the floor.

Alex stripped his shirt off and kicked his shoes to the side. They both unbuttoned their pants and unzipped at the same time. With a playful smile on her lips, Maya wiggled on the vanity, pushing her pants and panties to the floor, exposing the toned, smooth legs he wanted to stroke, kiss, and wrap around his waist for the next hour. Or week.

He didn't step out of his pants and boxers, just got

them far enough out of the way. She started to reach for him, then apparently remembered her promise. She gripped the edge of the counter and watched him roll on a condom.

He didn't even need to touch her to see her reactions to him. Her nipples were beaded into hard points, her skin was flushed, and she was breathing fast. Sex with Maya made him feel powerful in a way nothing else ever had. This woman used her body for so many things that gave her pleasure. But there was something about how they came together that made him believe she'd never felt this good before. And the high from making her feel that way was better than any drug on the market.

Suddenly ravenous for her, he took her mouth again in a hungry kiss as his hands stroked over her body. He played with her nipples, he ran his palms over her back and arms, he caressed her thighs, and then he teased her slick folds and the bundle of nerves that made her moan and shudder in his arms. He took her almost to the summit, then backed off, gentling his touch and his kisses. Then he worked her up again, almost to the peak, before slowing down. Finally, the third time, with her trembling and panting, he took her over the edge, relishing the look on her face, the way her body responded to him, the way she let him be in charge of her pleasure.

While she was still quivering, unable to help him even move her to the edge of the vanity, he cupped her ass in his hands and slid home. With the strongest woman he'd ever met boneless in his arms because of his love-making, Alex didn't last long. He thrust deep, trying to go slowly, but his need for her was too powerful, and he found himself climbing into his climax minutes later. He buried his face in the side of her neck, groaning her name as he found completion.

And he knew that he'd never feel complete without her again.

# *C*HAPTER ELEVEN

*C*harli's laughter from the next room washed over him, and he took a deep breath. The air in Rachel's kitchen smelled like lasagna, one of his favorite foods. His cousin Austin was here for dinner with them. Everything was good. But Alex felt like shit.

"I can't believe I didn't realize I was supposed to be there," he said for the third time.

"You'll have another chance, Alex. Let this go," Rachel said. For the third time.

"But it was the first one. I can't believe I missed it." Last night had been the first showing of the painting projects Charli had been working on with Rachel. The art studio where the classes were held did a showing every few weeks of the students' works. Apparently Rachel had mentioned it to Alex. But he'd missed it.

"Seriously, it's fine. There will be another one in a couple of months. You didn't promise to be there. She's not upset."

Alex watched Rachel drizzle dressing over the salad and toss it.

So this was why she always used the terms *might* and *maybe* and *we'll see* in regard to him, Alex realized. Clearly there had been a man, maybe a couple, who had said he wanted to be involved but hadn't followed through. But he was Charli's father. He was going to follow through. And then some.

"She doesn't even like the class," Rachel said, turning to pull the lasagna and garlic bread from the oven.

"What? Really?"

She shook her head. "Nope."

"Why are you having her do it, then?"

"Because I like it," Rachel said. "And I think it's an important lesson to learn that you sometimes do things because someone you care about loves them. It's also been great for her fine motor skills, and she's met some other girls her age." She placed the bread in a basket. "And she likes it more than she thinks she does. Of course, it's no bo workout." She gave him a small smile.

Damn. "Rach—"

"Alex, relax. I'm kidding. I love that you're doing bo with her. Honestly. She lights up on Tuesdays."

Tuesday was now the day that Rachel and Charli came to his place for dinner and they practiced the bo routines. Every time he saw Maya, she taught him a new move to add to the routine. Alex was working on putting them into patterns to teach Charli. But most of the time, he and Maya worked on the sword routine for the faux ember lances. He had the entire thing mostly memorized now.

And, of course, they also spent a lot of time naked and up against each other.

That was kind of unintentional. They didn't get together just for sex. But it seemed that thirty minutes of working out was about their limit before they were taking each other's clothes off and sweating for a whole other reason.

The reason that he'd missed Charli's art showing.

Well, not the whole reason. He'd been eating and bonding with her friends as well, becoming more a part of her life, deepening their relationship.

Alex pulled in a long breath, focusing on Rachel. "I love the bo stuff too," he admitted.

"But," Rachel said, picking up the lasagna pan with two oven mitts, "she lights up every day when she knows you're on your way over."

Alex felt happy surprise rock through him. "Yeah?"

"I thought you should know," she told him before turning and heading to the dining room.

He grabbed the salad and bread and followed her to the table, where Charli and Austin were already seated.

"You and Uncle Austin ready to eat?" Rachel asked, setting the lasagna on the table and interrupting their conversation about the new Supergirl TV show.

"Sure!" Charli said, turning to face the table enthusiastically.

She loved lasagna. It was number two on her list of favorite foods, behind cheeseburgers.

Alex had to cough to clear his throat as he took his chair and realized that he knew that about her without looking at his phone. It was a small detail, of course, but when he thought that three months ago he hadn't known anything about her—and that six months ago he hadn't even known she existed—the small details, the proof that he was getting to know her, mattered. A lot.

He would have really loved to be there for her painting class show.

But he refrained from saying so. He'd already told her how sorry he was and that he loved the paintings she'd done. He knew he was making a bigger deal out of it than it was to Charli. But he hated the idea that she might not count on him to be there for things that were important to her.

They talked and laughed through dinner. This wasn't the first time Austin had met Rachel and Charli, of course, but it still caught Alex in the chest to hear his cousin referred to as *uncle*. It was kind of like how Alex felt about the word *dad*. And Alex had to give Austin credit for having held up his end of the conversation about Supergirl.

"Charli, help me clear the table," Rachel said after everyone had finished.

"Let me help." Alex pushed his chair back. He had something he needed to ask Rachel about. Or to tell her about.

He followed her back into the kitchen and started loading the dishwasher. He was unable to keep his mind from wandering to the last kitchen he'd done dishes in. And of course to the woman he'd done them with. And then to the things he'd done with that woman in the powder room down the hall. Damn. Maya was on his mind constantly, and it was definitely interfering with his time with Rachel.

"Hey, I want to take Charli out next Saturday," he said as Rachel put the leftover lasagna into a plastic container.

"Oh, okay. Sure. I have kids in the morning, but—"

"Just me and Charli."

Rachel turned to face him. It would be the first time he and Charli spent the day together just the two of them. And Alex realized it was a big step. He hadn't asked for it before, letting Rachel take the lead. But she wasn't encouraging this, and... it was time.

"Are you sure?" Rachel asked.

He was. Definitely. And he was ready to push. *Sometimes pushing is okay. It means you care about something. It shows the other person you really want... whatever.* Maya's words came to him, and he knew it was time for him to show Charli that he wanted time with her. And that they didn't always have to be a trio.

"Yes, of course. I was thinking I'd take her to the comic book store that's down the street from the hospital. I think of her every time I go by."

Rachel nodded. "She'll like that."

"Great. I'll pick her up around nine."

"Sounds good."

"You think so?"

She smiled. "I think it's about time."

Alex felt as if he should say something else, but he had no idea what it would be. So he started the dishwasher and headed back into the dining room.

"Hey, kiddo, do you want to go to the comic book store next Saturday with me?" he asked, before he had time to think about it. Or overthink it.

Charli looked up at him. "Really?"

"Yeah. Just you and me. What do you think?"

Her eyes widened. "Yes. That would be so cool!"

Alex's heart thumped at her excitement and the fact that

she hadn't hesitated a bit over the idea of the two of them on their own. Maybe he had taken too long to get to this point. "Great. Maybe we can burgers afterward or something."

"Yes! Yay!" Charli exclaimed. "This will be awesome. I need to count my money. There's a whole set of *GR* comic books and I hope they have them!"

She popped up and ran to her room before Alex could say something stupid like that he'd buy her the whole store and anything else she wanted for the rest of her life as long as she said, "Yay!" and "Awesome!" about spending time with him forever.

"Hey, I'll go too. Maybe I can get Sam something," Austin said.

Rachel had come into the room. She shook her head before Alex could say anything. "This is the first one-on-one time for Alex and Charli," she said. "Let's let them go alone this time."

Alex wanted to hug her.

"I'm way cooler than Alex, though," Austin said, breaking into the moment. He leaned back in his seat. "Charli and I are completely clicking."

Alex, on the other hand, was trying to truly understand his daughter's obsession. He couldn't do the minimum with Charli the way Austin could.

"Alex is cool enough for Charli," Rachel told Austin, pulling Alex back into the moment.

Alex gave her a smile. "That's not exactly saying I'm cooler than Austin, though."

Austin snorted.

Rachel laughed. "Austin is cool. But you're her dad." She looked him in the eye. "That matters. It really does, I promise."

He valued her reassurance.

"Well, if you want, I can give you the superhero notes I studied for tonight that we never got to," Austin said.

Alex appreciated Austin's effort in looking facts up on fan sites online but was annoyed at the same time. "I'd prefer to talk to her about things I actually know and find interesting about *Galactic Renegades*."

"Suit yourself," Austin said with a shrug.

Alex hesitated. Then said, "But yeah, I could look at them, I guess."

Austin smirked but pulled out his note card and slid it across the table.

Rachel shook her head. "You don't need that," she told him as she walked behind Alex's chair on her way to Charli's room. She stopped and put her hand on his shoulder. "You're doing great. She loves you." Rachel leaned in and kissed Alex's cheek, then headed down the hallway.

Alex felt the tension in his shoulders increase as the feel of her kiss faded.

Austin watched her go before turning back to Alex, his eyes huge.

"What's going on there?" he asked suggestively.

Alex cleared his throat. "Um. Nothing." While thinking, *Crap*.

Austin gave him a disbelieving look. "Come on, Alex. Rachel just kissed you."

"On the cheek." Alex shifted uncomfortably. He couldn't help but flash back to the lip-to-lip kiss several days ago. He had moved quickly from thinking about how great it would be for him and Rachel to work out to thinking a solid friendship would be okay.

At least when he was with Maya. He was crazy about Maya.

But there was a definite dose of guilt and, unfortunately, a strong feeling of trepidation. Rachel was fully independent. She didn't need help. But didn't she deserve it? She was raising his daughter. Charli was amazing, mostly due to Rachel. He couldn't be more grateful. And he loved her for being an amazing mother to Charli.

But he couldn't not love Maya.

It wasn't fair to Rachel to love her only because of Charli. Without Charli, what would they have? Alex shoved a hand through his hair.

"Does that happen a lot?" Austin asked.

"What?"

"The kissing. On the cheek or otherwise?"

"No." He didn't elaborate.

"And you're not sleeping with her?" Austin asked.

"Rachel? No." Alex scowled at him. It wasn't a huge assumption. He and Rachel spent a lot of time together and obviously had a history—and a relationship that would last the rest of their lives. It was actually a totally fair question, assuming it was any of Austin's business, which it wasn't.

"Because you're sleeping with Supergirl?"

Alex felt his jaw tense. It was stupid, but he really hated hearing Austin call her that. Partly because it was his name for her. But also because, the way Austin said it, it sounded as if it were all . . . made up.

It wasn't Austin's business either, but the truth was, Maya was the reason he wasn't trying harder with Rachel. And he felt like shit about that. He didn't know if he and Rachel would work out even if Maya weren't in the picture, but he now had no interest in even trying.

"I am seeing Maya, yes," Alex finally said to Austin.

"Does Rachel know about Maya?"

Alex shot a look down the hall. "Keep it down."

"Ah." Austin nodded. "She doesn't know."

Alex didn't talk about personal stuff easily, even with Austin. "I don't know how to tell her," he admitted. "Or if I need to tell her."

Austin shrugged. "The fact that you're wondering about it probably means you should tell her."

Yeah, that's what he'd thought. Though there was a little voice in the back of his head that said, "What if it is made up?" He knew he wasn't imagining his feelings for Maya, but he couldn't deny that the way he'd met her, the way they spent a lot of their time together—with pretend swords and choreographed battles—the way she made him feel, all seemed more fantasy than reality. Reality was having dinner with his daughter and her mother, helping with homework, taking Charli out for the day on Saturday. A guy like him shouldn't be picking up a bo staff. At least not for real, not the way Maya did—in competitions and for a living. He wasn't a jump-into-the-deep-end-of-the-pool guy. Maya made him that guy.

And the thing was—to be a good dad to Charli, he wasn't sure he should be a jump-into-the-deep-end guy.

"The only way you wouldn't need to tell her is if you weren't going to keep seeing Maya," Austin said.

Pain stabbed him in the heart. And he didn't answer. Couldn't. How could he make this choice?

Austin read his face and chuckled. "Good luck with that." He pushed back from the table and stood.

Alex wanted to just let him go. What did Austin know about any of this? But he heard himself say, "How do you think Rachel will react?"

Austin paused. "Rachel? Or are you worried about Charli?"

Was it that Austin had become more insightful as he got older, or had he always been insightful and Alex just hadn't ever talked to him about anything like this?

"How do you think Charli will react?"

"To you having a girlfriend just after meeting you and thinking her family was getting back together?"

Alex narrowed his eyes. He knew Austin had said it that way to get a rise out of Alex. And it had worked. He felt his gut knotting even tighter.

"From what I know about Maya, I think Charli will love her."

Alex breathed out. Charli would love Maya. That was good. Probably.

"Hell, Charli will probably like Maya more than she likes Rachel."

Alex jerked his head up to look at Austin. "What?"

"Maya is cooler than Rachel," Austin said with a shrug. "She knows all this superhero stuff and is, literally, kick-ass. Rachel makes her put her book away and go to sleep, makes her study, tells her she can't do gymnastics with her friends. Of course Charli will like Maya more."

Alex felt his throat tightening. He'd thought he understood all the complications. "And that's bad, right?"

Austin laughed. "All kids resent their parents from time to time. If it's not Maya, it will be something else that makes Charli think Rachel is the meanest mom ever."

"But if it's me bringing something into the situation that makes things tense between them, that's bad."

Austin shrugged. "Maybe."

Fuck. Fuck, fuck, fuck. He couldn't do that to Rachel. Rachel didn't let Charli's pouting and temper get to her. Alex had already seen them butt heads, and Rachel just rolled with it. But that didn't mean that she wouldn't resent having someone to compete with for Charli's affection.

Charli would always love her mom. They were tight. But she was coming up on a tough phase of life—the teenage years. There would be rocky times anyway. Alex's role should be to help them both through it. Not make it worse.

"But I don't think you and Rachel need to be together or get married or anything," Austin said. "You have a terrific kid. I think Charli is going to be great no matter what. You can absolutely help raise her without being with her mom."

Alex let all of that spin in his head. Austin was right. But no matter what else he did, Alex needed to be a positive addition to Charli and Rachel's lives.

Austin straightened. "But what the hell do I know? I had two parents that lived in the same house and really seemed to like one another. It's not like I'm an expert on raising kids, and certainly not in a situation like this."

It was true that Austin was no child psychologist, but he knew Charli, and he was right. She was good. Doing better all the time. Things were great the way they were. And now they were just graduating to time alone. He couldn't mess with this.

Austin let himself out, leaving Alex with his thoughts.

They were, as usual, not far from Maya. He missed her. But now thinking of her made him feel completely conflicted. That wasn't fair to her either. She had every reason to think that they were moving forward. In a normal situation they would be.

But how would Rachel feel about her daughter spending time with another woman? A woman Charli might find cooler than Rachel? It might not even be okay with Charli. If Charli wanted more time with him, that didn't mean she'd want to share their time with someone else.

And he simply couldn't deny that he liked his time alone with Maya. It wasn't just about the sex. Though that was the best of his life. But it was her. He was trying to keep Maya and Charli in separate boxes, but the divider between them seemed to be getting thinner.

In Maya's life everything mixed with everything else and turned out bigger and more elaborate because of it. Alex wasn't sure there was any way to keep Maya's involvement in his life in just one contained box. He wasn't sure he wanted to.

"She's really excited about Saturday."

Alex looked up from his coffee cup. He smiled at Rachel. "Me too."

She took the chair at the table next to him and tucked a leg under her. "Yep. We both agreed that you would be the best one of us for a comic book store trip anyway."

Maya would be the best one of them. The thought ran through his head before he could stop it.

Rachel looked at him thoughtfully when he didn't reply. "Are you nervous?"

About introducing Charli to a woman who was so

bright and full of life and interesting that it would take Charli only five minutes to fall in love with her? Yes.

"About Saturday?" he asked.

Rachel nodded.

"Not really," he replied. But only because he hadn't thought much beyond how thrilled he was. "Should I be?"

Rachel smiled. "You'll be fine. You're great with her. She's really warmed up lately. She's sleeping better, her grades are coming up, she's smiling a lot more."

Alex felt warmth spread through his chest. Whatever it took to influence those kinds of changes, he'd keep doing it forever.

"So English is better?" he asked.

"Much."

"Do you think the bo stuff has made that much difference?"

"I think it's time with you that's made the difference," Rachel said. "And you showing such interest in her interests."

He hadn't even shown her the ember lances yet. He'd been saving them for her birthday. But he'd noticed that Charli had gotten more talkative each time they'd been at his house for the bo workouts. She had told him more about school and her friends and teachers here and back in Connecticut. He'd also learned a lot about her grandparents and cousins on Rachel's side of the family, some of their family vacations, and even a couple of Rachel's ex-boyfriends.

And every time, his heart ached over how much he'd missed, and he felt an equally strong gratitude toward Rachel for giving Charli ten such wonderful, love-filled years.

"Well, glad I thought of the comic book store then," he said.

"It will be great," Rachel agreed. She curled a strand of hair around a finger, a gesture Alex knew meant she was working up to something.

It looked as if he hadn't learned things just about Charli in the past few months.

"I was hoping you could do more than the bookstore, though," she said. "I liked your suggestion of burgers after."

"I'd love to do more."

"Good. Then maybe you can talk to her over lunch."

Alex knew Rachel didn't mean talking to Charli about whether Victoria Sampson, the actress who played Piper, was really dating Justin Bieber. A rumor Alex knew about only because, on a whim, he'd grabbed a copy of a teen magazine in the grocery store line the other night. "What's going on?"

"Gym class," Rachel said. "She was playing kickball and got a bloody nose."

Alex sat up and frowned. "How did that happen? Why didn't you tell me?"

"They handled it. The nurse at school is on top of it. It was a substitute gym teacher and Charli wanted to play."

Alex ran a hand over his face. Rachel was calm. But she'd dealt with all of this for almost ten years. She was a pro.

"Dammit," he muttered.

"She's fine."

He knew that. He'd seen her tonight. She was more than fine.

"But she's grounded from the computer for a week," Rachel added.

Alex hated this. Learning to be a dad to a nine-year-old would have been hard enough anyway, but this one had medical issues and a stubborn streak.

"I could use the help, Alex," Rachel said softly. "But I can't be the bad guy alone. I can't never be the fun one, you know?"

Yes, Alex knew that. He'd known eventually he'd have to step up this way. "You have fun together." He was trying, he supposed, to reassure Rachel. That was new. He wasn't sure he'd done more than promise he'd handle dinner and get Charli on his insurance plan. The rest of the time it was definitely Rachel reassuring him that things would be okay. That needed to change. He not only should help make things okay, he wanted to.

"We do," Rachel agreed. "But there's a limit. I still have to make sure she's going to bed and eating her vegetables and studying."

Alex nodded.

"It all used to be easier, before she had her own opinions," Rachel said, with a small smile. "But she's getting more independent and I've had to get stricter with her. Even before we moved. And then we came here and I introduced her to this guy who is completely cool and fun."

"I had to learn all of that. Just for her," he said. "None of that is natural to me."

"I know," she said, and smiled. "That all makes you even cooler. To me, anyway."

There was definitely something in her tone that made that a lot more suggestive than it sounded on the surface. Dammit.

Rachel reached out and covered his hand. "I love it. I love that she's getting closer to you and comfortable with you. I love that we're all getting comfortable being together."

There was definitely more underlying her words.

"Yeah, I can discuss gym class," he said. "It will come up on Saturday for sure."

"Thanks." Rachel squeezed his hand. "And one more thing."

"Anything." He meant it. This woman was his partner in the most important thing he'd ever done—raising Charli.

But her gaze dropped to his mouth. Then she leaned in. And for one second he thought about leaning in too.

"I can't," he finally said. "Part of me wants to. I know it would make things so much easier. Better in some ways. But I can't."

She sat back. "You're seeing someone."

He nodded. "Yeah. I didn't...mean to. I had no idea it was going to happen like this. I know the timing sucks."

Rachel blew out a breath. "Did you know her before we came to Boston?"

"No."

"Is it serious?"

Damn. What a question. "It's—surprising," he said. "So I don't know what it is exactly. It's happened pretty fast."

Rachel tipped her head. "Do you want it to be serious?"

*Yes.* The answer came to him swiftly, and he couldn't duck out of the way. "*Serious* means something different now than it did a few months ago," he said. "I have to consider more than just how I feel. It affects Charli. And you."

Rachel frowned. "Yeah, I guess so. I mean, I never thought about that part of it. The three of us are just figuring things out. I didn't think about how someone else might get involved."

He hadn't thought about it until Maya either. If he'd been serious with someone before finding out about Charli, if he'd been married or engaged, they all would have had to take that other person into consideration. But Maya was new. Their relationship was new. They were very much in those beginning stages where everything felt fun and easy. There was no way of knowing if it was going to last.

"Does she know about Charli?" Rachel asked.

"Yes. She's known from the beginning."

"But she doesn't want to meet her?" Rachel was clearly offended by that idea.

"I haven't offered," he said. "I'm sure she would love to meet Charli. But she knows that I basically just met Charli."

"Were you going to tell me about her?" Rachel asked. "I mean if I hadn't tried to make a move on you."

"Is that what you were doing?"

"Yes." She said it without hesitation. "I don't know if it's because I think us being together would be great for Charli, or it's just how attractive you are when you're being a great dad, or if it's that I actually have feelings for you, but yes, I was making a move because I've wondered what might happen."

The honesty was great. They needed honesty. But he really didn't know how to respond. "I've wondered too," he finally said. "I think that's natural."

"I'm concerned, more for Charli than me," Rachel

said. "I need you to know that. I mean, what if she wants to take Charli out for the day and they go rollerblading and Charli falls and—"

"Maya knows about Charli's condition," he said quickly, unable to keep from defending her. "She wouldn't let Charli do anything she shouldn't."

"Maya." Rachel seemed to be testing the name out. "She knows?"

He nodded. "About me too."

Rachel's eyes widened. "Oh."

He and Rachel had never talked about his hemophilia at length. But it would have been impossible to go through getting Charli's diagnosis and all the education and counseling that went with it and not figure out that he had to have given her the gene.

"I'm glad you told her," Rachel said. "That must mean you're kind of serious. You don't talk about it."

"She figured it out, actually, when she was researching it because of Charli."

"Oh." Rachel seemed surprised. "That was nice of her to take such an interest."

Alex nodded. "She's great. Smart, caring, adventurous but protective. She'd never do anything to hurt Charli."

He was defending Maya to Rachel. He hadn't expected that. Of course, "I hadn't expected that" had become his motto when it came to Maya Goodwin, it seemed.

"In fact, when you come to pick up Charli on Saturday, I'll show you what Maya made for her," he said.

"Maya made something for Charli?" Rachel asked.

He grinned. "Armor. And an ember lance."

Rachel seemed baffled. "Why would she do that?"

"Because she knows Charli likes *GR* but that the regular hard weapons she uses are dangerous. This is foam."

"Maya uses weapons?"

"At her studio. Martial arts plus bo and stuff," he explained.

"Oh." Understanding spread over Rachel's face. "She's your bo instructor."

Alex nodded. "Yes. She's the one I went to when I realized I wanted to learn this for Charli."

Rachel hesitated.

"What?"

"I just—want to be glad and impressed you did that, but—"

"But?" he prompted.

"You met Maya."

This was definitely uncomfortable.

"I'm—" Not *sorry*. He was sorry Rachel was disappointed, but not that he'd met Maya. "I'm sorry that complicates things," he finally said honestly. "And I know it does."

This was the definition of *complicated*.

"Me too," she finally said.

He pulled her in for a hug. No matter what else happened, he was going to be hugging this woman for the rest of his life. Charli wasn't his daughter only until age eighteen. She was their daughter forever. They'd go through all the big moments of her life together—accomplishments, disappointments, celebrations, and defeats. They'd see her graduate, get married, have kids. They'd be grandparents together. Alex's heart clenched at the realization of just how much had changed in the past two months, how much Rachel and Charli had brought to his life.

Rachel rose from the table, but he caught something in her eyes before she turned away.

"Are you okay?" he asked.

"Charli's going to love Maya, isn't she?"

She would. Alex couldn't deny that. Maya could never replace Rachel, but would Charli be in awe of Maya? For sure. "It's too soon for them to meet," he said, his chest aching even as he realized it was true.

He and Charli were going to spend time together alone for the first time Saturday. It was too soon to try to navigate all of this with another person who could end up getting hurt, and causing hurt. To Rachel now, to Charli if things didn't work out.

Rachel frowned. "Are you sure? I don't want to make this hard on you."

There was no help for that now. The only way this wouldn't be hard on him would be if he hadn't taken that last shot in the bar eleven years ago. Or if he hadn't taken that flyer at the mall.

And he wouldn't change either of those things now if he were given the chance.

# CHAPTER TWELVE

Alex had never been more nervous about a date in his life.

This girl meant everything to him. He wanted to impress her, ensure she had a great time, and guarantee that she'd want to go out again. She was beautiful and smart and funny and completely fascinating to him. But he didn't want to come on too strong. He also didn't want to make small talk. They were beyond that. But he wasn't sure what to talk about without a bo staff in hand or a *Galactic Renegades* reference handy. Or her mother in the room.

Charli had been quiet on the drive from his apartment to the comic book store. He wondered if she was nervous too. And he reminded himself for the fifth time that he was the grown-up and the burden of conversation and entertainment fell on him.

So he had asked her about school, to which she had replied that it was fine and that her English grade had come up. He'd gotten that information from Rachel, but he still praised Charli for working hard and taking it seriously. He'd asked her about her friends, and she'd told him that Toby had been in the hospital with pneumonia, but that he'd been back to their house for the past three days. He'd asked about her art class, and Charli had told him that she didn't like painting or the girl, Paige, that Rachel thought she should be friends with.

He'd been thrilled to be able to keep the conversation going, but he'd been relieved to pull up in front of the comic book store. Not something he would have ever expected to happen.

Alex was completely out of his element. And it wasn't because he was surrounded on all sides by comic books and comic book character posters, T-shirts, and bobbleheads. It was because he was one-on-one with his nine-year-old daughter.

Charli was running her fingertips lovingly over the tops of the comic books lined up in the bins. They were covered in plastic and were arranged facing forward, one behind the next, like old vinyl records in a record store. They were, no doubt, organized somehow, but Alex wasn't sure it was a way that would make sense to him.

He wasn't sure Charli really knew what she was looking at, but her eyes were wide and she seemed to have a permanent smile on her face.

Alex followed, just watching her take it all in.

"Did you read when you were my age?" Charli asked.

Alex was startled that she'd asked him a question, but he quickly recovered. "Yeah, I read a lot. I still do."

"I love to read," Charli said. She would occasionally

stop and pick a comic up to look at the cover with an expression of wonder.

It was adorable and made Alex's heart ache. He wanted to buy her the entire store.

"But Mom doesn't think comic books count as reading," Charli added.

"Hmm," Alex responded noncommittally. He wasn't sure how he felt about the subject of comic books as "real" reading. He'd never thought about it. Just as he hadn't thought about what a proper discipline should be for a kid not doing her chores. And just as he hadn't thought about what were appropriate chores for a nine-year-old. There were innumerable things he hadn't given much thought when it came to parenting.

"What do you like to read besides comic books?" he asked.

He knew that a few months ago he would have agreed that comic books didn't seem worthwhile, but he couldn't help but think that Maya would probably teach him otherwise. Maybe he should ask her about it and then he could share the information with Rachel. That would get him points with Charli.

"I like adventure stories," Charli told him. "*Hunger Games* and *Alice in Wonderland* and *The Lion, the Witch and the Wardrobe*, and *A Wrinkle in Time*."

Alex didn't know much about *The Hunger Games*, but the rest...

"I loved *A Wrinkle in Time*."

Charli looked up, making eye contact for the first time that morning. "Really?"

"I read it several times when I was growing up," he told her.

"Me too. Meg's awesome."

"I have a bunch of books that I've kept since I was a kid. You'll have to come look through them," Alex said.

Charli gave him a smile that sucked all the air from his lungs. "Okay."

Alex felt as if a string had wrapped around his heart and was pulling it toward the little girl in front of him. Much as he felt when they did bo. But better. This was organic. Real. This was something they both naturally loved. He didn't have to study and memorize these books.

He swallowed. He wanted more. He wanted Charli to know they had things in common that they could talk about and share that went beyond *Galactic Renegades* and superheroes. "I think I read adventure books because there were so many things I couldn't do in real life," he said.

Charli didn't respond. She'd found the *Galactic Renegades* section of the comic books and was holding one up in front of her as if gazing at a priceless painting in the Louvre.

"What do you think, Charli?" Alex asked. "Why do you like Meg and the other stories so much?"

She looked up, and Alex noted that he'd managed to pull her attention from the bright image of Piper, Beck Steele, and his ship, the *Horizon*, on the front of the comic book.

"Because they're fun," she said with a smile.

Alex nodded. "They are. It's fun to imagine doing that stuff, isn't it?"

"Definitely," she said enthusiastically, looking back to the comic.

Suddenly Alex wanted to press the subject. "I

couldn't do a lot of the adventurous things when I was growing up."

"Why not?" Charli asked, flipping through the comic.

"I had to be careful with jumping and climbing and play sword fighting and stuff. Like you."

"But you can play pretend in your head," she said. "Mom always says that. I used to lay on my bed and close my eyes and imagine I was running through Wonderland."

He smiled. He was ready and willing to talk about their condition, and she didn't even seem interested in how he was like her.

"That's true," he said with a nod. "But I always wanted to do more. Climb trees and jump off of rocks and pretend my bike was a spaceship. Things like that. Things my friends could do."

Charli was going through the comic books, pausing after every two or three to study a cover.

"Yeah, but at least you can walk and swim and run, right?"

Alex watched her face. "Yes. Why do you say that?"

"Toby can't even walk. So he would trade places with me if he could, even though I can't do everything."

"Did your mom tell you that?" he asked. Their being thankful for the things they could do was a very good thing, and he appreciated Rachel giving Charli that perspective.

"No, Toby told me," Charli said matter-of-factly. "He can't do most of the things I can, so he doesn't care about the things I can't do."

Toby had told her. Alex thought about that.

"But he pretends better than me," Charli went on.

"Does he?" Alex asked.

"He has to," she said with a little shrug. "He has to pretend almost everything since he doesn't really move. And he makes up great names for things," she added. "Because he doesn't talk very well. So he has to use words he can say. But they sound really cool for spaceships and aliens and things."

Alex stared at his daughter. He'd loved her from the moment he'd seen her. Feelings like pride, protectiveness, and amazement had been pretty constant. But he had never been prouder or more amazed than he was right now.

"His wheelchair makes a really great spaceship too," Charli said. "One time we made it a pirate ship and one time it was a race car. But it's best as a spaceship for sure. It's cool we can drive it. Lots of people don't get to do that when they pretend."

She was so accepting of her friend's limitations. Toby's disabilities were significant, but they didn't make him strange or hard to relate to in Charli's eyes. They made him even cooler.

"Is that why you like *Galactic Renegades* so much?" Alex asked, understanding dawning. "Because Toby can pretend space stuff the easiest?"

Charli shrugged. "Yeah. And it's super cool."

Alex touched her head, just needing a connection with her in the moment. "You're a good friend," he told her when she looked up at him.

"I'm a great pretender. Toby needs someone like that."

"It's nice that you spend time with Toby."

"Well, he likes me, so he talks to me."

"He doesn't talk to a lot of people?" Alex asked. He

knew Toby had profound issues and that it was more that Toby couldn't talk. Or so they all assumed.

"He doesn't try very hard with most people," Charli said. "He gets frustrated and mad."

Alex also knew the boy threw tantrums somewhat regularly.

"But I told him that if he wanted to pretend with me, he couldn't be like that. It's not his fault he doesn't talk very good, but it's not my fault he's hard to understand either."

Alex had to nod, still startled by his daughter's maturity. "I guess you're right."

"I told him we've all got stuff that isn't perfect, and that doesn't mean he can be a brat."

Alex's eyebrows went up as she moved to another bin and started sorting through comic books. "You did?"

"Yeah."

"That didn't make him mad or hurt his feelings?" Alex asked.

"He gets mad at me sometimes, but it was more before I told him about my bleeding. He didn't know that I have something special too. Now he knows, and it makes him not get as frustrated."

Alex took a deep breath. "So you telling him about your condition helped him?"

"Yeah, I don't like bleeding extra, and Toby hates his wheelchair sometimes. We can talk about that."

Alex swallowed hard. He'd expected her to hate it, but hearing it made his chest feel tight. "I bleed extra too," he made himself say. "Did you know that?"

Charli looked up from the comics. "Really?"

He nodded, feeling as if he were standing on the edge

of a cliff. Once he jumped, he couldn't take it back. "Hemophilia," he managed. "Just like you."

Charli looked surprised for only two seconds.

"And I don't like it a lot of the time either," he told her.

She nodded. Then said, "But I don't think that's why
we like adventure stories."

Alex blinked. They were back to the first part of the
conversation. Okay. She'd taken the news of his hemophilia in stride. "People were always telling me the things
I couldn't do," he said. "I think that added to why I liked
those stories."

"Well, yeah," Charli said. "But lots of people who
don't have hemophilia or a wheelchair like those stories."

She had a point.

"You're pretty smart."

She shrugged. "I probably get that from you."

That slammed into Alex harder than anything.
"Really?"

"Well, you're a doctor. You're obviously really smart."

He was stupidly pleased that she thought so. "Your
mom's really smart too."

"Yeah, but she said that you have to work really hard
to be a doctor and she could never have paid attention to
everything you have to know."

Alex had no idea why it hadn't occurred to him that
Rachel and Charli might talk about him when he wasn't
around. He appreciated Rachel building him up in
Charli's eyes. "Well, I think you can do anything if it's
important to you," he said.

Charli nodded, but her attention was back on the books
in front of her.

Alex just watched her for a moment. He didn't miss

the fact that, while they were in a comic book store, they'd just moved well beyond comics and superheroes. He couldn't wait to tell Maya.

Again his thoughts went automatically to the other female he'd recently gone beyond superheroes with.

"Is this the first one?" Charli asked, holding up a *Galactic Renegades* comic book.

Alex took it from her and scanned the cover. The full title was *Galactic Renegades: Millennium*. The comic was marked "Series Two, Volume One" in the corner.

"I don't think so." He moved in behind her and flipped through the bin. There was a single copy each of volumes two to fourteen in series two. There were also volumes one, two, five, eight, and nine in series three. Finally he found a series one, volume one, but this title was *Galactic Renegades: Enforcers*.

"I don't know," he finally confessed.

He looked around and spotted someone who worked in the store. The kid looked to be about nineteen and was flipping through a comic book behind the front counter. Alex could ask him, of course. He could also probably Google the answer on his phone. But he didn't want to.

He pulled his phone out. "But I can get the answer, easily."

\* \* \*

Maya nearly knocked Kiera over as she lunged for her phone. Kiera and Sophie were at the studio with her to go over the details for Sophie's upcoming play—and trying to keep Maya's mind off Alex's day out with Charli. Her heart thumped when she saw it was him. It was only eleven. Surely their date wasn't over already. *Please let it be going well.*

"Hello?"

"There are different series in the *GR* comic book universe?"

He'd been so excited and nervous about the outing. She'd been thinking about them all morning. "How did it go?"

"We're still here."

"Oh." That meant Charli was with him as he was talking to her. "So here's the code," Maya said. "Sunny and warm means it's going well, cold and rainy means not so much."

"Sunny and warm."

She could hear the smile in his voice, and she felt herself grin. "Thank goodness." Maya gave Kiera and Sophie a thumbs-up when they looked at her questioningly. Everyone knew today was big for Alex and Charli.

"But we do need your help," he said.

Maya straightened. Was he going to ask her to come meet them? Did he have a flat tire? Or did they need help navigating the store? "Of course." She turned toward the door. She could be there in thirty minutes.

"Charli wants to start with the first of the *Galactic Renegades* comics, and I want to check out the first Spider-Man, but I can't figure out where they all start."

"I can come down and look at them with you and explain how they work together," she offered, breathlessly.

"You don't have to do that. Just give me a title."

Oh. Maya felt her shoulders slump and worked on pushing her disappointment down. This was his day with

Charli. His first outing with her one-on-one. Maya shouldn't have even considered joining them.

Maya boosted herself up onto the front desk and crisscrossed her legs. "It's confusing," she agreed. "And there's not a great answer. The series kind of run simultaneously, and some of them branch off into story arcs that are totally separate from the movies."

"Why do they do that?"

She smiled in spite of the fact that she hadn't gotten the disappointment squashed down as far as she would have liked. "Well, there are various writers, and they're developing a world even bigger than the movies. It's fun. Until they start contradicting each other, of course."

He groaned, then chuckled. "So the series are different story lines?"

"Right."

"Charli, Maya says that there's not really a first one. We need to just figure out which series you want to read first."

Maya felt her throat tighten. Charli was right there. Talking to him while he talked to her.

"Charli wants to know which series you think would be best to start with," Alex said in her ear.

Maya had to clear her throat before replying. "Does she want to pick up right from where the movies left off or does she want to read some stuff from before the movies started?"

"There were comics before there were movies?" he asked.

"No. But there is a series that's kind of a prequel to the movies."

He explained that to Charli while Maya listened.

"Which one does she like best?" Maya heard Charli ask.

Maya felt a weird flutter in her chest. That was Alex's daughter. The whole reason Maya had met him in the first place. The reason behind...so much.

"Which one do you like best?" Alex asked her.

"Um..." Maya had to swallow again before she could go on. "Well, I liked the prequel series. It's called *Beginnings*. But I liked the series that came before that one even more. It's called *Foundations*, and there are, I think, ten volumes or so. That's even more fun because then it leads to *Beginnings*."

"Look for *Foundations*," Alex said to Charli. "And then volume one."

Maya felt warm that he was taking her recommendation.

He lowered his voice. "It's appropriate for her? Not too violent or anything?"

"Should be okay. There's a civil war in it, and some planets being annihilated. But it's all important to the story."

"Okay."

But it went really far back in the timeline for *GR*. Maya thought quickly. "Maybe *Beginnings* would be more interesting, though. She's only nine. I don't know how much history she really wants or needs."

"*Foundations* goes way back, no Piper or Arietis IV," Alex told Charli. "You want to start there?"

"Actually, Arietis IV is in *Foundations*," Maya corrected. "It's part of the galaxy. The stories are about three generations before Piper. Everyone generally believes that the two main characters in that series are

Piper's great-grandparents, but that's never specified. It doesn't talk about anything in the movies. It's kind of like studying the Revolutionary War in American history. It sets up a lot of—"

"Maya," Alex interrupted, "this would be a time I'd kiss you if you were here in person."

Rambling. Right. But her heart thumped anyway with even the suggestion of kissing. "I just don't know if she wants to go that far back," Maya finished weakly.

He chuckled, the deep sound rolling through her. "Charli, the people in *Foundations* might be Piper's great-grandparents. Do you want to go that far back?"

"Does Maya think it's important to know?" Charli asked.

"Do you think it's important to know?" Alex repeated dutifully.

Maya made herself really think about the question. Not in relation to Alex's nine-year-old daughter, who Maya wanted to impress—and she never worried about impressing the kids she interacted with—but as one *Galactic Renegades* fan to another.

"Yes. I think it adds a lot to the world," she finally said. "If someone wants to really appreciate all of the details and enjoy the little threads they've dropped in the movies that don't feel like they go anywhere, then the comics, going way back to *Foundations*, are really fun."

"Okay!"

That was Charli's voice, and it was right in Maya's ear.

Before she could respond, Alex was back on the line. "Sounds like we're doing *Foundations*."

"You put her on the phone?" Maya asked.

"Easier for her to hear it straight from you," he said.

She'd been talking to Charli without knowing it. Maya swallowed and hoped she hadn't sounded stupid. Maya rubbed her forehead. She was worried about a nine-year-old thinking she'd sounded stupid. She definitely had it bad.

"This cover is amazing!" she heard Charli gush in the background.

"She found it." Alex's voice was filled with amusement.

"You could, of course, read through it before she does," she suggested as her mind flashed through the first issue of *Foundations*.

"I totally trust you here, Maya," he said.

Her heart thumped and then missed a beat. That was so nice. And made her feel a little panicky at the same time. She did not want to screw up the first time Alex asked her for advice on something having to do with Charli. "Well, I was just thinking, it's been a while since I read that one, and I don't—"

"She's very excited. It will be fine. I'll be sure to ask you any questions she has."

Maya smiled too, even as her stomach felt crampy.

"Can I get the first three, Dad?" Charli asked. "I know I'll read this so fast."

"Sure. I don't mind."

The gruffness in his voice made Maya's eyes sting. She knew how much this day meant to him and she wondered if Charli calling him Dad hit him the way it did her. It was strange, but that made it all so real.

Sophie gave her a concerned look from where she and Kiera were pretending to go through some of the sword-fighting choreography. They were actually eavesdropping.

Maya just shook her head. She was sure she looked as if she were about to burst into tears. Or throw up. But it was all actually really good.

"Has Maya seen all the movies?" Charli asked.

Okay, so Alex hadn't talked about her and her expertise in *GR* before this.

"Maya is my go-to girl for *GR*," Alex said.

The damn tears stung again. She was his girl...for something, anyway.

"Do any of the comic series talk about what happened after Benni left the City of Daxxu? Does she think he took the orb with him? Is he going to come back in future movies?"

There was a beat of silence from Alex, then he said to Maya, "Uh, Charli has some more questions."

Maya laughed. "I heard."

"Thank goodness," Alex muttered.

She laughed again. "Tell her that the *Galaxy Beyond* series has Benni in it, but it doesn't actually refer to anything that happened in the movies. Most people accept that the *Beyond* series is kind of an alternate universe thing. And yes, I do think he took the orb, and I really hope he comes back."

Again there was a moment of silence, then Alex said, "Benni is in *Galaxy Beyond*, and yes to the orb thing."

Maya rolled her eyes. "You're not a very good go-between."

"I don't speak the language," he said.

Maya held her breath, waiting for him to offer to let her talk directly to Charli again and biting back asking to.

"I think so too, about the orb," Charli said.

"Okay, so we got that cleared up," Alex said drily. Then he lowered his voice. "Thank you."

"For what?"

"Being there for me to call."

Maya bit her lip, wondering how much she should say. Finally she settled on, "Anytime. I mean it. It's my pleasure."

His voice dropped even further. "I owe you."

He didn't. He really didn't. She wanted to do this. She wanted to do more. But she couldn't push. She was trying so hard not to charge in here as she did with everything else.

"How are you going to pay me back?" she asked, purposefully putting a teasing note into her voice.

"What do you want?"

That deep, delicious tone made goose bumps chase each other over her skin.

Maya wanted dinner with him and Charli. But she couldn't freaking say that. She'd never realized how much she just went for it. She wasn't very good at holding back—words, emotions, actions.

"How about grabbing a costume, and we can do some role playing?" she said, deliberately making her tone light.

"I would give so much to see you in a Supergirl costume," he told her in a hushed voice.

Clearly Charli wasn't too far away.

"Can do." And she could. She had one in the attic.

"And who am I in this scenario?" he asked. "I'm not seeing any Spider-Man costumes here."

"Would you actually wear a costume for me?" she asked.

"As long as I'm guaranteed to be getting out of the costume with you too," he said.

It was just silly-sexy teasing, but Maya knew that Dr. Alex Nolan hadn't worn a costume since Halloween when he was a kid. If then. The idea that he would for her, even if it was to get lucky, made her smile.

"You'll have to order something online," she said.

"Even better. No one has to see me buy it then. Text me some websites."

She hit send. "Already did."

"Does Spidey come with webs I can use to tie Supergirl up?"

She grinned. "Just hit the purchase button on the page I sent you."

There was a pause on his end, and she figured he was looking at his text and clicking through to the website.

"Ah, Captain America," he said when he came back on the line. "Of course."

"You're not going to need webs to keep me where you want me," she told him.

"Captain America it is."

Maya hesitated over her next words, but she'd been swallowing a lot of things over the past few weeks with Alex. She needed to say this. She was ready to move past the superhero stuff. It was sexy and fun to tease about the role playing, but she wanted things to be more than sexy and fun. "Actually...," she said.

"Yeah?"

"You know what I would most like you to dress up as?"

"What?" His voice dropped again, telling her that he was still teasing.

She took a breath. "Just you."

There was a long pause, and Maya made herself wait him out.

Finally he said, "Just me?"

She nodded, then realized he couldn't see her. "Yes, Alex," she said. "You. That's what I want." *And everything that comes with you.* But she knew that would be too much.

Alex cleared his throat. "I'm kind of hating that we're on the phone right now."

"Really?"

"That's a throw-you-over-my-shoulder thing to say, Maya."

She pressed her hand to her hammering heart. So she hadn't stepped over any line getting serious there. Good to know. "Well, you know where to find me."

"I, and my shoulder, will see you later."

Maya knew she was grinning like an idiot as she disconnected.

"Wow," Kiera said.

Maya looked up to find Kiera and Sophie staring at her. "What?"

"That was really . . ."

"You're in love with him," Sophie said when Kiera trailed off. "You got all teary about him and Charli, and you don't want him to dress up as Captain America."

"That's the definition of being in love?" Maya asked sarcastically, trying to ignore how she could feel her heart beating throughout her whole body.

"For you?" Kiera asked. She and Sophie exchanged a look. "Yeah," they said together.

Well...crap. They were right. She was falling in love with Alex Nolan. "Oops."

Kiera and Sophie smiled at her.

"I didn't mean to," she said.

"That's how it often happens," Kiera said with a laugh.

Maya shook her head, feeling emotions tumbling over one another in her chest. Happiness, worry, excitement, possessiveness...fear. "I am in love with him," she admitted. It wasn't her style to deny what she wanted.

Sophie and Kiera both beamed at her. "I'm so happy for you, sweetie," Sophie said.

Maya nodded. Happy. Yeah. She felt that too. Among other things. "You guys have to help me," she said, letting her worry show.

Kiera frowned and reached for her hand. "What's going on?"

"I want to make him a foam board weapon and put on my Supergirl costume and get the same pizza we had the first night and show up on his doorstep to declare my feelings."

Kiera let that sink in. Then she laughed and sat back. "Of course you do."

"I do," Maya said, leaning in. "I want to go way overboard. I want to go straight to him right this minute and gush all over him. I want to make a huge public scene. I'm talking a billboard along the interstate or a skywriter or...worse."

"What would be worse?" Kiera asked, clearly delighted by all of this.

"A Captain America–themed surprise party," Maya told her.

Kiera laughed. "Yep, that would be worse."

"Or showing up at his office in the Supergirl costume with pizza."

Kiera nodded. "Yep, that too."

"Kiera, this is serious. I don't know how to go easy and take things slow. I'm in love for the first time in my life, and I want to make a big deal out of it."

Kiera's expression softened. "Sweetie, Alex is in love with you too. I'm thinking you making a big deal out of it wouldn't surprise him."

Maya looked from one of her friends to the other. "You think he's in love with me too?"

Sophie nodded. "I do."

Maya started shaking her head. "No. I don't think so. I haven't even met Charli yet."

Sophie shrugged. "Well, if it helps, I don't think he meant to fall in love either."

Maya groaned. "Should I stop seeing him?"

"No!" Sophie's protest was quick and loud.

Maya looked at her in surprise. "No?"

"Maya Goodwin, you are a go-for-it girl. You live big and you grab opportunities and you work for the things you want. You want Alex. You need to go for it."

Maya didn't know what to say. Sophie looked serious. And the things she'd said were true. Maya did go for it. She prided herself on that.

The first time Alex was in class at the studio, she'd felt a humming in her body that reminded her of precompetition butterflies. That excitement helped her know that what she was about to do really mattered to her. She felt them now too.

*Dammit.* She didn't want to push and end up pushing him away. She didn't want to rush something that just needed a little more time. But holding back all the things she wanted to say to him was getting tough.

"Excuse me?"

They all jumped slightly at the new voice. Maya swung around to see that someone had come into the studio. But not just someone—Kelsey, the girl from the mall the day Maya had met Alex. She had two girls with her.

"Kelsey, hi," Maya said, sliding to the floor. "I'm so glad to see you."

Kelsey gave her a little smile. "I'm glad. I'm sorry I haven't come before this."

Maya had helped Kelsey buy her dress, and the girl had texted her some photos of her in it before the big school dance. But she hadn't taken Maya up on the offer of self-defense classes. Yet.

"It's fine. I'm glad you're here now."

Kelsey nodded. "I decided I wanted to get some lessons. And these are my friends, Lucy and Anna. Can they come too?"

Maya smiled at the other girls. "Of course. Definitely." She studied Kelsey's face closer. "Is everything okay?"

The girl sighed and glanced at her friends. "Yeah. Mostly. I just . . . wish we'd come before this."

Maya moved closer. "What happened?"

"Nothing," Kelsey said quickly. She looked at her friends again. "But something . . . almost did."

Maya felt anger rush through her. Someone had done something to one of these girls. But she kept her expression and tone of voice relaxed. "Tell me about it."

"Anna went to the dance with a new kid. He was really nice, everything was good. But then the next time he took her out, they went to a party and he got drunk and . . . she locked herself in the bathroom and called us to come and get her. We did. But it was scary."

Maya worked on keeping herself calm. Or appearing calm, at least. "I'm glad you were there for her to call. And anytime you need help, you can call me."

Kelsey nodded. "Thanks. I'll remember that. But I was thinking that it would also be nice to know some ways of keeping ourselves safe. We'd feel more confident."

"Absolutely," Maya said with feeling. "Self-defense is just that—it's being able to take care of yourself. It's not about starting anything or using force if you don't need it, but no one should be scared like that."

"So we can do some classes?"

"Yes. Do you want to start now?" Maya asked.

Kelsey smiled. "I can't. I have to go to work. But we can start whenever you're available next week."

"I'm available anytime." Alex would totally understand if she needed to take some of his class time for the girls. "I could even do tomorrow night." Tomorrow was Sunday, but Maya practically lived at the studio anyway.

"Okay, we could come tomorrow night," Kelsey agreed as her friends nodded.

"I'll be here at seven," Maya told them.

"See you then." Kelsey started to turn toward the door, but she swung back around. "Thanks, Maya. I feel so lucky that you were at the mall and willing to help me out that day."

Maya felt her throat tighten. "Me too," she said sincerely. "And I expect you to pay it forward. You three need to step in when someone needs you."

They all nodded solemnly.

"Okay, see you tomorrow," she said with a smile.

The girls smiled back, and they seemed lighter than when they'd come in.

"I love you," Sophie said to Maya as she watched the girls leave. "You're the epitome of girl power, you know that."

"That's one of the nicest things you've ever said to me," Maya told her. She gave Sophie a half hug around her shoulders.

"I agree," Kiera said. "You walk the walk."

"Thanks." She appreciated the compliments. Her mind was whirring, though. She had stepped in for Kelsey. That ripple effect was now positively affecting Kelsey's friends. Maya was proud of that. She was pushy and she got involved and she stuck her nose into things and she made things happen. Was it sometimes fast and even a little overwhelming or intimidating? Maybe. But she wouldn't change it. Nine times out of ten it was the right thing to do.

With Alex it was the right thing to do. She'd been hanging back, biting her tongue, taking it easy. But she wanted this. She wanted him.

Maya took a deep breath. "Okay, so I'm going to go for it with Alex. The only way I know how...all in."

"Great." Kiera gave her a huge smile. "I'm so happy for you."

"And I'm going to buy him a ferret."

Kiera's smile turned into a puzzled frown. Sophie blinked at her.

"Did you say a ferret?" Kiera asked.

"Yep."

"If *ferret* is a euphemism, you really need to work on those," Sophie told her.

Maya shook her head as her plan began to form. "Not a euphemism. A real ferret. Charli wants a cat, but Rachel is allergic."

"Why do you have to be the one to get the ferret?" Sophie asked.

"I don't have to be. That's the point. I want to be. I want to be involved. I want to show him that I get his situation and I'm supportive."

Sophie nodded. "Okay, I get it."

"So no Supergirl costume and pizza?" Kiera asked.

Maya gave her a grin. "I didn't say that."

# CHAPTER THIRTEEN

$\mathcal{I}$ love it so much!"

Charli was in her new Piper costume, which Alex had finally gotten around to asking Sophie about. She'd put the outfit together in two days and had refused to take money for anything other than the material she'd purchased. Alex was going to find a way to pay her back. The smile on Charli's face at the moment was worth millions.

"You better take it off while you eat your cupcakes," Rachel told her. "You don't want to get frosting all over it."

"I'm never taking it off. Ever," Charli informed her.

Alex couldn't help but smile smugly. Perfect gift for her first birthday with him—check.

Rachel had agreed to let him have the birthday celebration at his place. Austin had come over for dinner, as had Alex's parents. He usually called them once a week and saw them at least once a month, but since Charli had come into his life—and their lives—they'd been in closer contact, and they'd been to visit more often. Alex's mother loved having a little girl to spoil. But now everyone was gone, leaving Alex, Rachel, and Charli together. The evening wasn't over, though. Charli was spending the night with him for the first time ever.

That plan had come together quickly the night before and had been Charli's idea. She'd claimed that Alex's large living room and big sectional sofa would make for an "epic" blanket fort. One of her wishes for her birthday was to build the fort and sleep in it overnight. Alex had been so surprised and happy to know that she wanted to stay that he'd readily agreed. Rachel had been agreeable but had warned him that it might not be as easy as it seemed. Charli had slept overnight with Rachel's parents only twice. The one time she'd tried a sleepover with a friend, she'd called at midnight to come home. The last thing he wanted was for Charli to have a bad experience staying over, but he'd also really wanted it to happen, so he'd suggested that Rachel stay too. He had a guest room, after all.

Now the three of them were in the living room, the smell of popcorn lingering in the air, and Charli was running around gathering every blanket and sheet that Alex owned.

It should have been completely satisfying. It seemed like the perfect family evening. Charli was officially ten years old, and she was with both of her parents. As it should be. But he couldn't help but feel restless. Something was missing. Someone was missing. Except she wasn't. Maya wasn't a part of this. At least not in person. Not directly. This part of his life, Charli and his family, didn't include her. But it felt as if it did. Or should. Maya was a huge part of how close he'd gotten to Charli and the things that were making Charli so happy tonight.

His chest ached, and he shifted on the sofa, trying to find that comfortable spot where he could relax and just let the contentment settle in.

But as Charli ran past, her red scarf flapping behind her, his eyes went to the closet door where he had the ember lances from Maya stored away. They were supposed to be part of Charli's gift, but Charli had gotten another bloody nose just yesterday from the bo staff. She'd been using it unsupervised, swinging it around in a made-up technique, and had accidently hit herself in the face. It hadn't been an overly serious situation, but Rachel had asked that he hold off on the ember lances until Charli consistently showed she would be careful with all these new things they were letting her try. Alex rubbed a hand over his chest, surprised by how disappointed he was not to be giving them to her tonight. It was probably a good thing Maya didn't know Charli's birthday was today. She'd have wanted to know all about Charli's reaction to the gift.

Somehow he managed to make small talk with Rachel as they watched Charli build her fort. He helped her drape the biggest blankets and brought extra chairs in from his dining room to support one side. He even crawled inside with her, wanting to throw himself into the activity and focus on this female and her happiness so that he could forget the one he was missing.

But when he heard a knock on his door twenty minutes later and peered through the peephole to see Maya standing on the other side, any surprise he felt was quickly replaced by pure happiness.

He pulled the door open, his breath jammed in his throat.

"Hi," she said brightly.

He assumed she was smiling just as brightly, but his eyes hadn't quite made it to her face.

She was dressed in a Supergirl costume. Tight blue top, short red skirt with a gold belt, and red leather boots that went just past her knee. And a matching red cape.

She was also holding a pizza box in one hand and a pet carrier in the other.

"Alex?"

He forced his gaze to her face. "Hi."

She smiled. "Surprise."

"Uh...yeah."

"I brought you a ferret."

Lust and affection flooded through him just looking at her. His brain was still processing the long, smooth expanse of bare thigh between the tops of the boots and the bottom of the skirt. Those thighs were two of his favorite things in the world. But her words slowly penetrated. And he frowned.

"A...ferret?" he repeated dumbly.

She nodded. "It's not for you. It belongs to a friend of mine. But this way you can see what you think without making a commitment. It's an option, anyway—since Charli wants a pet and Rachel is allergic to cats."

She'd brought him a ferret. Because of Charli and Rachel. Who were right down the hall.

*Fuuuck.*

His synapses started firing again immediately. He stepped forward, forcing her farther back into the hallway. He closed the door behind him, and her eyes widened.

"And the costume?" he asked.

"All for you. You said you wanted to see me in it. And this is the same pizza we had the first night we ate together." But she didn't give him the flirtatious smile that would have usually followed. She was frowning. "What's going on, Alex?"

"Charli and Rachel are here."

And he'd just put Maya in the hallway with a door between them. His first instinct had been to shut her out. Literally. Dammit. This was bad.

Maya's gaze traveled over him, clearly noting the worn T-shirt and baggy sweatpants. Alex felt his shoulders tense. He was obviously in for the evening, relaxing. It was late. And he hadn't asked her in.

"Charli's here?" Maya repeated. "This late?"

"Yes."

"You didn't tell me why you couldn't come over tonight," Maya said. "I guess I figured it was work and that you'd surely be home by now."

He nodded. All of that made sense. Considering he hadn't told her anything. "It's her birthday," he said, trying to explain.

"Charli's?"

"Yeah."

"Oh." Hurt filled her eyes.

Alex clenched his fists, needing, wanting to reach out for her but not at all sure what to do or say.

"I didn't realize it was today."

"Yeah." He didn't know what else to add to that.

"How's it been?"

"Good. Really good." He almost winced after he said it. He was so mixed up. He hated telling her that he'd had a good time doing something that hadn't included her. But he had. The day with Charli had been great. And that was a good thing. It was what he'd been working for.

Still, he'd wanted Maya there. It would have been even better if he could have shared it with her. But he couldn't say that either because he wasn't sure how to explain that he couldn't include her.

"I'm glad. This first one together is... big."

She still looked and sounded hurt, and Alex felt his gut burning with the need to comfort her, reassure her, promise her... whatever she wanted. And he couldn't do any of it. Because he couldn't let her through his front door.

But maybe she understood. She got that this birthday was a big deal for him and Charli.

And then he feared she did understand. Completely. That she wasn't invited inside. Into this big moment with his daughter.

Alex cleared his throat. "Yeah." He wasn't even sure what he was saying yeah to at this point.

"Okay, so then... I should go." Maya looked around, as if unsure how to do that.

Alex wanted to say she wasn't interrupting. That she should stay. That she looked amazing and that her bringing him a ferret had made him fall even more in love with her. But how could he tell her he loved her while at the same time keeping her firmly out of a huge part of his life?

"Maya—"

The door swung open, and Maya's gaze focused

behind him. Charli stood on the threshold, staring at them both.

"Dad?" she asked. But her eyes were taking in every detail of the woman dressed as Supergirl and holding a ferret. "Mom wants to know if everything is okay?"

Alex coughed and nodded. "Yeah." *No, nothing is okay right now.* "Tell her I'll be right back in."

"She wanted to know if she should take the pillows off your bed for the tent. She said she doesn't need all of those in there."

Fuck. This was going from disastrous to the worst night of his life really quickly. It was his first birthday with Charli. It was supposed to be one of the best nights. Son of a bitch.

"That's fine," he said. "Yes. Any of them are fine."

Okay, he had to let Maya know the truth. Rachel was spending the night at his place. If she didn't trust that it was nothing, he didn't know what he could do about it. Once Charli was back inside, he'd explain and apologize and whatever else he could think of and then . . . pray. Pray that Maya knew how he felt about her and would trust him.

"I'm Charli. Who are you?" Charli finally said, addressing Maya directly. And definitely not going back inside.

"I'm Maya." To her credit Maya gave Charli what seemed like a very genuine smile.

If he hadn't known her, he might not have been able to hear that she was barely holding back her emotions. But he did know her. And Maya Goodwin was choked up.

Alex finally did the one thing he really didn't want to do—he looked at Maya again.

There was love and heartbreak in her eyes. And she wasn't looking at him. She was staring at his daughter.

And he fell the rest of the way in love with her in that moment.

"Are you the Maya we called from the comic book store?" Charli asked.

Maya smiled. "Yep."

"Your friend made me my Piper costume!" Charli spun around to show it off.

Maya nodded. "Right. And I'm the one that made your ember lances. With my friends Sophie and Kiera."

Charli froze, her eyes growing huge in her face. And Alex groaned.

"What ember lances?" Charli asked.

Maya looked at Alex for the first time since Charli had opened the door.

"We'll talk about it inside," Alex said. "Go on in. I'll be right there."

"Is that a cat?" Charli asked, pointing at the animal carrier Maya still held. Apparently, to this point, she'd been as dazzled by the costume as her dad.

"A ferret, actually," Maya said.

"Why did you bring my dad a ferret?"

*Please don't tell her it's for her.*

"Oh, I didn't bring your dad anything," Maya said. "It's my friend's ferret. Thought your dad had probably never seen one before, and I thought I'd show it to him."

Alex breathed out in relief.

"And you come over to see him dressed as Supergirl?" Charli asked.

Maya shook her head. "No. I'm pretty sure your dad

won't be seeing me in any costumes again. It's a one-time thing."

The wave of disappointment was entirely inappropriate, but it was undeniable. This was getting all kinds of fucked up.

Alex ran a hand over his face. "Charli, go back inside, please. We're almost—"

"Not almost," Maya said before he could finish. "We are done. Now."

Charli turned to go inside, but then things got even worse. Rachel showed up in the doorway. In her pajamas.

"What's go—oh." Her eyes widened at the Supergirl impersonator with the ferret as well. "I'm sorry to interrupt."

Alex groaned silently. Neither of the women should feel as if she were interrupting, and yet both of them were.

"No, I'm very sorry to show up like this on family night. I'm going to go," Maya said. "Happy birthday, Charli."

"Thanks." But even the ten-year-old's response sounded awkward.

Rachel took Charli's hand and led her back inside. Alex flinched as the door shut behind them.

"Maya—"

"You didn't tell me today was her birthday," she said over the top of whatever he'd planned to say.

"I know."

"You could have avoided all of this if you'd told me."

"I guess."

Maya's eyes narrowed. "I never would have showed up here if I'd known what tonight was and what you were doing."

He nodded. "I know."

"Do you? Or were you worried about this exact thing? That I would just butt my way into things? It's not like this is the first time I've showed up somewhere uninvited."

Alex stepped toward her. "No, that is not what I thought."

"And you didn't give her the ember lances? I never would have said that if I'd known you didn't want her to have them." It was obvious that the thought he wouldn't want to give them to Charli hurt her even more than not telling her it was Charli's birthday.

"She got a bloody nose playing kickball in school the other day and then messing around with the bo staff last night. Rachel wanted to wait on the lances."

"Does Rachel know they're from me?"

He nodded, feeling miserable.

"The lances are safer than the bo. I told you that."

Her eyes were shimmering, and Alex felt as if his heart were cracking in two. "I know. The nose just happened. Rachel will come around."

Maya was holding herself stiffly, and Alex was struck by how different that was from usual. She was so relaxed and happy all the time. Even when she was working out, her body was coiled and tight at times, but never stiff and hard. Not like this.

"You didn't tell me about Charli's nose either," Maya said. "There's a lot you don't tell me, isn't there? I thought we were talking and sharing, but... you don't really let me close."

He drew a big breath. "I guess... I didn't think you needed to know." That sounded a lot worse out loud.

Maya drew in a breath. "Got it."

He saw the flash of pain cross her face. Then he saw something far worse—she closed off. The most outgoing, live-life-to-the-fullest, wear-her-heart-on-her-sleeve person he'd ever met closed herself off from him.

And he deserved it.

"I'm going to go." She turned on the heel of her red boot and started for the elevator.

"Maya—" He followed, reaching out and grasping her elbow. He had no idea what to say, but he couldn't just let her go.

But Maya jerked her arm from his grasp. When she whirled to face him, the anger in her eyes reminded him that she could put him on his ass really easily.

"Don't," she told him firmly.

"I just don't want you to be hurt."

She shook her head. "That's the thing you haven't realized yet, Alex. Getting hurt is part of living. What you should be worried about is that you're not hurt. And that's because you don't take risks. You've been doing all of this, thinking you're protecting me and Rachel and Charli, but really you've just been keeping yourself from having to make some hard decisions."

"I can't take a risk with Charli," he said firmly.

"Charli's not going to get hurt. Having one more person in her life who loves her and wants her to be happy? Even if I never saw you again, I would want that for her, and I would do what I could. Even from the sidelines. I think I've proven that."

She turned away, strode to the elevator, and pushed the button as Alex tried to get air past the tightness in his throat. She was right. This was his moment to make a decision that would change him forever. The elevator arrived quickly, and the doors swooshed open.

"Maya—"

She faced him from inside. "This is your burning car, Alex. You know that it's going to change you. It might hurt some too. But sometimes to get to what you need, you have to break a window and use a crowbar and then you have to be willing to reach in."

Numb, Alex watched the doors slide shut between them.

* * *

In the two days after ripping her heart out and leaving it on Alex's doorstep, Maya finally understood the appeal of not sharing every damned detail of her life with everyone. She had always been an open book. But the book had always been happy and entertaining and interesting. Even her shoulder injury hadn't been all bad. Because she'd known it was going to improve. It wasn't always going to suck as badly as it did at first. And through it all, her friends had cheered her on, listened to her bitch—and then told her to quit whining and to get back to work.

Losing Alex, on the other hand, was always going to suck. Not having him in her life was always going to hurt.

Where Alex wasn't willing to reach into that metaphorical burning car, she had. Again. She'd pushed right in. She'd gone full steam ahead in falling for Alex. She hadn't hesitated to give him her heart. And now she was left with more scars that were always going to ache.

So this was all her own fault. Typical.

"Why can't my friends be the type to drown their

broken hearts in chocolate and liquor?" Sophie huffed from several feet below Maya on the rock wall.

"I like chocolate and liquor," Kiera panted. She wasn't as far behind as Sophie, but she wasn't even with Maya either.

Whether that was because of Maya's superb climbing skills or because they didn't want to be any closer to Maya's mood, she didn't know.

"But you're madly in love with no chance for heartbreak," Sophie told Kiera.

"True," Kiera agreed.

"That's not helping," Maya shot down to them. She should have come alone.

"And the rock wall is?" Sophie asked.

Well, Maya had been looking for something that would challenge her and make her shoulder hurt enough to take her mind off the frustration and pain caused by Alex. So yeah, it was kind of helping. Because every time she reached overhead with her left arm, she was irritated by her limited motion and strength, and every time she tried to pull herself up, it hurt like a bitch.

But she kept going. She didn't have a choice. Ben couldn't spar with her because of his concussion, and no one else would agree to face off with her after her last session with Rob, when he'd called uncle after only twenty minutes. She needed some outlet for all the emotions.

It had been two days since Alex had blocked her way into his apartment and, essentially, his life. He hadn't been willing to take a chance on her. He hadn't been able to trust what they had.

Maya forced her arm overhead, stretching for the outcropping above her. She gritted her teeth and pulled. Her hand slipped as pain shot down the length of her arm and into her neck. She cursed, took a deep breath, and reached again. She tightened her grip on the fake rock and pulled. But she had nothing left in the arm. Tears sprang to her eyes. She was done.

She glared at the rock. No, dammit. She could make this happen. She couldn't make Alex love her. She couldn't make him try harder or push through. But she could push. She could control this.

Maya lifted her left foot to the next tiny ledge and strained upward, sliding her arm up the face of the wall, breathing through the fire that streaked down her arm. She grabbed the rock above her again and held on. She pulled with her arm as she extended her leg and managed to move several inches.

Then it all went to hell.

Her grip loosened, and her fingers refused to obey her command to flex. She felt her weight shift and her shoe slide off the foothold. She realized she was about to fall a split second before she slipped off the wall.

Of course her harness caught her.

But she felt as if what was left of her composure plummeted to the floor and shattered into a million pieces.

"Maya!" Kiera gasped as Maya swung out from the wall.

"For fuck's sake," she heard Ben curse from below. Then she felt herself being lowered. She had her hands over her eyes, covering the tears that suddenly wouldn't stop no matter how many deep breaths she took or pep talk phrases she tried.

She was tough. She was strong. But she was not unbreakable.

She felt Rob's arms around her a moment later and then heard Sophie's soothing voice as hands—she assumed Kiera's but didn't really care—unhooked her harness.

"No more," Rob said. "No more sparring sessions where you try to kill us all, no more three-hour workouts, no more kickboxing until you can't lift your arm, and no more climbing. Or anything else. This sucks. We get it. Physical pain is better than emotional pain. Totally understood. But we need you whole. We need you healthy."

Maya shook her head. "I don't know if I can be whole. My arm will never be good enough again."

"Bullshit," Sophie said firmly. "Your arm is good enough. For things better than being a cop. Your arm makes other people realize that they can be strong anyway. And your broken heart will do the same."

"Everyone has heartbreak," Kiera agreed. "The strongest people aren't the ones who've never gotten hurt or taken a fall. They're the ones who get back up and keep loving because they know love, even for a short time, is better than no love."

Maya felt her heart clench hard in her chest.

"You remember who said that?" Kiera asked.

Maya nodded.

"You did," Kiera said anyway. "And a thousand other things just like it. You know that getting back up again matters more than staying on your feet all the time."

Maya did know that. Coming back from her injury had given her pride and confidence she'd never had before. It had helped her relate to people she had only sympathized with before. It was a part of her, of who she was. It was never going to be 100 percent. It was going to be weaker. It was going to hurt. And she wasn't getting back on the force.

She knew that. She'd probably always known that. But she was finally admitting it. She'd fought the idea because she hadn't wanted to give up the goal of helping people, of protecting people and making their lives better. But now she'd realized that she was doing that. Her arm had changed how she did it, but she was now helping people help themselves feel stronger and more confident and even safer. The kids in her classes, Kelsey and her friends, even Alex and Charli.

So she wouldn't change it.

And she wouldn't change her time with Alex either. Even if it hadn't turned out the way she'd hoped.

She'd be okay. She'd find out what she was made of. She'd make adjustments. And there would be something better. Eventually.

"Okay, you're right. I'm going to be okay."

They all seemed relieved.

"But," she added, "I'd really love to try the chocolate-and-liquor thing."

Two hours later they were on the sofa at their house and well into the brownies and Kahlúa when Zach came in. Maya looked up and frowned as she realized there were one and a half of him.

"You've been at work a long time," Kiera said. "I thought you'd be off an hour ago."

He nodded. "Last-minute call that we needed to take."

Even with sugar and alcohol coursing through her blood, Maya could tell that Zach was far more serious than usual.

"Are you okay?" Kiera asked him, coming off the couch and crossing to him.

He folded her in his arms, but he kept looking at Maya. "Uh, Maya—"

She went cold and sobered up instantly. "What is it?"

"I saw Alex at the hospital."

Okay, that was nothing. Alex worked at the hospital. Obviously. It wasn't that crazy to think someone might see him there.

"I saw him in the ER," Zach added.

The ER. So that was…different. Why would Alex be in the ER?

Then she went completely still. There were some very good reasons why Alex might be in an ER. Her heart lodged in her throat and completely quit beating as she asked, "Is he okay?"

"Yes. He's fine. Physically. The patient was his daughter."

There had been a patient. Alex had been at the hospital in the ER because of a patient…who was his daughter. Maya suddenly felt as if she was going to be sick, and it had nothing to do with the Kahlúa. She felt Sophie grab her hand.

"What happened?" Kiera asked. Thankfully. Because Maya was afraid that if she opened her mouth, she'd either throw up or start sobbing.

"I don't know exactly. I didn't have a chance to get details, but it's…"

"What?" Kiera asked when Zach trailed off.

"A head injury."

Maya felt dizzy, and her stomach definitely roiled. A head injury in a hemophiliac could be catastrophic. Zach crossed the room quickly, and when he grabbed her upper arms, Maya realized she was on her feet and swaying. Zach lowered her to the couch and pushed her head between her knees. Sophie and Kiera were there then, on either side, rubbing her back and telling her to breathe.

She tried. She really did. But her chest was too tight. Charli was hurt. Really hurt. Maya felt a tear run down her cheek. "The ember lance," she said.

"What? Honey, what?" Sophie asked.

Maya made herself sit up. "She got hurt because of the ember lance we gave her. Something happened with the bo staff the other night too."

"You don't know that," Kiera said. "It could have been something else."

It could have. But all Maya could see in her mind was Charli dressed as Piper. And swinging an ember lance around that Alex had given her because Maya had opened her big mouth and told Charli about it. She'd probably been jumping off the couch, in full Piper mode.

Maya suddenly stood. "I have to go to the hospital." She had to see Charli. She had to be sure she was okay. She needed to see Alex and make sure he was okay. She had to help. Do something. Anything.

"Maya," Sophie said gently, "hang on."

Maya spun to face her friends. "I have to go."

Kiera rose, nodding. "Okay, we'll go too."

Maya felt tears stinging her eyes. "Thank you."

"Of course," Kiera said. "But remember, they might not tell you anything. You're not . . ." She glanced at Zach.

"You're not family," Zach said. "They might not be able to tell you anything."

Maya nodded. "I know. I just need to be there." She

grabbed Zach's hand. "You know everyone. You can find out what's happening."

Zach looked at Kiera.

Kiera stepped in front of Maya. "Honey, maybe—"

"What?" Maya looked back and forth between them.

"Maybe you should call Alex first. See if . . . it's a good time," Kiera said.

And the truth hit Maya directly between the eyes. And in the heart. This was a family issue. Rachel and Alex would be there with Charli. Together. The last time Maya had just shown up—

She hadn't been invited to Charli's birthday party, and no one had requested her presence at the hospital. No matter how much she wanted to be there for Charli and Alex.

She swallowed. "You're right. He could call me if he wanted me there."

"Maybe he will—" Kiera started.

"But I'm going anyway."

Kiera didn't look surprised. "You sure?"

"Yes. I don't need to be asked to do the right thing. In fact, most of the time I'm not invited to get involved. But I almost never regret it."

Almost.

But the risk was worth it.

# CHAPTER FOURTEEN

$\mathcal{Y}$es, she's going to be fine."

"Oh, thank God."

Alex felt his throat tighten at the emotion in his mother's voice. He had called his parents earlier to tell them that Charli was in the hospital, and he was incredibly relieved to be able to call with this update. "They're going to keep her overnight, just to be sure, but the bleeding has resolved, and she has no abnormal signs," Alex told her.

"Well." His mom sniffed. "Okay. Maybe we can come down this weekend."

"That would be nice," Alex told her with a smile.

He knew she was busy planning a huge, gushy get-well-soon-gift delivery as soon as Charli was home. And he was going to let her go completely overboard. This was her only grandchild, and she was dealing with everything Alex was dealing with—getting used to the idea of Charli, realizing she'd missed ten years, and trying to catch up without overwhelming the little girl. She was also trying really hard not to fuss and be overprotective of her one and only granddaughter. Alex had needed to ask her to pull back in the beginning, and to her credit she had done so.

But he wasn't going to ask her to do that anymore. She loved Charli, she worried about Charli, and she knew something about raising a child with hemophilia. She hadn't done everything perfectly, but it had all been done out of love and concern. He got that now more than ever.

Alex took a deep breath. This hospitalization had shown him a lot of things. "Hey, Mom," he said, as she started to say good-bye.

"Yes, Alex?"

"I just wanted to say thank you. And I'm sorry."

"For what, honey?"

"For thinking you were too strict. For thinking that you worried too much. For…resenting you sometimes," he added honestly.

His mother laughed softly. "Sweetie, everything you felt was normal. You were a kid, and I was telling you no at nearly every turn. None of that was easy for any of us."

Alex wished he were there to give her a hug. "I'm sorry I didn't make it easier, though," he said. "I should have listened better. You were just doing your job as a parent. I get that now."

"Well, that's nice. That's just one of many wonderful things about having Charlotte in our lives now," she said, and Alex could hear the smile in her voice. "But Alex, it wasn't your place to make things easier for me. You were the kid."

"It's not a two-way street?" he asked, wondering why

he hadn't talked to his mother more about parenting in the past few months.

"Not really," she said. "The love and respect and trust go both ways, hopefully. And as your child gets older, it becomes a different type of relationship. But it's more like a really long one-way street that just keeps going. You take care of your kids, and then they take care of your grandkids. And believe me, that matters. You're a wonderful father. That makes me even happier than it would have if you had obeyed every single one of my rules one hundred percent."

Alex felt his chest tighten. "Thanks, Mom."

"And you'll really understand someday when Charli has children," she said gently. "Seeing your child as a loving, caring, involved parent is when you really know that you did something right."

The emotions of the last few days rose up and threatened to choke him as he nodded, even though she couldn't see it. "Thanks, Mom," he said again. "I love you."

"I love you too. We'll see you soon. Tell Charli we're thinking of her."

"I will."

They disconnected, and Alex sucked in a big breath. Then he turned toward his daughter's hospital room. His mom thought he was doing a good job. That made him feel great. But he knew he could be doing a better job. And that needed to start right now.

He met Rachel in the hallway outside Charli's room. Rachel had a cup of coffee in one hand, her cell phone in the other.

"You okay?" she asked, looking up into his face.

He nodded. "Yeah. But I need a minute alone with Charli."

Rachel lifted a brow, but she nodded. "Yeah. Sure."

"I need to lay down some rules. And some consequences if she doesn't follow them."

"Okay," Rachel agreed easily. "It's about time."

Yeah, it was.

"I'll go call my mom back then," she said. "See you in a little bit."

He pushed the door to Charli's room open. She looked away from the TV and smiled when she saw him.

"Hey," he greeted her, crossing to the side of her bed. "How's your headache?"

"Better. The pudding helped."

Alex smiled. If only pudding could help everything. "Dr. Warner says you're going to be fine. Home tomorrow."

"Okay."

He sat on the edge of the mattress near her feet. "Grandma Nolan said to tell you hi and they want to see you soon."

Her smile got bigger. "Okay."

He hated to kill that smile. "Charli, we need to talk."

She sighed, and her smile did disappear. "I knew the vacation wouldn't last."

"The vacation?"

"Having a dad who didn't get upset."

Alex frowned slightly. "What do you mean?"

Charli shrugged. "Mom's the only one who gets upset about things like kickball in PE class and me jumping around the house."

"That's not true," he told her. "I don't like those things either."

Charli frowned at him. "But you never say that."

No, he didn't. He shifted on the mattress. "That's one of the things we need to talk about. That's going to change. Your mom isn't the only one who's going to have rules and consequences now."

Charli slumped against her pillows. "Because I slipped by the pool?"

He shook his head. "No. Because you have a serious medical issue, and you're not being careful enough to make me feel like you're safe."

Charli chewed on her bottom lip.

"You have to be more careful," he said, more firmly than he'd ever said anything to her.

"I know."

"I think you do know," he agreed. "But you're not acting like you know. You remind me of—" He broke off, a sharp pang in his heart suddenly.

Charli lifted her head. "Who? You?"

He wished it were him. He'd rebelled against his mother's rules at times growing up, but he'd never taken his condition lightly. "No. A friend of mine. She, um—" He cleared his throat. Even thinking of Maya made him ache. "She has a bad injury. She got hurt doing her job. And it keeps her from doing some of the stuff she really loves doing. So sometimes she does that stuff anyway. And she pushes it too hard, and she ends up getting even more hurt from it."

Charli was watching him carefully. "And it bothers you when she does that?"

"Yes."

"How come?"

"Because..." He took a deep breath. "Because I love

her. And I want her to be safe and healthy. And I hate that there are things she wants to do that she can't, but it hurts me to see her hurt."

Charli was quiet for a moment. Then she asked, "And it hurts you when I'm hurt?"

He reached out and laid a hand on her knee. "Very much."

"Mom too?"

"Definitely."

"So I need to be more careful so it doesn't bother you guys?"

He shook his head at that. "No, Charli. You need to be more careful so you are safe and healthy. We can give you lots of rules and even punishments, but the truth is, you are the one in charge of your body. If you do risky things and get hurt, we can be mad and take your comic books away, but you've still done damage. All the punishments in the world can't take that back."

She frowned. "You would take my comic books away?"

Okay, she was ten. She understood what he was saying, but she wasn't fully embracing that she was the one ultimately in charge of taking care of herself. Fine. They could have this conversation another million times as she grew up. She'd get it eventually. "Yes, I will definitely take your comic books away. And your ember lance. And TV. Whatever it takes to make it clear that the rules are serious and you have to follow them."

She nodded, staring at the bedspread instead of him.

He gave it a minute to sink in. Then he said, "I don't like saying you can't do something. Because I know how that feels. My friends asked me to play basketball with them the other day, and I had to say no."

Charli looked up. "You did?"

"Yep. I wanted to play, but they're grown men and they play hard. It just wasn't a good situation for me. It stinks, but sometimes with hemophilia we have to make tough choices."

"Couldn't they just be more careful?"

He shrugged. "Sure, I guess they could try. But it's kind of like when you have sword fights with Toby. Do you like asking him to be more careful?"

"No," she admitted. "That wouldn't be as fun for him."

"Right. But the thing is," he said, "when you're hanging out with friends, it's about being together, not what you're doing. So I invited my friends to do something else that I can do. We're going to play pool. And cards. I might even teach them chess."

Charli sighed again. "Do I have to play chess with you?"

He smiled. "No." Though someday he hoped she'd change her mind. "We can still do bo stuff and ember lance stuff. But that's because we're in the same boat. We have to make some adjustments."

"Toby will make adjustments," she said after a moment. "He just wants to spend time with me. It's not about what we do."

Alex nodded. "Lots of people will feel that way."

"What about Maya? Does she make adjustments for you?"

His heart squeezed so hard he had to pause for a moment. Just hearing her name was like a knife. There was no way he could have expected Charli to forget about

Maya. Rachel had kept Charli from asking him about Maya the night she showed up at his door, but he'd known she'd want to know more eventually. He hadn't, however, been prepared for how much it would hurt. He made himself nod. "Yeah."

"Because she just wants to be with you."

Damn.

Maya had definitely made adjustments for him. She'd stayed after hours for him, she'd adapted routines for him, she'd taken the few hours he'd given her and made the most of them. She'd let him into her life. She'd let him be a part of everything that mattered to her, even when he wasn't giving her much in return.

He was the one who hadn't adjusted. He hadn't made any changes. He'd made her fit into his schedule around the other things. He had happily become a part of her life, but he hadn't let her into his, hadn't let her be a part of things that mattered to him.

Alex's chest felt tight, and he had to force his lungs to expand. "Yeah," he told Charli simply. "Because she just wants to be with me."

"That's nice," Charli said.

Alex almost laughed at the gross understatement. But he just nodded again. Maya hadn't been far from his thoughts since she'd left his apartment the other night. Hell, since he'd first met her. But he'd been trying to push his feelings and regrets away while he focused on Charli. Now it seemed he couldn't stop the images of Maya, the memories, the feelings. "There are things you can always do—chess, cards, swimming. There are things you can sometimes do— like bo and swords and even kickball—all with modifications. But there are things you just can't. Like gymnastics."

"And running by the pool."

He leveled a serious look at her. "Right."

She nodded solemnly. "Okay."

"I don't want to take your comics away, Charli. Help me out. Just follow the rules so I don't have to."

"Okay." After a pause she said, "But it's okay if you have to sometimes."

"It is?"

Charli shrugged. "Mom gets upset because she loves me. So I knew, after you started loving me, that you would start getting upset too. And I understand."

Alex stared at his daughter. His heart pounded, and he battled the urge to . . . he wasn't sure what. "I have loved you since the very second I knew about you," he finally said, his voice a little scratchy.

Charli tipped her head. "Really?"

"Really."

She seemed to be thinking. "I started loving you the first time we watched TV together. You laughed at something that I thought was really funny too."

Alex had to blow out a breath before he said, "The first time we watched TV was pretty early on."

Charli nodded. "I loved you pretty early on."

She slew him. She did. She had such a strong grip on his heart that Alex didn't think it would ever beat again without an extra thump because of Charli. "Well, I'm very sorry that you thought I wasn't upset because I didn't love you yet." His voice almost cracked, and he had to clear his throat again.

She smiled. "I kind of liked not having you upset at me."

"I wanted us to be friends first. But I've realized that I need to be your dad first."

"You're the only dad I have," she said softly.

And he lost the battle with his emotions. He leaned in and wrapped his arms around her. She didn't even hesitate. Her arms reached around his neck, and she hugged him hard.

Alex couldn't speak for a long moment, even after they parted. As he looked at his daughter, he realized that everything he'd been afraid of had been keeping him from what he wanted—and needed. Keeping lines between and around each segment of his life had made things easier in some ways. But...had it really?

If he'd just mixed everything up from the start—if he'd just lived his life as one big messy, fun, amazing, hard, and happy thing—Charli would have known he wanted to be her dad from day one, he would have been an actual help to Rachel, and Maya would be here right now. And he never would have hurt Maya. Hell, he would have told her he loved her the moment he realized it.

"Hey." Rachel poked her head in the door. "How are things in here?"

Alex and Charli both said, "Great," at the same time.

Rachel smiled. "Awesome. Um, hey, can I talk to you out here for a second, Alex?"

He looked at Charli. "We're good?"

"Totally good."

She gave him a big smile, and sure enough, his heart thumped extra hard. He pushed up off the bed.

"I'll be right back," Rachel told Charli.

"Okay." She turned back to her TV show as if one of the biggest moments in Alex's life hadn't just happened.

He grinned and headed for the door. "I laid down the rules and the consequences," he told Rachel as the door shut.

"Great."

"I'm in. All in. On all of it."

Rachel tipped her head. "I know that, Alex. I've always known that."

Relief swept through him. "Good."

"So, have you called Maya?"

Alex was taken aback by the question. "No. I've been...focused on Charli."

Rachel nodded. "Yeah. I know. But..."

"But what?"

"You know you can love Charli and love Maya at the same time, right?"

Rachel knew him. That shouldn't surprise him, he supposed. She was a loving, generous, sweet, and hopeful person. She was also incredibly insightful. Or he was really easy to read. "I'm hoping that's true."

"Then call her."

"I don't know if I should."

"I'm okay with it," Rachel said, echoing what she'd told him at his apartment after Maya had left the other night.

He sighed. "I'm not hesitating because of you, Rach," he said honestly.

She nodded. "Good. I know...I had to see if there was anything between us. I couldn't wonder what if. You know?"

"I do. Completely."

"But even if Maya wasn't in the picture, I don't think it would have worked with us romantically."

She really was amazing. "I do love you, Rach."

"Ditto. In a very platonic, you're-my-kid's-dad way," she said with a smile.

"And maybe even in a you're-one-of-my-best-friends way," he told her.

She seemed a little surprised, and a lot pleased, by that. "That sounds perfect."

So things were good with his mom, his daughter, and Rachel. Now there was just one more woman he needed to fix things with. And this one was a doozy.

"So, as one of your best friends, I'm going to insist that you call Maya," Rachel said. "You need her here."

Hell yeah, he needed her here. Why couldn't she just barge in and demand he let her be there and help him? He scrubbed a hand over his face. "What right do I have to call her after I pushed her away? I kept her away from Charli. How can I call her now and say that I need her, I'll let her in?"

"Calling her now will matter a lot, Alex," Rachel said.

"I left her out. I purposely didn't let her get close."

"So you messed up. Now you know you want her here. Tell her that."

"I don't know if she'll forgive me," he said.

"She will. That's how love works," Rachel told him. "You get mad and hurt but you'd rather be with the person than without, so you forgive them."

"You've got a lot of experience with that?"

"With giving my whole heart to someone?" Rachel asked with a smile. "Yeah, your daughter. Love is worth going through all the heartache and mistakes."

Yeah. He got that. Alex took a deep breath. "If I call her, she's going to be a part of this. Of me. And everything."

Rachel nodded and gave him a small smile. "She already is."

His heart thumped. She was. "I really tried to keep everything separated and easy. But it all got mixed up anyway."

"That's because your heart is finally involved. You can put your time and your energy and even your mind into different boxes, but the heart doesn't work that way. It's a part of everything."

"You don't think I had my heart in my work and my personal relationships before this?" Alex asked her.

Rachel shook her head. "I think maybe you've had things or people who'd almost opened you up, but with Charli and Maya, it's the first time you couldn't fight it."

He realized she was right. And that it was wonderful, and crazy, that Rachel was the one giving him this advice. "I'm warning you. Maya is...a lot."

"A lot of what?"

He smiled. "Everything. Life. Love."

Rachel laughed. "I got that impression when she showed up in a Supergirl costume with a ferret, Alex. She sounds awesome."

"She is. She's...Charli in eighteen years."

"Then I already love her." Rachel reached over and squeezed his hand. "Not that what I think matters. You love her. That's what's important."

"I do." He did. With every fiber of his being. And he couldn't wait to tell her. He would grovel, he'd beg, he'd...push. He'd channel Maya herself and go after her with everything he had, and he'd keep at it until she believed him and agreed to spend her life with him.

"But I also really like her," Rachel said. "She's the

woman who researched hemophilia because of Charli and made her armor and swords, taught you bo, helped you with the comic books, and rushed down here to see if Charli was okay even though you were a real asshole to her."

Alex was nodding along with everything she said. It was great that Rachel liked her. That would make his life easier, for sure. Maya was amazing...And then Rachel's last words sunk in. "Rushed down here?"

"She's up at the front desk raising hell because no one will come and get you for her," Rachel said. "We had a little talk."

"You and Maya had a little talk?"

"I told her Charli's status, and I thanked her for caring about my daughter so much. And I told her about your status and thanked her for loving you too."

"You told her about my status? What status?"

"That you're miserable without her."

He turned on his heel. "Front desk?"

"Yep. She's the one in the Captain America pajamas."

He spun back to face her. "She's in—"

Rachel laughed. "Of course she is."

Of course she was.

A minute later Alex was striding for the front of the ER. He could hear Maya hassling whoever was at the front desk. "I know I'm not family. I don't need to see the patient. I just need to see her dad. Or if you want to, you can take a note back to him."

"You didn't even change out of your pajamas?" he interrupted, walking right up behind her.

She spun and launched herself into his arms without warning. "Oh my God, Alex! Are you okay? Zach told

me he saw you, and I know I shouldn't be here. But
Rachel said it was okay, and she said Charli's okay, but is
she really? I know that I'm just barging in again, but I had
to be here. I thought maybe it was the ember lance. Or the
bo again. But Rachel said she slipped by the pool. But oh
my God, that's so scary! And no matter what, I need you
and Charli to know that I love you and I'm here and if you
need—"

He covered her mouth with his, squeezing her tight and
just absorbing her. Her being here. Her energy, her love,
her never-quit. She hadn't let him push her away. Not for
good. And he would never deserve her. But he was going
to spend his life trying to.

When he finally let her breathe, he was careful not to
let her start talking again. "Thank you."

"For—"

He covered her mouth with his hand. "Thank you for
being here. For knowing I needed you. For not letting
me push you away. Thank you for loving Charli. And no,
it wasn't the bo or the lances. She was running on the
wet deck of the pool and slipped and fell. She was with
Rachel."

Maya's eyes got wide, and he slowly took his hand
away. "But she's okay?"

"She is. She's staying overnight, but things are going
to be fine."

A tear slipped down Maya's cheek, and his heart
turned over in his chest. He wiped it away with his thumb.
"I love you," he told her.

"But...I push. I barge in."

"Yes, you do. Please, keep pushing."

She pressed her lips together, her eyes sparkly. Her feet

dangled off the floor, because he still had an arm banded tightly around her waist and she was hanging on to him as if she'd never let go.

Lord, he hoped she never let go.

"I love you too," she finally said.

"Thank God."

"And keep pushing? Really?" she asked.

"Yes. You've made me push—to get closer to Charli, to try new things, to finally say what I'm feeling. Keep pushing me. Please."

Maya searched his face for a moment. Slowly she nodded. "Okay, but you might need to tell me if I step on toes or butt in where I'm not wanted."

"There's nowhere in my life where you're not wanted. I'm so sorry about the other night."

She nodded. "I forgive you."

And that was it. She forgave him. Just as Rachel had said she would. Because she loved him.

"Do you want to see Charli?" he asked.

"So much."

He set her on the floor but didn't let go of her hand on the way to Charli's room. When they got there, he reached to open it, but suddenly felt Maya pulling back.

He looked at her with an eyebrow up. "Really, Supergirl?"

"I just—"

"You just need a little push." And he nudged her into his daughter's room.

# EPILOGUE

*Three months later*

Alex looked out over the roomful of people. He was in the Imperial Ballroom at the Boston Park Plaza Hotel. Onstage. Preparing to address a huge group of physicians, patients, and families affected by hemophilia as the keynote speaker for the evening.

He looked down at the table where Maya was seated with Charli and Rachel and felt his chest expand with love and confidence. He was up here because of them. And he was incredibly grateful they'd pushed him to do this.

"Good evening, everyone," he said into the microphone. "Welcome. I'm Dr. Alex Nolan, and over the next thirty minutes, I'm going to be sharing with you several thoughts about hemophilia. Some of you have heard me speak before. Some of you in my office as patients. Some of you on panels and at conferences as physicians and colleagues. Some of you have heard me speak to families of those affected. But tonight is a little different. For you. And for me. Tonight I will be speaking to you for the first time as a patient, and a father, rather than a physician."

He let his introduction sink in for a few moments. He knew that the physicians in the room, as well as the patients he'd worked with, were going to be shocked by the news of his hemophilia. And his daughter's.

When the murmuring died down, he resumed his speech. "I've lived with the condition for thirty-two years. I became an expert in more than the research, diagnosis, and treatment of the condition. I became an expert at living with it. And in hiding it. But that ends tonight. In part because my daughter recently came into my life and is living with hemophilia as a carrier with symptoms. In part because I met a woman who challenged me to see my limitations as strengths and as a way of helping others. And in part because it's who I am. No matter how much I'd like to keep it only in the back of my mind, I can't. It's part of my life, and our lives aren't meant to be lived in carefully delineated boxes with things separated and never influencing anything else."

Alex again caught Maya's eye and saw her beaming with pride and love. And then he looked at Charli. She was eating her chocolate mousse and fiddling with her knife and fork—no doubt imagining some fantastic ember lance battle in her mind—and fidgeting on her seat because the lace on her dress was scratchy. She was completely oblivious to the big moment in her dad's life. And that was as it should be. Her condition was a part of her too. No big deal. Nothing that needed a stage and a spotlight and an audience.

He smiled and continued his speech, talking about his history, some anecdotes from his childhood with an over-protective mother, a few more stories about his daring daughter, and some of the things he'd had to learn as a dad, and then he wrapped up.

"Vulnerability. It's something hemophiliacs know well. As a physician, I understand vulnerability, risk, and consequences. But there's another word I've recently learned a lot about. *Passion.*" He smiled at Maya and saw her wipe a tear away. "Before I came out about my condition and saw it in my daughter's life, I never really understood passion. Passion for work or interests, and for other people and happiness and dreams. Because my condition made me feel vulnerable, I let that hold me back from going after some of the things I wanted. But now I've learned that there's a place for both words in our lives, even with hemophilia.

"A few months ago, I would have told you that you need to balance the two, but that's not true. And you may think I'm going to tell you that passion is the most important, but it's not. Vulnerability. That's where you're the strongest.

"I'm not saying to go out and put yourself at risk and do things you know you can't or shouldn't. But I am saying don't let your condition, your vulnerability, make you feel weak or small or less. It is what's going to help you appreciate the brave moments and the challenges. So embrace it. Don't hide it. Don't whisper about it. Don't push it down deep. It's a part of you, and it makes you amazing."

He gave Charli a wink as he used her favorite word and then, as the room applauded, he descended the steps and joined his family at their table.

Maya leaned in as the next speaker took the stage. "That was awesome."

He looked at her. "Yeah?"

"Definitely."

"That's it?" he asked when she failed to elaborate.

"What do you mean?"

"No gushing, rambling speech that I have to stop with a kiss?"

"Oh," she said with a grin. "Sure. You were great. I'm so proud. I love you so much. I have Supergirl panties on. Blah, blah, blah, blah."

He leaned in.

But she wasn't quite done. "Blah, blah, blah. You should marry me."

He brushed his lips against hers but then quickly pulled back. "Seriously?" he asked. He rolled his eyes. "You just had to push it. You couldn't wait for me to do it?"

"You've been taking forever!"

"We've known each other just over six months," he said with a chuckle. Maya wanting him so much would never, ever get old.

She grinned and took the lapels of his tux in her hands, pulling him close. "I know. I've been waiting and waiting."

"Uh-huh. So impatient." He put his mouth against hers.

"Yeah, well, get ready. The next thing I'm going to push is for you to speak at that conference in London. And then I'm going to push for you to edit that big paper for the university. Then I'm going to push for a fast wedding. And then I'm going to push for a honeymoon right away."

He did cut her off with a kiss finally. But when he lifted his head, he looked into her eyes, and felt more love than he'd ever known was possible. "You just keep on pushing me, Maya."

"Forever," she promised.

He kissed her once more, then settled back in his chair, his arm over the back of hers. "I love this dress," he told her.

"You do like me in this color, don't you?"

He grinned. He sure did.

The answer to his prayers was in bright purple. Again.

Theater geek Sophia Birch has put everything into running her own playhouse—until she almost loses everything. But smokin'-hot cop Finn Kelly is staging a play of his own...starring a sexy drama nerd as his leading lady.

A preview of *Totally His* follows.

# CHAPTER ONE

$\mathcal{F}$inn would have noticed her even if she hadn't been wearing hot pink lingerie. And nothing else.

He really would have. She was totally his type—brunette and curvy and, apparently, a little crazy. As evidenced by the fact that she was trying to sneak into a burning building. He did seem to be attracted to crazy. No matter how hard he tried not to be.

But maybe she wasn't actually trying to get back into the building. All he knew for sure was that the building was definitely burning and she was definitely acting sneaky. As she pulled apart from the crowd, she moved slowly, looking over her shoulder and from side to side, as if checking to see if anyone was watching. She obviously didn't notice Finn. Because he was absolutely watching as she made her way across the street, acting as if she were just casually strolling along. Toward a burning building. In nothing but a bra and panties.

It made sense that he hadn't seen her before now. For

one, he'd been a little busy evacuating a hundred people, give or take, from the buildings on the block. For another, if she'd been huddled with the crowd, she could have easily been blocked by some of the other spectators. No one seemed inclined to leave, all choosing instead to stand around and watch the real-life drama unfold. She was short, and there were two women in enormous skirts that stood out several inches on each side, a woman dressed in a full-length fur coat and hat—in spite of it being a pleasantly warm September night—and a man dressed as a cow. He was on two legs, but otherwise he was clearly a cow. So there were plenty of big, distracting people to hide behind.

Which might all have seemed peculiar at any other scene, but considering that the burning building was the Birch Community Playhouse and that they had been in the middle of a production when the alarms went off, it wasn't so strange. Finn had no idea what the play was called or what it was about, but it explained the cow. He hoped.

He watched the woman stop at the east corner of the building, the one farthest from where the firefighters were working. Then he frowned as she slipped into the shadows along the side of the building and out of sight.

Dammit.

He started after her.

As one of the cops on the scene, it was his job to keep the area clear for the firefighters and to keep the crowd of onlookers safe. If one of them happened to have a great body and be dressed in nothing but a pink bra-and-panty set, well, he'd just call that a perk. And as he jogged across the street, Finn couldn't help but wonder if she was in costume or if the alarm had caught her in the midst of a wardrobe change. If that was her outfit for the show, he might need to buy a ticket.

His foot hit the sidewalk as his cell phone rang. He glanced at the display, then shook his head and answered, "What?"

"You saw her too, you bastard."

The voice on the other end belonged to his best friend and partner, Tripp. Finn grinned. "Who?"

"Seriously?"

Finn laughed. Tripp had a radar for beautiful women. Finn shouldn't have been surprised that he'd noticed the brunette too. "Do we need to flip a coin to see who checks her out?"

"Nah. You go be the mean guy that says she can't play by the burning building. I'll be the good cop later. If you know what I mean."

Finn definitely knew what he meant. And he ignored it. Tripp was a notorious flirt and had plenty of women, but he was also a big talker.

Finn rounded the corner of the building. The streetlights didn't quite reach along the entire length of the building on this side, and it took his eyes a second to adjust. Just in time to see her duck around the back.

Finn sighed. "You sure you don't want to be the bad cop this one time?" he asked his friend, who was out front helping control the theater crowd that had decided to stick around.

"Why's that?" Tripp sounded amused.

"I think she's trying to get back into the building."

"That's perfect," Tripp said.

"Perfect?" Finn asked, heading toward the back of the building after her.

"Sure. 'Hey, you can't go in there' is better than trying to come up with some charming line to start a conversation, right?" Tripp asked, sounding as if he was enjoying himself. "And maybe you'll get to use your handcuffs."

Finn could practically hear Tripp's eyebrows wagging. He turned the corner to the back of the building and looked around. He didn't see her. "Damn. She either went inside or she has the power of invisibility."

"Maybe she can fly," Tripp suggested, chuckling as he said it.

Finn couldn't have gotten that lucky. She'd gone inside. Dammit. He climbed up the four steps that led to the back door of the theater.

The theater was only one story and wasn't very big. He'd never been inside it, the art studio next door, the trendy new bar on the other end of the block, or any of the twenty luxury apartments that occupied the upper two stories of the building. This was the artsy part of downtown, just a few blocks off the true theater district. Finn was more the type to hang out at sports bars and, better yet, the sporting complexes around the great city of Boston.

Finn touched the back door and found it cool. It seemed that the flames were still limited to the wall on the other end of the theater, but it was a mistake to assume anything when fire was involved.

Finn yanked the door open and paused.

"You're going in, right?" Tripp asked in his ear, suddenly more serious.

"Yep."

"Okay, talk to me. What's going on? Where are you?"

Tripp was a good guy and a great partner. He was a

smartass and a man whore, but he was a hell of a cop and knew exactly when to be serious.

"Back door. West end. No smoke. No noise," Finn reported, referring to the lack of crackling or other sounds that would alert him to fire nearby.

He stepped inside and pulled the flashlight from his belt to shine it back and forth. In the center of the room was a huge wooden table cluttered with tape measures, ribbon, lace, and other stuff. There were sewing machines, and the room was filled nearly to bursting with bolts of fabric, mannequins, racks of clothing, and shelves of hats, purses, shoes, gloves, and other accessories. "Looks like this is where they make and store costumes," he told Tripp.

Finn shined the flashlight around, located the door on the other side of the room, and started in that direction. His foot hit something as he rounded the table, and he stumbled. He gritted his teeth, his irritation growing.

"You ever been in a play?" Tripp asked in his ear.

"When I was like six," Finn replied without thinking.

"Yeah?" Tripp sounded delighted at the news. "What part?"

"I don't remember." Finn totally remembered. He'd been a Dalmatian in his school production of *101 Dalmatians*.

"I bet Angie has pictures."

Finn could hear Tripp's huge grin. And he knew his friend was right. His mother most definitely still had pictures. And would happily show Tripp every damned one of them over roasted chicken and potatoes one night without Tripp needing to do anything more than mention the play.

Damn. "You ask my mom about that play and I might forget to block Duncan next time we play." Tripp was the quarterback for their rec league football team, and Duncan was the huge lineman for the firefighters. Duncan had a tally on the inside of his locker of the number of times he'd sacked Tripp. The number was significantly lower than it would have been if Tripp hadn't had Finn on his offensive line.

"Yeah, well, my ass would tell you that you're not as great at that as you'd like to think."

"Let's find out how great I am," Finn challenged as he touched the door, found it cool, and pushed it open. He stepped into a hallway. It was lit, which was helpful. It was also empty, which was not helpful. Fuck. Now which way? He looked up and down the hall. There were several doors. She could be anywhere.

"Okay, okay, don't get your panties in a wad," Tripp said. "I'm just giving you shit."

Finn grinned. Tripp knew damned well that he needed Finn blocking for him. "I'm in a hallway with a bunch of doors," he said. "And I'm feeling like fucking Alice in Wonderland here."

"Okay," Tripp said slowly.

"Jesus, man, read a book once in a while," Finn said. Though he probably should have known Tripp wouldn't know *Alice in Wonderland*. At least not in any detail. Finn had been the only kid in his class who had read the original Lewis Carroll version—or had it read to him. Three times. It was his mother's favorite. Which totally fit Angie. Angela Kelly was a dreamer, and Finn's dad had always said that she lived in her own wonderland.

"I read," Tripp protested.

"*ESPN Magazine* doesn't count," Finn told him. "Okay, these are probably dressing rooms and stuff," he said, eyeing the doors. "Maybe she came back in to get dressed." That would make a little sense, even though it was stupid.

"Or to get something," Tripp said.

Yeah, maybe. People always did shit like that.

*Dammit.* She was one of those. Convinced that material possessions were worth risking her life for. Finn had no choice but to start searching. He moved up and down the hallway throwing doors open. "Nothing. And yeah, these are dressing rooms," he reported to Tripp. The lights were all on, and there were clothing pieces scattered everywhere in all of them. "Looks like a tornado hit."

"Well, they were in the middle of a show," Tripp said.

"Yeah, at least everyone bailed and left their stuff behind." That was incredibly intelligent. With the one exception who'd come back in, of course.

After he'd opened every door to every dressing room, a storeroom, and a bathroom, Finn swore. No woman in pink panties. Or panties of any other color.

"Where the fuck is she?" he muttered out loud.

"Keep going," Tripp said. "I haven't seen her come back out."

"I'm heading south. There's an exit sign up here." He headed down the hallway for the door at the end.

"You're at the front?" Tripp asked.

"No. There's no way this door opens to the outside." A moment later he stepped into the outer lobby of the theater. The empty outer lobby.

"Box office to my left, doors into the theater to my right," he told Tripp.

"Got you."

Finn looked to his left again. "The box office," he repeated. Where the money would be. And the computers.

"You think she's looting the place?" Tripp asked.

"Money or clothes," Finn said. "People also go back in for scrapbooks and photographs, but she wouldn't have any of that here. Why else would she come back in?"

"Check it out," Tripp agreed.

"How are things going out there?" Finn didn't see or smell anything that made him worry right now, but he had no way of knowing if the flames were, at that very moment, licking along the rafters or crawling through walls in other rooms. Finn scowled as he stomped toward the front offices. He might be making an arrest here. If nothing else, he was going to chew this lady's ass but good. The ass in the hot pink...

*Fuck.* He shoved the office door open, but as it banged against an interior wall, he realized the room was empty. The lights were on, the computer was still running, but there was no one in sight. He also smelled smoke.

Definitely *fuck.*

He turned a full circle, not sure where to go next. It was a typical office, and there was a safe under the desk in front of him. So she hadn't come for the money. Well, what the hell?

"She's not here."

"She's in there somewhere."

Just then Finn heard a door slam shut somewhere behind him. He swung toward the sound. "Hang on." He moved back into the lobby just in time to see the woman step out from a room behind the coffee machine.

Her eyes went wide when she saw him.

"Boston PD! Stop!" Finn shouted.

She had covered up. Kind of. She now wore a robe, short, sheer, and unbelted. Which really did nothing to cover his view of her panties and bra. Or all that skin.

And maybe that was why she suddenly took off at a run.

Finn stared after her for a moment, a little stunned. She was actually running from him?

"She's running," he told Tripp grimly.

"You need backup?" Tripp still sounded amused. The bastard.

"Maybe. You know anyone good?" Finn asked, starting after her.

"Ha ha. You need to hang up so you can run? If you huff and puff into the phone, I'll make fun of you."

"If you make fun of me, I'll kick your ass on our next run. Again."

"Go get the girl," Tripp said.

Finn disconnected, mentally calling his friend names. But nothing he hadn't called him out loud and in person.

The woman made it to the other end of the lobby and through one of the doors leading into the main theater before Finn got to her. He grabbed the door as it was swinging shut, nearly smashing his fingers. The lights were off in the inner theater, but as he plunged into the darkness, he got a big whiff of whatever body spray or perfume she wore. He took a deep breath. It was nice. Lemony. Sweet and...

*Jesus.* Finn scowled and turned his flashlight back on. He was thinking about how she smelled? How about the smell of smoke that was going to be chasing them both pretty soon?

"Hey!" he called into the theater. "You can't be in here. Just come out with me now. No problem. You're not in trouble."

He heard what sounded like papers rustling behind him, and he swung around. He had to lift the beam of light above his eye level. The sound was coming from the room up behind the rows of theater seats, where the lighting and sound equipment were. The door to the booth was hanging open, and he heard muttered swearing in addition to the papers.

He started in that direction, but suddenly the door slammed shut.

He strode to the door and banged his fist against it. "You have to come out, ma'am. It's not safe for you to stay in the building."

"Just give me a damned minute!" she shouted through the door.

"I'm sorry, ma'am, I can't do that," Finn said.

"I have to find something. Then I'm coming right out."

"Ma'am, the fire could be spreading. You need to evacuate the building." Finn shined his flashlight on the door, wondering if he could break it down.

"I will!" she called back. "I promise."

"Ma'am, I will have to remove you myself if you don't come out immediately."

"Oh, for fuck's sake!" he heard her exclaim. Something in the room banged—a file cabinet closing, if he had to guess. Then it sounded as if she slid something across the floor. Like a chair or a table.

As something heavy thumped against the other side of the door, Finn frowned and grabbed the doorknob, turning it easily. It wasn't locked. He started to push it open and realized that yes, she'd slid something across the floor—and put whatever it was in front of the door. He shoved hard, moving the object several inches. He could see now that she was bent over a short filing cabinet, a small flashlight held in her teeth as she rifled through the folders frantically.

Maybe she wasn't going for the safe in the front office, but she was clearly messing with someone's stuff. "Ma'am, this is your last warning. Stop what you're doing and come with me."

She took the flashlight from her teeth and glanced over, her eyes meeting his. She didn't look scared. She looked irritated. Her dark hair lay against her cheek, her mouth was a grim line, and the beam from his flashlight easily penetrated the sheer fabric of her robe, highlighting the curves of her right breast and hip. They stared at one another for several beats, and Finn felt heat sweep through him. Damn, that was stupid. And careless. He was working here.

But she broke the spell a moment later when she bent back over the files, her fingers flying over the folders. Okay, well, he'd warned her. Whatever she'd been able to move in front of the door wouldn't slow Finn down much. He put his shoulder against the door and shoved. The table scraped across the floor, and as soon as the opening was wide enough, Finn slipped inside.

She straightened, looking even more irritated now. "I have to check one more place."

He shook his head. "No way. Let's go."

"Officer, I understand what you're doing. But I promise you that I'm not going near the fire. I just need to—"

*Enough of this.* Finn stalked to her, put a hand around

her upper arm, and turned to remove her from the sound booth. And the building.

She dug her heels in, though, pulling against his hold. "Hey, you can't—"

"Oh yes I can," he told her calmly, careful to keep his eyes off her body. The heat from her skin had immediately soaked through the thin robe, and Finn felt it traveling from his palm up his arm. "I've given you several opportunities to cooperate."

"You're arresting me?" she asked.

"Are you doing something that you need to be arrested for?" he asked, moving her toward the door, despite her resistance.

"No! I need to get something. It's very important. It belongs to a friend of mine. It's irreplaceable."

"Ma'am," he said calmly, "don't make me carry you out of here."

He really didn't want to carry her out. That would involve him touching a lot more of her. And the fact that she was barely clothed would become even more of an issue. As it was, he was far too aware not only of her body heat and how much skin was on display, but also that the scent surrounding her was definitely lemony. And it was completely inappropriate to acknowledge how badly he wanted to take a really big, deep breath.

"You can't give me two more minutes?" she asked.

"Absolutely not." Finn took a risk and glanced at her. Then gritted his teeth against the sheen in her eyes. It wasn't as if he'd never had someone cry when he was trying to get them to do something they didn't want to do. But sometimes it got to him and sometimes it didn't. This time it did.

She pulled against his grip and leaned all her weight into fighting the forward motion across the room.

Well, shit. He'd kind of figured it would come to this, but he wasn't sure he was ready to touch her more. Still, it didn't look as if he had a lot of choice. Reminding himself that he was a professional, he bent and hooked an arm behind her knees, looped the other around her back, and lifted her.

She gasped, and for a moment she didn't fight. And he thought maybe the hard part was over. But as he headed out the door, trying to ignore how warm and soft and fucking lemony she was, she started to wiggle.

\* \* \*

"Knock it off."

Sophie frowned up at the cop who was carrying her out of the theater. *Carrying* her. Out of *her* theater. "You can't force me to leave."

"The fuck I can't."

Of course he could. Obviously. And she'd known going back in had been a stupid, risky thing to do, but she'd thought she'd known exactly where the script was.

She had to get that script.

Angela had finally finished it. And it was amazing. And it was handwritten on pink notebook paper with purple ink. And somewhere in the theater that was possibly burning down.

Sophie squirmed in the cop's arms again. It was the only copy in the world. There was no way Angela could rewrite it if it burned. It had taken her three years to write it as it was.

The arms holding her tightened, and with a sigh Sophie gave up trying to get loose. The cop was far bigger and stronger than her. And under any other circumstances, she would have been enjoying being this close to him. A hot guy carrying her away from danger? Oh yeah, that was good stuff. If only carrying her from danger weren't also carrying her away from the most beautiful independent script she'd ever read.

Well, if she was going to be carried away—literally—she might as well enjoy it. While she came up with a plan.

She looked up at him. The cop had dark hair, cut very short, and dark eyes. With the lack of light she couldn't tell the exact color, but she felt their intensity. He had a strong jaw, because of course he did—just like all the great save-the-day heroes. He also had wide shoulders, large biceps, and big hands. Not that she minded.

She was acutely aware that she was pressed up against his solid, very warm chest. And that one of those big hands was curled around her thigh. Her bare thigh. Which reminded her of what she was wearing. Or what she wasn't wearing. In act two she was in the bra, panties, and robe—until she slipped out of the robe just as the curtain came down. She'd been in the dressing room, about to pull her dress on for act three, when the alarm had gone off. She was smart enough to know that you got out when a fire alarm sounded. But as soon as she'd determined where the fire was and that the firefighters were on it, she'd truly thought she could slip back in, grab the script, and get out again without anyone knowing. No harm, no foul.

She'd kind of forgotten about her lack of clothing. As crazy as that sounded. She certainly wasn't the type to run around in barely there clothes, and definitely not in her underwear. It was the theater that made her forget the real world. And the wig. Sophie lifted her hand and touched the wig of straight black hair that covered her own blond waves. She really did love wigs and costumes. They allowed her to do all kinds of things she wouldn't normally do.

The cop started for the front doors of the theater.

"Wait!"

He frowned down at her. "What?"

"How about the side door?" she asked. Maybe if she was cooperative and sweet, he'd let her down. And maybe relax a little. And then leave her alone once they were outside.

Then she could slip back into the costume shop, the only other place in the building where the script might be. She'd gone in through that room, but it hadn't occurred to her to stop and look there. Angela had given the script to her in the sound booth, saying it was finally done, but Sophie knew that Angie had sneaked it back and been tinkering with it over the past couple of days. No matter how many times Sophie assured her that the script was wonderful, Angie was having a hard time letting it go.

"Why the side door?" he asked, but at least he'd stopped walking.

That was good. That was very good.

"Less attention. I don't want to freak anyone out when they see me with the big, bad cop."

He sighed. "If I was so big and bad, you'd be in handcuffs right now."

# ABOUT THE AUTHOR

Erin Nicholas is the author of sexy contemporary romances. Her stories have been described as "toe-curling," "enchanting," "steamy," and "fun." She loves to write about reluctant heroes, imperfect heroines, and happily-ever-afters. She lives in the Midwest with her husband, who only wants to read the sex scenes in her books, her kids, who will never read the sex scenes in her books, and family and friends who say they're shocked by the sex scenes in her books (yeah, right!).

You can find Erin on the Web at:
    ErinNicholas.com
    Twitter @ErinNicholas
    Facebook.com/ErinNicholasBooks

*Fall in Love with Forever Romance*

### HOLDING FIRE
### By April Hunt

Alpha Security operative Trey Hanson is ready to settle down. When he meets a gorgeous blonde in a bar, and the connection between them is off the charts, he thinks he's finally found the one. But after their night together ends in a hail of gunfire and she disappears in the chaos, Trey's reasons for tracking her down are personal...until he learns she's his next assignment. Fans of Rebecca Zanetti and Julie Ann Walker will love the newest romantic suspense novel from April Hunt!

### THE HIGHLAND DUKE
### By Amy Jarecki

Fans of *Outlander* will love this sweeping Scottish epic from award-winning author Amy Jarecki. When Akira Ayres finds a brawny Scot with a musket ball in his thigh, the healer will do whatever it takes to save his life...even fleeing with him across the Highlands. Geordie knows if Akira discovers his true identity, both their lives will be jeopardized. The only way to protect the lass is to keep her by his side. But the longer he's with her, the harder it becomes to imagine letting her go...

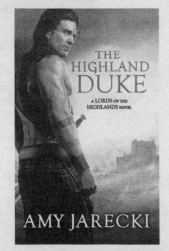

## Fall in Love with Forever Romance

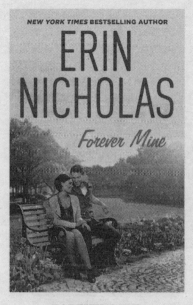

**FOREVER MINE**
**By Erin Nicholas**

**The newest book in *New York Times* bestselling author Erin Nicholas's Opposites Attract series!**

Maya Goodwin doesn't believe in holding back. Ever. As a cop, she never hesitated to throw herself into harm's way to save someone. As a doctor, Alex Nolan knows all too well that risks can have deadly consequences. So Maya—daring and spontaneous—is the exact opposite of who he's looking for. But he can't resist exploring their sizzling attraction, even though falling for Maya might just be way too hazardous for his heart.

RACHEL
LACEY

"Rachel Lacey
is a sure-fire star."
—LORI WILDE,
*New York Times*
bestselling author

CRAZY *for* YOU
*A Risking It All Novel*

**CRAZY FOR YOU**
**By Rachel Lacey**

Emma Rush can't remember a time when she didn't have a thing for Ryan Blake. The small town's resident bad boy is just so freakin' hot—with tattoos, a motorcycle, and enough rough-around-the-edges sexiness to melt all her self-control. Now that Emma's over being a "good girl," she needs a little help being naughty...and Ryan is the perfect place to start.